D1258294

CONVERGENCE

Thomas Settimi

Sky Scientific Press
PO Box 184
Skyforest, California 92385
convergence@skyscientific.com

Cover design and cover art adapted by Anthony Settimi
anthony@emagimotion.com

CONVERGENCE

ISBN-10 1-4196-6151-5
ISBN-13 978-1-4196-6151-8

Additional copies available from:

BookSurge, LLC
www.booksurge.com
1-866-308-6235
orders@booksurge.com

Special Thanks . . .

. . . to Kham Do for his review and input on issues related to Vietnamese culture, language and history. Thanks also to my wife, Charlotte, for encouraging me to begin—and to complete—this project and for providing suggestions for improvement throughout the process.

Thomas Settimi
Lake Arrowhead, California

ONE

"I HAVE NO IDEA, Cap'n. But whatever they are, they're back." Lieutenant Richardson answers the half-rhetorical question posed by his commanding officer, then lowers the pair of eight power field glasses to his side and unfastens the case on his belt. He secures the glasses and continues, not removing his gaze from the spectacle high in the evening twilight sky that has captured the attention of every man in Company B. "They seem to linger up there for a while, then spread out and disappear. Always movin' north."

Feathery white ribbons in the sky, vapor trails from the Pratt & Whitney J57 engines that power the giant American B52s, were a common sight from Quang Tri Province, Vietnam, in the summer of 1968. But from this location and time they were a puzzlement. What could ordinary soldiers comprehend of the strange apparitions in the eastern Pennsylvania sky, near Gettysburg, during the last days of June 1863?

Sergeant Wyatt, removing his hat and scratching his scalp with fingers of the same hand, offers an unsolicited opinion, "If you ask me, sir, I'd say it's a good omen—of our impending victory engaging the Federals."

William Wilson, the twenty-two-year-old captain of Company B, acknowledges the comment with a grunt of skepticism. Perhaps the upcoming battle would result in a favorable and conclusive outcome for the Confederacy, but he had serious doubts. The last two years of the war had taken much from the young captain. Not only had he abandoned his once held certain belief in a quick victory for the Southern cause, but he now began to wonder if the stalemated struggle might never end.

Within a few days, nearly every soldier on the road to Gettysburg that day would come to accept the notion that the strange sightings were indeed an omen. But for most of the brave members of that North Carolina regiment, including Captain Wilson from Union County and Sergeant Wyatt from Wilkes County, that omen would prove to be one of carnage and doom, and not victory. Indeed, history records that of the 800 men of the entire 26th Regiment North Carolina Troops, 588 would be killed or wounded at Gettysburg on July 1, 1863. More than half of the survivors would suffer a similar fate two days later on July 3$^{rd.}$.

But for one man watching from his sanctuary near the road, hidden from the rest by the brush and brambles, the white trails in the sky promised neither good fortune nor the foreboding of evil. The vapor trail evidence of high-flying aircraft was a common sight for him and he took no particular notice. But what left him nearly breathless as he watched from his hiding place was the very procession of soldiers before him: like movie extras assembling for a battle scene in a great Civil War film epic. What were they doing and why was he here, a reluctant witness to it all?

TWO

J UST ONE WEEK before the end of the spring term and Professor Roger Atwood was way behind schedule. The syllabus for American History 102 at Gettysburg College called for the subject this week to be "Appomattox and the End of the War". But today was Friday and with only a few minutes before the bell, Professor Atwood was at the white board with a diagram of the Union and Confederate battlefield positions of July 3, 1863. He had spent the whole week on the events leading up to the Battle of Gettysburg and the first two days of the fighting. For the students in the class, this could have been expected because of the local historical importance of the Gettysburg battle. Just as significant was Professor Atwood's reputation as a Civil War expert; well known to everyone present. Author, lecturer, consulting expert for the History Channel and network television specials, the Professor had declined attractive offers from the largest universities in the country, favoring instead the freedom of expression and activity that came with his position at a smaller school. Administration officials were content to let him do pretty much as he pleased as his presence on the staff brought much prestige to Gettysburg College.

Atwood continued his lecture. "Remember the South's overall strategy here: General Lee knew that he couldn't sustain a long war effort against the North's manpower and resources. His only hope was to grind down morale; inflicting such high casualties that public opinion in the North would force an end to the war and acceptance of an independent Confederacy. Lee decided to press his luck on the third day of the fighting because he knew that routing the Union forces here in their own backyard would be a huge psychological victory. He had reason to be optimistic because, as we have seen, his forces had inflicted heavy casualties on the Union army during the previous two days."

"The Confederate artillery barrage began at one PM on July 3rd. Unfortunately for the South, much of their fire was misdirected over the Union lines." Atwood paused to pose a question to the class. "Now, who knows—from your reading—the names of the two key Confederate generals involved in the infantry assault that followed?"

"Pickett!" One of the students called out.

"And who else?" He waited a moment. "Does anyone know?" Professor Atwood scanned the expressionless faces looking back at him. After a few seconds, it was clear that he wasn't going to get an answer from any of the regular students—the nineteen and twenty-year-olds—in the class. He directed his attention to the attractive female sitting on the far right side of the room in the front row. She did not look up.

"Ms. Marshall?"

Amanda Marshall was only auditing this class, but was clearly his most knowledgeable student. The thirty-six year old redhead pulled nervously at a lock of hair behind her ear as she raised her eyes. She was certain that everyone in class was staring at her.

As had happened several times before during this semester, she didn't volunteer any answers, but nonetheless knew them when called upon. She spoke softly. "That would be General Pettigrew."

Professor Atwood turned back to the board, quickly scrawling an X on the battlefield diagram.

"Correct!" he exclaimed. "Pickett on the right and Pettigrew here—" Another X. "—on the left below Seminary Ridge."

Amanda Marshall looked down at her notebook once again, trying to appear as inconspicuous as possible.

"Twelve thousand Confederate troops started the advance toward the Union lines." Atwood joined the scene he was describing to the class, strutting behind the lectern with arms outstretched, fist upon fist as if he were clutching the staff flying the regimental colors. "They marched almost a mile across open ground under tremendous fire from protected Union positions. A few soldiers actually succeeded in breaching the Federal line briefly at one point, but they were driven back and the overall assault was doomed."

Professor Atwood tossed the marking pen into the board tray and turned to face the class in the large amphitheater-style room. "General Lee's gamble had failed. The South lost several thousand more men killed or wounded that day, and Gettysburg became the turning point of the war against the Confederacy."

At that moment, the bell signaled the end of the class period. Professor Atwood struggled to maintain the attention of the class by raising his voice over the commotion of rustling feet, books and papers. "Don't forget—final exam one week from today. Last day of class—next Wednesday. Any of you needing extra credit points, be sure to show up tomorrow at 9 AM at the excavation site. I have maps here if you need them. Have a good weekend."

Amanda Marshall had already gathered her books and reached the first step up in the exit aisle of the lecture hall when she heard Professor Atwood call out. "Ms. Marshall—Ms. Marshall. Do you have a minute?" Amanda turned and walked back toward the lectern at which Professor Atwood was standing. Roger couldn't keep his eyes off her as she approached. "Yes, Professor?"

"I—uh, well I understand that you are auditing this class, Ms. Marshall, and so you don't need the extra credit points. But I wanted you to know that you, too, are welcome to come by the excavation site tomorrow." Nervously, he raised his left hand to his head and plunged his fingers through the thick mop of graying black hair, leaving it more disheveled than before. "I think that you might find it interesting if you are into—uh—dirt and shovels and—you know—old stuff."

Amanda swallowed hard and then smiled, trying desperately not to laugh at the Professor's awkwardness. "You make it sound almost irresistible, Professor." Her words were still in the air when she realized she had embarrassed him. Roger forced a weak smile, but then looked away.

Immediately regretting her smart aleck response, Amanda reached out with her right hand and touched the arm of Roger's sport coat. "I didn't mean that the way it sounded, Professor. I'm sorry. I really appreciate the invitation and I will try my best to be there." She gathered her things and turned to leave without waiting for a response.

Roger watched her walk off. Amanda was nearly out of the amphitheater when he finally called out, almost shouting, "Very good, then. We'll see you tomorrow." Amanda turned her head back towards him and flashed a smile and continued toward the exit.

On her way to the school parking lot, Amanda was struggling in an effort to square her curious exchange with the Professor with what she knew as fact about him. Between his bio and her observation during the last few weeks of class, she knew Roger Atwood to be a distinguished and confident professor of history, author of several books, and accomplished lecturer who could extemporize for an hour before a class of 100 students without uttering a single "um" or an "ah". The problem she was having was reconciling what she thought she knew about the man with the reality of the painfully embarrassing episode in the lecture hall, only minutes before. She couldn't now help but add "socially inept" to her composite opinion of this professor of history. Did it make any difference to her? No, probably not. She still found him very intriguing.

On the way to his office in the adjoining building, Roger Atwood felt a wave of depression attempting to overtake his consciousness. He was castigating himself for acting like a complete idiot, tongue-tied while attempting to exchange in a simple conversation with Amanda Marshall. How pathetic! Slowly he was able to shake off the dark cloud that attempted to overwhelm him. As it lifted, he couldn't help but think about the new Amanda Marshall he had seen for the first time today. She had seemed so shy and withdrawn in class when in the presence of the other students and even during their brief meeting before the first class session when she needed his signature on an audit approval form. But today he was surprised to find her so self-confident.

At almost the same instant in time, Roger and Amanda, now several miles apart, each had the same independent thought: Was it possible? Could two people that were so different have a successful relationship together, or was it simply a hopeless fantasy?

Three

THE EXCAVATION to which Professor Atwood had invited the students in his class was the archaeological dig at a newly discovered location at Gettysburg National Military Park, site of one of the largest engagements of the American Civil War. The park is also important for President Lincoln's address at the dedication of the Cemetery at Gettysburg. This speech proclaimed the site to be of special historical significance for all American citizens, North and South. Less than one year after the historic battle, the Gettysburg Battlefield Memorial Association was granted a corporate charter from the State of Pennsylvania. Gettysburg then became the first Civil War battlefield to become a memorial park. After the war, Gettysburg was a popular travel location for war veterans and their families from both sides. Throughout its history, the park suffered through periods of political controversy and mixed popularity, but by the 1980s it attracted up to two million visitors per year. In more recent years, there had been a serious effort to restore the grounds to their original historical state. This preservation effort, which included grading to restore original topography, had unearthed artifacts and even skeletal remains at a few locations.

Professor Atwood, the forty-two year old head of the History Department at Gettysburg College, was well known and respected by park officials. He had been called upon numerous times to assist in the identification and interpretation of unearthed artifacts. It was his close association with the park managers that led them to agree, with some reservation, to allow students from his class at the local college to assist at one of the new excavation sites. The Professor was the first to arrive at the site, about 8:30 AM.

The perimeter of the dig area was laid out with bright yellow tape, printed every few feet with the words "RESTRICTED AREA — DO NOT CROSS" in bold black type as a warning for regular park visitors to keep away. As a consequence, the location more resembled a crime scene investigation than an archaeological one. The restricted zone was essentially rectangular in shape, about seventy-five feet long and forty feet wide.

By 9 AM, there were ten people inside the perimeter. Four male students were using picks to cut into the base of a clay wall, revealing multiple gravel-laden strata. Despite the coolness of the morning, two of the young men, who appeared to have spent more time at the local gym than in the classroom, had removed their shirts. For this blatant act of male exhibitionism, two attractive coeds working a sifter near by had secretly dubbed them 'Pecks' and 'Abs'. Professor Atwood and a third female student were shoveling loosened earth from the pick work on to the mesh of the sifter as the coeds sifted. Amanda Marshall chatted quietly with Gary Knowles, the Park Ranger who was officially in charge of the excavation work. Today, the ranger was overseeing the work of this group of volunteers. He was to make sure that any significant discoveries were properly logged and added to the inventory of park artifacts, tagging each with its exact discovery location relative to a survey stake at one corner of the perimeter. It was clear that Ranger Knowles was taking his role as overseer quite seriously. He was unlikely to engage in any heavy lifting today and was careful not to get any dirt on his ranger's uniform. The rest of the group was dressed in jeans and a sweatshirt or T-shirt, except of course, for 'Abs' and 'Pecks'.

The low wall at which they were digging was created during a grading operation about three weeks earlier. The work was temporarily suspended when the blade operator unearthed pieces of a rotted wooden crate and five Enfield rifles. The metal parts were severely rusted and the hardwood stocks were partially decomposed, but the weapons were complete with no components missing and were most likely in new condition when they were buried 140 years earlier. The discovery was unusual in that it was at the extreme northwest end of the park, a considerable distance from the center of the Gettysburg fighting. The area may have been the location of a Confederate brigade command post prior to the outbreak of hostilities. It was thought that retreating Southerners abandoned this position in haste on the last day of the battle. Historical commentaries recorded that heavy rains drenched the area on July 4, 1863, the day after the fighting ended. The site was most likely spared from scavengers by a thick layer of mud.

By eleven-thirty, the early exuberance of the volunteer group had begun to wane. So far this day, the sifters had recovered only a half dozen Minie balls, the bullets that were used with Springfield and Enfield rifles in the conflict, and the rusted barrel and rotating chamber of a Colt revolver. This side arm had a missing grip and trigger assembly. 'Abs' and 'Pecks', failing to gain any serious attention from the coeds, had packed it in after only two hours, apologetically citing the need to study for upcoming final exams.

Roger walked to the perimeter tape and called out to the group, "How about some lunch? I have sandwiches and cold drinks in the car."

Shovels and picks dropped to the ground as the professor raised the yellow tape to pass under it and jogged to the dusty, white mid-1980s Carerra Coupe parked on a nearby access road. He removed a Coleman cooler from the vehicle and returned to the group.

"Ham or turkey? And here are some chips." No one passed on the sandwiches. They were all hungry.

"We haven't found much, Professor." One of the coeds remarked after setting her can of cola on a convenient flat rock at her side. A few of the others murmured in agreement.

Amanda Marshall offered some encouragement. "I think the gun piece you recovered is quite interesting, Jennifer. Besides, we still have a few hours, right Professor?"

"In the words of that ancient archaeologist: you can never tell what might be in that next shovel full of dirt! I'll stay out here as long as any of you want to work."

But by 3 PM all of the younger students had left the excavation site, feeling somewhat discouraged that they were unable to recover anything else of significance. The Professor and Ms. Marshall were digging further down the length of the wall at the point where the students had stopped their work. When Amanda sat down to rest for a minute, Roger turned and directed his attention towards the park ranger. Roger couldn't help but notice that something was troubling Ranger Knowles. The ranger had already moved the few recovered artifacts to his truck. Now he was pacing up and down one edge of the perimeter, repeatedly checking his watch.

"Do we need to stop work for today?" Roger was looking over the top of his sunglasses at Ranger Knowles.

Knowles replied, "I was hoping to get out early today. I have a dinner date."

"Not a problem, we can pack up right now if you wish." Roger glanced over at Amanda, then back at the Ranger.

"Look, Professor. I really don't want to rush you. I think it would be O.K. if you two want to work a little longer. If you find anything else, mark the location with a stake and bring the piece by the office on Monday."

With that, Knowles promptly left the perimeter, jumped into his truck and was gone.

Now alone with Roger, Amanda was surprised to discover that she was feeling slightly uncomfortable. "I should probably be leaving, too, Professor." She looked around for her purse.

But before she could rise, Roger came over and sat down on the dirt, cross-legged and facing her. "If I promise not to act like such a complete ditz like yesterday, would you stay a little longer, Ms. Marshall?"

"I think you are being too hard on yourself, Professor." She lied. "And please call me Amanda."

Roger nervously fumbled with some blades of grass and bits of wood he found on the ground in front of him. Without looking up he spoke. "You know, when I'm around someone especially attractive—as you are—I get sort of inept."

She smiled, accepting the complement without even a trace of a blush. "You don't seem inept today." Amanda stretched her arm towards Roger and, without thinking, he raised his right hand to meet her left.

After several seconds with palms and fingers touching, Roger came to a surprised awareness of what had happened. With an almost involuntary reaction, the hand dropped to his lap and his eyes darted to the side. He was clearly uncomfortable with the silence and intimacy of the moment.

Roger cleared his throat before he spoke. "I remember, Amanda, when you signed up for my class, you told me that you were working on a magazine article. How is it going?" The apparently contrived question had an immediate and chilling impact. The closeness of the moment that they had shared only seconds before was lost. In subconscious retreat, Amanda turned on to her side, supporting herself with her left hip and elbow.

"I finished it a month ago, but my editor wants me to totally rewrite it. It's kind of discouraging."

"What was the problem? Can I help?"

"I don't think so. The article was intended as a response to a national poll conducted last year. The poll showed that younger Americans are remarkably ignorant about our history. You've heard the stories. For example, most college students couldn't name the President of the United States during the Civil War. And thirty percent thought the Russians attacked us at Pearl Harbor—that sort of thing. Anyway, my assignment was to write a basic, easy-to-understand article about the Civil War and the events that led up to it."

"For you, Amanda, that should have been a piece of cake."

She laughed. "Well, Roger. I had no trouble writing the article, but my editor felt that I should have stuck to the conventional wisdom that still maintains that slavery was the one and only issue responsible for the war. I wrote instead that the South had many other legitimate grievances that led to secession. And—"

"And that was politically incorrect?" Roger interrupted her.

"Exactly. But after attending your classes, I just can't do it. I won't rewrite it."

"That's very noble, Amanda, but sometimes you have to bend a little, if need be, to keep the wolf from the door."

"Bend, yes. I can bend a little, but I refuse to bend over!" She embarrassed herself with the remark. "Anyway, you are to blame, Professor—I mean, Roger. You've had a big influence on my thinking. I find your perspective on history really fascinating and I always look forward to your class lectures."

"That's very kind of you to say." He squints at her and asks with a tone of mock interrogation, complete with fake German accent, "Are you sure you're just auditing? You 'vouldn't be trying to flatter the professor for a good grade, 'vould you?"

She laughed again. Roger rose and helped Amanda to her feet. Grasping both of her hands, he hoped to reestablish a connection. "Look, Amanda, I need to finish searching the edge of the perimeter so that this site can be closed and the park people can get back to their landscape work next week. It shouldn't take too long. If you can wait, I can drive you to your car and we can get something to eat later. O.K.?"

"Roger, that!"

Smiling broadly, he floated back to the perimeter line. "Well, that worked out better than I expected," he thought to himself.

Roger resumed his spadework, carefully shaving about an inch of soil at a time off the surface on which he was working near the edge of the perimeter. He had only a few more square feet to search.

Meanwhile, Amanda had taken it upon herself to move some of the tools that the students had been using to a portable metal storage shed nearby, just inside the perimeter tape. By the time Amanda returned from her last trip to the shed, she noticed that Professor Atwood had set the spade aside and was now on his hands and knees.

"What have you found, Roger?" She hurried to where he was working. His strokes using a coarse-bristled paintbrush made the dirt fly from the top and sides of some object buried in the dirt.

"I don't know yet, but it looks interesting. Here's another brush. Give me a hand."

Within a minute, they had cleared all the loose soil from the top of a rectangular metal object, about twenty by thirty inches with a convex bow in one dimension. It was shaped like the top of a country mailbox, only larger.

"It looks like a footlocker," cried Amanda excitedly. The revealed surface was mottled black, brown and blue-green. A metal framework bordered the surface and two parallel cross pieces divided it into three equal parts. Rivets fastened the framework to what appeared to be a single underlying panel.

"Can you open it?"

Roger didn't look up. "We need to get it out of the ground first. I'm going to use the spade."

It took no more than a minute or two to dig completely around the metal box. There was evidence that it was originally fitted with leather handles on the two shortest sides, but now only remnants were visible. Roger applied some light sideways force to the footlocker in an attempt to loosen it from the earth underneath. He was concerned that the rivets around the base might give way if he forced it. Fortunately, the entire box yielded to the pressure he applied and remained completely intact. Within seconds, he had lifted the heavy box out of the hole and placed it on a piece of burlap.

"See all this green stuff? It looks like sulfate corrosion. The framework is some wrought metal, but these panels must be made out of copper sheeting."

They worked quickly with the brushes, whisking the remaining soil from all four sides. A small brass plate on the front panel had been crudely stamped with the words "24th NCT — Company B".

"NCT stands for 'North Carolina Troops'. Those guys were virtually annihilated at Gettysburg. I believe they lost something like ninety percent of their men." Just above the brass plate there was a hasp, but no lock.

Amanda took a deep breath, then exhaled with the words, "Open it!"

FOUR

THE ROAD TRIP from Gettysburg, Pennsylvania, to Richmond, Virginia, is about three hours on a good day. It was 9:30 AM when Roger merged from Exit 4C on Interstate 495 to I-95 South. They had crossed the state line from Maryland into Virginia only a few minutes before.

Today was Thursday, and in the five days since the time they shared together at the excavation site, Roger and Amanda had seen each other three times. Clearly, the arms length teacher-student relationship they maintained throughout the class term had given way to something closer. Neither had any misgivings about it, especially as yesterday was the last official day of the semester.

"Will I be seeing you in class tomorrow for the final exam?"

"I was planning to take your final, Roger, but I decided to schedule a root canal instead. Do you mind?" He laughed.

Amanda's thoughts returned to the purpose of their trip. "Seriously, Roger, I still think you should have tried to call him first."

"Call who?" Atwood was toying with her.

"Roger, stop it! He may not even live there anymore. He may have died—or moved to Arizona. This whole trip may be a waste of time."

"Let me remind you, Amanda," Roger's tone was playfully accusatory. "It was *your* father who got his address from the Naval Institute. He said it was current."

"Besides," Roger continued, "what could I possibly have told the man on the phone that wouldn't have made me sound like some kind of lunatic?"

"That's just fine." Her tone was one of feigned resignation. "Now instead of you sounding like a lunatic, we show up at his door looking like a pair of lunatics."

Roger replied, "Somehow, I think there will be a great deal more to this story than even Commander Hayes can tell us, but for now, he is definitely the central figure in this mystery. I didn't want to risk losing the trail at square one with a phone conversation gone badly."

Apparently satisfied with his explanation, Amanda turned away to look out on the Virginia countryside from the passenger window of the Carerra Coupe. Roger turned up the volume on the FM radio and continued down the interstate.

But after only a minute, Roger switched off the radio and glanced toward Amanda, placing his hand lightly on her left knee. "You know, I'm so glad that you stayed with me at the excavation site on Saturday. These last few days with you have been really special."

"I'm glad, too." Amanda leaned in toward Roger and kissed him below the ear.

FIVE

IT WAS AN HOUR later when they turned off I-95 on to Parham Road and then into the rural suburb known as Chamberlayne Farms. This middle-class development in Northern Henrico County dated back to the 1950s. Mature sycamore trees bridging over the clean streets and well-kept front yards contributed to the peaceful air of the entire neighborhood. Roger parked on the street in front of a two-story brick Southern Colonial. As they exited the Porsche, he grabbed the nylon tote bag from behind the front seat.

"Hi, there." Roger called out to the mid-sixtyish man tending the rose bushes in front of the porch. "Are you Commander Hayes?"

The man turned slowly. Roger and Amanda looked at his soft blue eyes and noticed his thinning gray hair with streaks of blonde.

"No, sir. but I believe he's in the house." The man spoke very slowly. As Roger and Amanda glanced momentarily at each other, he continued. "Did you want me to git him for you?"

His speech and mannerisms suggested a mild case of mental retardation. Amanda asked, "What's your name?"

"Junius", was the one word reply.

"That's O.K., Junius. We'll just go to the door. You continue on with your work. Your roses are absolutely beautiful."

"Thank you, ma'am." As Junius directed his attention back to a stunning yellow tree rose, Roger and Amanda mounted the single step up to the porch and crossed to the front door. Amanda took a deep breath, grabbed the large brass knocker and struck the door twice and waited. After thirty seconds, they got a response.

"Who is it?" The deep voice came from behind the massive door.

Roger answered with some hesitation, "Commander Hayes, my name is Roger Atwood and I have Amanda Marshall here with me. I teach history at Gettysburg College in Pennsylvania. Can you—would you—tell me: Are you the Commander Hayes attached to the air wing of the *USS Enterprise* during the Vietnam conflict?"

"Conflict?" The one-word question seems to rush through the door, confronting Roger like a finger poking at his breastbone. "Is that what you history pukes call it now?" He paused for a few seconds. The ex-Navy officer got no response, but didn't really expect one. "Yes, that's me, but I was a lieutenant then. And I don't give any damn interviews. Please go away."

"Just give us a minute, Commander. We've got something that belongs to you." Roger and Amanda looked at each other for a few seconds of silence, waiting for an answer from behind the door.

"What is it?" The door opened slightly. Amanda could see an intensely serious look on the face of the black man behind the narrow opening of the large door. He was about six feet tall. When he bent over, the top of his nearly white crew cut hair showed some thinning. She could see a wide scar in his scalp on the right side of his head, about two inches above the ear.

"What do you have there?" He asked again.

"Here, Commander—see for yourself." Roger unzipped the tote bag and passed it through the door opening.

"Where in the hell did you find this?" Hayes bellowed as he opened the door wide.

"May we come in?"

Hayes gestured them forward and led them through a darkened hallway to the dining room. The Commander had removed an airman's helmet from the tote bag and placed it on the center of the table. The helmet was in less than perfect condition. A section about four inches long and an inch wide was missing on the right side, revealing the torn lining below. The hard white surface of the helmet had yellowed, but the words stenciled on it in block letters couldn't be clearer: LT. L.R. "LINK" HAYES - VA-35.

The three sat down at the dining room table. Hayes stared at the helmet for a minute. "You found this at—", he paused.

"—at Gettysburg," Roger completed the sentence. "We found it buried on the park grounds just last Saturday." Hayes dropped his chin to his clasped hands that were resting on the table and closed his eyes. Roger's attention was now drawn to the scar on the black man's scalp, taking note of it for the first time since they entered Hayes' home.

"Ms. Marshall and I found your helmet last Saturday in an antique trunk buried near the Gettysburg battlefield. It was wrapped up in a piece of parachute material."

After a minute, Hayes opened his eyes, sat back and asked, "You didn't find another helmet, did you?"

"No sir, just yours," replied Amanda.

"I can give you an explanation, how I lost this helmet, but you won't believe it." Hayes stared at Roger Atwood.

"Look, Commander. All the evidence suggests that the trunk we uncovered last Saturday had been buried, untouched, for 140 years. Unless you are about to tell us that you were kidnapped by alien time travelers, we'll believe just about any story you have to tell."

Commander Hayes rose from the table and walked to the window facing the manicured backyard. Junius was now trimming a boxwood hedge that ran around the border of the property. Hayes exhaled with an audible sigh, then began slowly to relate the story of his last air mission launched from the *USS Enterprise* off the coast of Vietnam in June 1968.

SIX

"**H**OW MANY MORE missions, do you think, for this cruise?" Bombardier and Navigator Lieutenant Lincoln Hayes queries the pilot of the Grumman A-6A Intruder over the aircraft ICS, the Internal Communication System. They were returning to the aircraft carrier *USS Enterprise* from an overnight bombing mission, hitting a truck convoy on the Ho Chi Minh Trail in Laos. The mission was successful, no thanks to the fact that the second aircraft in the flight of the two Intruders had to turn back to the carrier prior to the strike due to engine trouble encountered before crossing the Laotian frontier.

Pilot, Lieutenant Commander Nat Booth, answers his B/N, Bombardier/Navigator, the man in the right seat. "Word is that we'll be out of here in two weeks. You count the missions."

Enterprise, designated CVAN-65 with the 'N' for 'nuclear powered', was nearing the end of her third WESTPAC deployment. Commissioned nearly seven years earlier, in November 1961, the ship shared her name with a famed warship of World War II. *Enterprise (CV-6)* was commissioned in 1938. When the Japanese carrier fleet destroyed or severely damaged most of the high-value U.S. Navy ships anchored at Pearl Harbor early on the morning of December 7, 1941, the *Enterprise* was 150 miles west of Oahu, returning from a mission ferrying Marine aircraft and pilots to Wake Island. She had been expected to return to Pearl on December 6, but fate, in the form of a storm system, intervened and the ship was delayed, probably saving her from the Japanese bombs and torpedoes. Subsequently, *Enterprise* and her aircrew were able to contribute enormously to the war effort in the Pacific at such historic battles as Guadalcanal, Midway, Leyte Gulf, Iwo Jima and Okinawa. After the end of the war, *Enterprise (CV-6)* was decommissioned in 1947. When it became clear that there would be no place for her in jet-powered naval aviation, the *CV-6* was sold for scrap in July 1958.

The new *USS Enterprise*, actually the ninth naval ship to bear that name, was much larger than her predecessor, displacing nearly three times the tonnage. *CVAN-65* began her third Vietnam deployment in the Gulf of Tonkin in January 1968. In addition to the "Black Panthers" A6 Intruder Attack Squadron, VA-35, the air wing consisted of two squadrons each of F-4 Phantoms and A-4 Skyraiders. The deployment had been a costly one in terms of aircraft and aircrew losses, a fact clearly on the mind of Lincoln "Link" Hayes.

Hayes and Booth had flown out of the heavy weather first encountered within minutes of leaving the target area and were now less than thirty minutes from the deck of the "Big E". Some scattered lightning was still present, though it was not nearly as visible now in the early morning twilight. No moon this early morning; it had set shortly after dark, long before the start of their mission.

To Nat Booth, the view outside the canopy was serene. The lower layer of clouds displayed a beautiful and regular tuck and roll upholstery-like pattern as far as the eye could see.

But instantly and without prior warning, that state of calm was irrevocably broken. Nat announces to his B/N, "We've got some electrical problem—instruments jumping all over the place."

Seconds later, the aircraft began to shake violently.

Navigator Hayes calls out, "Have we been hit?"

"I don't think so. This area was supposed to be clear of enemy Triple-A and no indication we were lit up." Pilot Booth was stating that they had no advance warning of possible anti-aircraft artillery units in the area and that no enemy surface-to-air missile site had been illuminating the Intruder with tracking radar. Seconds later, a new situation had Nat's undivided attention.

"We've lost both engines!" The crew could feel the plane decelerate and begin to fall. Nat pointed the nose down to gain some airspeed and prevent a stall. With a tone of matter-of-fact bravado in the face of the most serious situation an aircrew will ever find itself, Nat makes an announcement. "Prepare to depart the aircraft!"

The brightening blue-gray sky was gone once the Intruder mushed downward into the lower bank of clouds. Suddenly, a blinding white light permeated the aircraft canopy from every direction at once. Eyes squinted in response to the overwhelming glare. Nat had heard firsthand stories from pilots who had experienced temporary flash blindness from lightning strikes, but this was not what he expected. The electrical outage occurred *before* the lightning glare. Besides, Nat's present visual impairment was not due to some neuro-visual response to an instantaneous flash, but because there was still a persistent penetrating brightness coming from outside the aircraft canopy. Nat called out, "What the hell is this—light?"

Several interminably long seconds passed. Shielding his eyes from the bright white, Nat could see that the needles in his instrument cluster had slowly begun to move from their pegged positions. "Looks like I've got power again! I'm going to try to restart the engines." He glanced to his right and noticed Link nodding in acknowledgement. Instantly, the engines came to life with a roar, and a reassuring sense of acceleration pressed them back into their seats. Link released the death grip he had held on the ejection seat handle ever since Nat first declared that abandoning the aircraft was an imminent possibility. Slowly at first, the blinding white began to subside, then vanished completely after several more seconds. Straight ahead Nat could see blue sky below a distant horizon. The aircraft was inverted, but flying level.

As the pilot rolled the aircraft over, Hayes calls out, "Weren't we just about to leave the coast? I don't see any water down there."

"I'm going to bring her down to get our bearings." Nat Booth brought the aircraft to the 2,000-foot level. The airspeed indicator read 250 knots.

"I don't see any jungle down there, either," Hayes announces over the ICS. The thick, tropical foliage they expected to see was gone. Instead, they saw open land, dirt trails and woods. "Look, there's a goddamn farmhouse—and a corn field!"

The pilot banked the aircraft for a better view below of the small white painted farmhouse, a weathered wooden barn nearby and split rail corrals containing a few horses and a half-dozen cows.

"I'm going in lower." The aircraft was vectored directly along a straight dirt road. The countryside below was now a patchwork of wooded groves separated by crop fields and farmhouses. No rice paddies, no villages with thatch-roofed huts.

Up ahead, the wooded area was more expansive and they could see what appeared to be a military encampment. In seconds they were upon it. Tents, horses, ancient artillery pieces, a few dozen soldiers in gray uniforms and some without shirts, but all with expressionless faces looking up at the Intruder as it screamed over them above the treetops.

Nat maneuvered the aircraft into a steep banked climb to the left and exclaimed with a tone of unbelief, "I gotta see that again. Either the boys in Three Corps are into Civil War reenactment, or something terribly strange has just happened."

SEVEN

THE SCENE ON THE GROUND was expectedly chaotic. Most of the men of the 26th Regiment North Carolina Troops encamped in the woods a few miles northwest of Gettysburg that morning were awakened by the whining roar of jet engines only seconds before the Intruder passed overhead. Some fifty men were already awake and about, tending to morning rituals. Not knowing what their eyes and ears were witnessing, fear had gripped them and most could do nothing but simply stand in place, stunned. A few ran for the cover of the trees. They could only assume that this was some kind of Yankee contraption designed to do them physical harm.

As the aircraft climbed to the southeast, a few soldiers aimed their muskets and fired. Fortunately for Hayes and Booth, the Intruder was a half-mile away before the first volleys resounded. Even the modern Intruder could have been vulnerable to a barrage of this archaic ground fire coming from a closer range.

Captain Wilson yelled at his men nearby, "Hold your fire now. Don't waste your ammunition. Sergeant, get over to Captain Manley's position and tell them to get ready to direct battery fire to the west at their highest possible elevation. That thing may be coming back over us."

Captain Manley was in charge of Company A of the 1st North Carolina Artillery. His men and weapons were situated on a hillock about 50 yards from Captain Wilson. The battery consisted of two 12-pounder howitzers and two 3-inch ordnance "rifles"; the dimension indicated the bore of the muzzle-loaded weapon. Before Sergeant Wyatt had covered half the distance to Company A at a dead run, Captain Manley had independently evaluated the threat and had already ordered his men to turn and line up the artillery pieces to fire in a direction due west. Each pair of guns was commanded by a lieutenant; each gun under the direction of a sergeant, with two corporals doing the heavy work.

The lieutenants barked out the order, "Load!" One man at each gun reached into his limber chest—the wooden ammunition storage box carried with each artillery caisson—and pulled out a round of ammunition. For the howitzers, this consisted of a hollow iron shell filled with black powder and a paper fuse to set it off. The two 3-inch rifles used a "Read Bolt" projectile with a copper sabot to engage the rifling of the cannon barrel upon firing. Each round included an attached powder bag so that the ammunition could be loaded quickly in a single motion. The rounds were placed in the muzzle bore and a rammer at each gun rammed the round down the length of the barrel.

"Set for maximum range." The order was called out and the gunner at each position adjusted the elevating screw of his gun to the maximum elevation, which was about 15 degrees from horizontal. At this elevation, the howitzers had a range of 1,100 yards and the 3-inch projectiles would travel over a mile. The order was passed to the men down range to clear out of the line of fire. Captain Manley could not be sure that the strange flying object would return for another pass, but if it did, he would be ready. With their greater range, the 3-inch rifles would be fired first, then the howitzers.

EIGHT

IT TOOK LIEUTENANT Commander Nat Booth two full minutes to complete the wide, 360-degree turn and approach the encampment a second time from the west. With the nose of the Intruder pointed down, the aircrew could now see many more men on the ground in the open scurrying about; looking for more substantial cover than was afforded by their canvas tents.

Lieutenant Hayes declared, "This is no reenactment. Those boys on that hill on the right look like they're ready to engage us. We should take 'em out."

"I'm not about to fire on anyone until I know who they are, or until they fire first," was the reply.

Just then they could see two puffs of smoke from the far right pair of cannon on the ground below. The artillery pieces rolled back on their six-foot high spoke wheels as the carriage of the guns absorbed the recoil. "Oh, shit!" Nat banked the aircraft hard to the left and pulled the nose up under maximum power. At that instant, they could see a third and fourth puff of smoke and seconds later an explosion in the air in front of the aircraft on the right side. The Intruder shuddered from the blast.

"I repeat, shit. Now we've really lost an engine."

"Damn." Lincoln Hayes spit out the word with disgust. "Fifty missions without a scratch and we're taken out with a lucky hit from a 19th century artillery piece!"

A large section of the right wing near the air intake was damaged. The aircraft was still climbing, but slowly now due to the loss of power.

"We have to punch out, Link. Eject, eject, now."

Lincoln Hayes did not hesitate. He pulled the face curtain ejection handle on his seat back. The rocket motor beneath him ignited and instantly propelled the seat and occupant through the Plexiglas canopy of the A-6. Nat looked over his shoulder in time to see Link's drogue chute deploy. He was about to eject himself when he noticed that the aircraft was quickly coming up upon a cluster of farm buildings. Although unlikely that the Intruder would hit one of them, Nat figured he still had time to direct the aircraft safely off to the right.

Seconds after Link's drogue chute had deployed to stabilize his descent, his main parachute opened and the seat with which he had been shot out of the aircraft fell away toward the ground. He could see the crippled Intruder continue to the east in a banked turn, but he was concerned because there was no sign of Nat's parachute. He could barely make out the letters "A" and "J" on tail of the aircraft, above and below the painted image of an attacking panther. On the ground below, a large contingent of soldiers set off in his direction. A moderate wind was pushing him further east and he estimated a landing point about a mile east of the encampment.

The Intruder was still in the air, now several miles away. Link could see the smoke, but it was too distant to tell whether or not his pilot had ejected safely. Suddenly, Link's heart sank as he saw an orange ball of flames; the Intruder had exploded in the sky.

Now with about a thousand feet left in his parachute descent, a dozen soldiers gathered directly below him. Half of them had their weapons up and trained upon Link. He saw one soldier, obviously in charge, reach out to pull down the barrel of one of the raised muskets, preventing the man from firing. But in the same instant Link saw the nearly simultaneous discharge from the other weapons. He felt a crashing blow on the right side of head. Link was straining to see, but he had only tunnel vision, and the tunnel was getting smaller and smaller. After a few seconds, his chin dropped to his chest; he was out cold.

NINE

I N AIR OPS aboard *Enterprise*, the mood was grim. Over an hour before, a brief message had been received from the A6, call sign 'Apple Two', reporting that Booth and Hayes had successfully completed their mission and were returning to the carrier, but nothing after that. Since then the weather conditions began to degrade precipitously and now the ship's air search radar displays showed only clutter covering the expected return path of the aircraft. They were way over due, but before a search and rescue operation could be mounted, all Navy air operations in the Gulf were cancelled due to the weather.

At noon, *Enterprise* received a message that the heavy rains had dissipated in the area south of the Intruder's target site. An HH-3E Sikorsky "Jolly Green" helicopter from the 40th Air Rescue/Recovery Squadron at Udorn Royal Thai AFB in Thailand was dispatched to the area. Two A-1E Skyraiders accompanied the helicopter to provide fire suppression, but after an hour of surveillance with no voice or beacon signals, the search and rescue operation was cancelled: The Air Force promised to try again the next day.

TEN

LINCOLN HAYES AWOKE to find a bayonet staring him in the face. He was flat on his back. One of the enlisted men behind him had unfastened his parachute, and two others were removing his helmet and facemask in a not-so-gentle manner. Link winced from the renewed pain in his head.

"Do you believe that? It's a black Yankee bastard!" The rebel troops had encountered black Union soldiers before, but usually as infantrymen. The soldiers around him crowded in closer. Those in the back craned their necks for a better view.

"And who the hell are you people, and why were you firing on me?" Link's brain had difficulty processing the notion that anyone who looked and sounded like Americans would fire upon his aircraft or his person.

The soldier holding the bayonet on Link drew the musket back and prepared to take a swing at Link's head with the butt of the weapon. Sergeant Wyatt grabbed the musket from behind before the man could swing, then looked directly at Lincoln Hayes. "You keep a civil tongue in your head, boy, or you will regret it."

Hayes was bewildered. By the time his brain had convinced himself that he was not dreaming, he decided it was best to keep further thoughts to himself until someone of higher rank appeared; someone who could sort this all out and provide a rational explanation.

The two men who had wrestled off his helmet pulled him to his feet, one under each arm. One had taken his Smith & Wesson 38 and began to examine it while the other searched his flight suit. Captain Wilson and Lieutenant Richardson arrived on the scene just as one of the men recovered Link's emergency radio.

"Look'ee this fine weapon, Cap'n." The soldier handed the revolver to Captain Wilson, grip first.

"What d'ya 'spose this is?" The other soldier was displaying Link's PRC-49 emergency radio.

"What's your name, soldier?" Captain Wilson stared at the strangely dressed black man in front of him.

"Lieutenant Lincoln Hayes, U.S. Navy." Hayes announces his name and rank, not even considering offering his military ID number. After all, the men around him looked and spoke like Americans.

"Lincoln? Say what?" One of the enlisted men spoke up. "I say we shoot him just for his name, Cap'n."

Captain Wilson ignored the remark. Link raised his right hand to the side of his head and touched the wound that still stung badly, but at least it had stopped bleeding. The blood on the side of his face was sticky.

"Navy, eh? So that was your ship then, Lieutenant?" Several of the soldiers chuckled at the Captain's words. "Where is the rest of your crew?"

Link didn't know what had happened to his pilot, but he didn't want to jeopardize Nat's chances to evade capture in the event that Nat had ejected in time. He also knew that the Captain was unlikely to believe that Link was the only one in the airplane.

"You saw the explosion. I'm the only one who got out."

"We'll see about that. Sergeant, get some of your men together and search the area where that thing came down. Bring back any bodies—or pieces—that you find. Someone get a dressing bandage on this man's head."

"Yes, sir!" Sergeant Wyatt selected four men from Company B and headed off to the east. Another soldier pulled a stained roll of gauze from a backpack and wrapped it around Link's head. When the man had finished covering the wound, the Captain ordered everyone back to camp. He walked alongside his captive, holding Link's Smith & Wesson. Two soldiers directly behind them held their muskets at waist level, directed at Link's back. The rest of the assemblage followed behind.

Link turned his head to the Captain and asked, "Seriously, sir, who are you guys?"

Captain Wilson responded, "You have been captured by a detachment of the North Carolina, 26th Regiment, Confederate States of America. And I am Captain Wilson."

As he walked, Link began to consider all of the sights and sounds that he had witnessed since he and Nat Booth had been fired upon less than an hour before: the rural American countryside, horse drawn artillery pieces with spoke wheels, awestruck men in strange gray uniforms carrying muskets, and the sincerely sounding words of the very young officer walking beside him. He didn't know exactly when or where he was, but of this he was certain: This was not Southeast Asia on the day after yesterday.

ELEVEN

THE 26TH REGIMENT North Carolina command post consisted of three tents surrounding a sprawling oak tree. Two sentries stood guard at the entrance to the largest tent. Inside, Captain Wilson poured coffee into a china cup from a silver server and offered it to his prisoner who sat at a square wooden table.

"Thank you, Captain." Link was grateful for the offering.

"You know, Lieutenant, that I could have you shot as a spy, even here in Union territory." This was Link's first definite clue as to where he was. His mind raced back to the coursework on military history and strategy from his days at the Naval Academy at Annapolis; then even further back to high school American History. God, how he wished he had paid more attention in class. But he remembered that the South had not made many forays into the Northern States during the war. He guessed he was near Gettysburg, and since his captors did not seem to be in retreat, but appeared to be preparing for a fight, he presumed that the battle had not yet begun. If he was correct, the year was 1863, but he couldn't remember the month or day. Not that it mattered much. It was enough to know that he was a long ways in distance and time from where he wanted to be. He needed to escape from his captors, find his pilot, and get back—or rather, forward—to 1968 and the *USS Enterprise*.

"We were over the town—"

The Captain interrupted, "You mean, Cashtown? Or Gettysburg?"

"Yes—Gettysburg—and we got off course and lost our bearings. When we made that second pass over your camp, we were just trying to figure out where we were and how to get home."

"I see. And your mission?"

"I guess you could call it—uh—advanced training."

"And you expect me to believe that you were not sent by General Meade—maybe to destroy the entire regiment with that flying machine? Or to find our troop positions and strength and probe for weaknesses in our lines?" The vein in Captain Wilson's forehead was bulging; he was losing his temper. Link raised his cup to his lips, making no attempt to respond to the tirade. Apparent that he was not going to get an admission from his captive, the Captain's voice became more subdued. "Tell me, then, more about your ship."

"How about some more coffee?" Link held out the empty cup and the Captain filled it. Link had decided in the last few minutes that his duty as a captured U.S. Naval aviator not to volunteer information or cooperate with the enemy in any way did not entirely apply in this case. He would continue to claim that he was the only survivor of the downed aircraft in an effort to not compromise Nat's chances to evade capture in the event that he was still alive. Other than that, Link didn't believe that anything he could tell the Captain would constitute collaboration with the enemy.

"Look, Captain, I won't try to blow smoke up your ass."

"Pardon me?"

"I'm not going to lie to you. My ship, as you call it, is a U.S. Navy A6 attack aircraft. The Grumman Aircraft

Company in Bethpage, New York, made it. It flies over 600 miles per hour and burns JP5—that's kerosene. It takes off and lands on a large flat top ship named the *USS Enterprise* which itself runs on steam generated in a nuclear reactor. This morning, I was on a bombing mission in support of the war in Vietnam, a country on the other side of the world. It was June 30th; the year was 1968. Do you hear that? Nineteen-sixty-eight! We were on our way back to our ship and ended up here. I don't know how or why it happened. I have nothing to do with this war you are engaged in. I am not your enemy; I just want to get back home." The words were blurted out in a staccato stream of conviction.

"Lieutenant, excuse me but I failed to understand even half of the words you just rattled off." Wilson, nonplussed, simply shook his head. He didn't know if the man across the table from him was a liar, or just plain crazy. The third possibility, that Lincoln Hayes was truly a man from the future, was utterly out of the question. Leaning toward the notion of a mental condition, perhaps aggravated by the head wound, Captain Wilson decides to humor his captive. "If what you say is true, then you should be able to tell me if we can expect to do battle with the Yankees here at Gettysburg soon, and if so, what the outcome of this battle will be. In fact, you should be able to tell me when and how this whole war will end."

Link could have blown off the comment as rhetorical sarcasm, but instead he was determined to answer the Captain as best he could. "History was not my strongest subject in school, but as I recall, both sides sustained terrible losses at Gettysburg. Your forces will end up in retreat. The Battle of Gettysburg will be the turning point of the war against the South. In less than two years, General Robert E. Lee will surrender to General Grant at a place called Appomattox Court House. Despite all your efforts, America will remain as one country and my people—black people everywhere in America will finally be—well, almost—free."

Captain Wilson, now standing, picked up Link's Smith & Wesson from the side table just inside the entrance to the tent. Examining the barrel and spinning the cylinder, he reflects, "This piece wasn't made by any arms factory in this country, North or South. And I've never seen nor heard of anything like that craft you were flying in." Captain Wilson pointed at Link's chest. "Never seen a suit of clothes like that, either. Very fine fabric—and your boots are strange, too. But your story, Lieutenant, is beyond belief." Captain Wilson decided not to divulge his true personal expectations about the war as he continued. "And your prognostication concerning the outcome of this war cannot be supported by the facts. Our forces have performed remarkably well. Despite the strength of the enemy, we have bested them in nearly every engagement. You are clearly tiring of the fight."

"As I stated earlier, Captain, this is not my fight, but the outcome that I described will be clear to every survivor of the Gettysburg battle that is about to begin."

Captain Wilson stared across the table at his prisoner; the prediction on the war, at least, sounded plausible. "You mentioned earlier about some war you were fighting . . . ?"

"Yes, in Vietnam."

"Where is this place, Vee-et-nahm, and why would America be fighting there?"

"It's a country south of China, near the Sea of Japan. During this century—your century—it came under the control of the French. It was called French Indo-China. After the big war in the 1940s, the Vietnamese wanted their independence from France, but our president screwed them over and supported the French instead. The northern half of the country aligned itself with our enemies, China and Russia, and drove out the French in 1954. After the French were gone, people in the North wanted to bring the South under their control—to make one country, but South Vietnam wanted no part of it. A civil war was the result, and we sided with the South." The words were hardly out of Link's mouth when he noticed a curious expression suddenly appearing on Captain Wilson's face.

"That's pretty funny, Hayes. You are telling me that the United States Government, your government, will send men to fight on the other side of the world to help some folks in the South country, who are trying to be independent from the North country?"

The discussion was interrupted by an aide, who brought in the Captain's lunch: a bowl of beef and vegetable stew and a large piece of corn bread. "Don't be rude, Johnson, please bring some lunch for our guest—and more coffee, please." The aide acknowledged the order and set out immediately to bring back a similar meal for Link Hayes.

"Thank you, Captain. But regarding your comment, the situation is simply not the same. In Vietnam, we are dealing with a despotic government that has no respect for human rights, trying to extend their power over people in the South. In the American Civil War, the Confederacy was—or is—the despotic government; having no regard for the human rights of black people."

Captain Wilson began to laugh. "You need to check your history, Lieutenant. The President of the United States has issued something called the E-man-ci-pa-tion Proclamation. Slavery is no longer permitted in the South, according to your President Lincoln. Of course, in the Union states of Missouri, Kentucky, Maryland, and Delaware, nothing has changed. Slavery is still the law of the land."

Lincoln Hayes felt his ears getting hot. Captain Wilson made a good point. The Emancipation Proclamation issued by Abraham Lincoln freed the slaves only in those states that had seceded from the Union. The North could not risk driving the four "border" states into the Southern

Confederacy given the uncertainty surrounding the outcome
of the war that prevailed at the time the proclamation was
issued.

"To your credit, Cap'n, a hundred years from now
Americans will still be debating whether the war you are now
engaged in was fought over the issue of slavery, or over
state's rights."

"Here! Here! But now, tell me, how is *your* war
progressing?"

Link put his spoon down and placed both hands, palms
down and fingers outstretched, on the table. He took a deep
breath. "Not as good as we hoped. Americans have been in
Vietnam for about six years, with a big build up of forces
starting three years ago. We can't seem to stop the movement
and resupply of men and matériel coming from the North.
Not to mention plenty of folks in the South who wave at us
in the daytime, then try to kill us at night. Lots of turmoil at
home with demonstrations against the war nearly every day.
Many, even in the military, are asking the question, 'If the
South Vietnamese don't give a shit about their country, then
why should we?' Three months ago, President Johnson
announced that he would serve only one term because of the
unrest. He would not be running for reelection."

"With any luck—perhaps with a well-aimed bullet—
Lincoln will likewise not be running for President in sixty-
four and I can go home to my family in a free South!"
Lincoln Hayes winced at the words—not simply due to the
prescience of the Captain's offhand remark regarding the
President—but because only three weeks earlier, Link had
been shocked and saddened to learn that Bobby Kennedy,
someone for whom Link had the greatest admiration, had
been assassinated in Los Angeles.

As they finished the stew and corn bread, Captain
Wilson brought a close to their conversation. "You know, I
find you to be a likeable fellow, Mr. Hayes, for a person of

the Negro race, and a Yankee to boot. Reflecting upon your story, I have no doubt now that you believe what you're telling me as truth. I can detect no hint of insincerity in your words, but my considered opinion, sir, is that you are mentally deranged. Hopefully, it is only a temporary condition, caused by the head wound that you sustained. Perhaps we can speak again, when you are feeling better."

One of the sentries entered the tent. Saluting the Captain, he announces, "Sergeant Wyatt is outside, Captain, and has a report for you."

"Send him in. And hold that wagon with Private Cooper for a minute. I want our prisoner sent back to the supply camp also."

A stray musket round fired during the artillery engagement against the Intruder had hit Private Cooper, now lying outside in the bed of a horse-drawn wagon. His stomach wound didn't look particularly bad, but in most cases like his, the available medical treatment was of little help. Victims of such injuries usually lingered for a day or two and then died.

The guard left the tent and Sergeant Wyatt entered. He looked at the seated prisoner, then at the Captain.

"You may speak freely, Sergeant. What did you find?"

"It looks like that thing broke up over the creek 'bout a half-mile beyond the pond. Didn't find much but small pieces of metal." Sergeant Wyatt emptied the contents of a backpack on the floor of the tent. Out spilled a collection of aircraft parts including pieces of the instrument cluster and scraps of partially melted Plexiglas. "This is typical of what we found, but there may be some bigger pieces under the water. No sign of anyone dead or alive. We had to quit lookin' when we saw a Yankee patrol comin' over the ridge." Captain Wilson bent down, looking closely at the collection of junk, and picked up the torn portion of a map displaying Laos, North Vietnam and the Gulf of Tonkin.

"Very well, Sergeant. Private Cooper is in the wagon outside. See if the doctors can do anything for him back at the supply area. I want you to take Lieutenant Hayes with you and have someone look at his head wound; then lock him up." He paused, then added, "And have a good day, Lieutenant." As Lincoln Hayes was escorted out of the tent, he nodded at the Captain. When he was alone, Captain Wilson unfolded the map on his table and began to study it.

TWELVE

PROFESSOR ATWOOD and Amanda Marshall had sat silently for the last half-hour while they listened to Commander Hayes relate his tale.

Roger spoke up. "You are telling us that you were sitting in a tent outside of Gettysburg in 1863 with an officer who was about to participate in one of the greatest military engagements of all time?"

"I warned you that you wouldn't believe it, and as I suggested, the Captain really wasn't buying my story either. As for me, all I could think about was how I could get out of there. I could see no upside to being a black man stuck in the year 1863. Especially one held as a spy by the Confederate Army."

"Commander, it's a remarkable story and—you are correct—impossible to believe, but. . . " Amanda and the Commander were waiting for Roger to finish his sentence, but his thoughts seemed to have escaped him, and he simply shook his head. Finally, Amanda prompted him.

"But, what, Roger?"

"I just don't know. Ever since we found that helmet, I've tried to consider every plausible explanation for how it got there. I hate to admit it, but so far, the Commander's explanation is the most reasonable—if we can rule out a hoax!"

For Amanda, there was no doubt in her mind. She believed the Commander's story. Amanda asked him, "You must have been back at Gettysburg since then. Were you able to reconstruct where any of this took place?"

Lincoln Hayes walked over to the china cabinet in the dining room and removed a map from the top drawer, unfolded it carefully and placed it on the table. "After I got home I made several trips, but it was hard to identify any landmarks. Things can change a lot in a hundred plus years."

Hayes stood over the map and pointed at some pencil markings. "This is where I baled out of the aircraft, and here is where I think it came down. A creek runs through the area, but I couldn't find any pond there. The artillery detachment was camped on a small hill. I marked it with an 'H'." Hayes then pointed at another location on the map. "The infantry command post with the three tents must have been about here."

Professor Atwood added, "And that is just about where we found the trunk with your helmet. What is *this* area?" Roger was pointing to an 'x' marked on the map about 5 miles west of the command post location.

For the first time since they met him that morning, Commander Hayes smiled broadly. "That's where I was rescued. When we left the command post, they bound up my hands with rope and put me in the wagon next to the driver. The Sergeant was in the back of the wagon with the kid who was hurt. He was wrapped up in a blanket and was talking, but he looked pretty bad. One of the sentries, a corporal from the command post was back there also. After a few minutes, it became clear that the sentry was the kid's brother."

"The Corporal was really upset and was trying to comfort his brother, but the way he was talking to him—well, it was obvious that the kid wasn't very bright. Probably shouldn't have been in the army at all. The sentry wasn't very happy with me, either. He clearly blamed me for his brother's condition. The Captain had kept my side arm and helmet when we left the command post, but I was happy to see that the Sergeant had brought along my survival pack, including my emergency radio and pen flares. We traveled for about half an hour. The driver was pretty talkative. I found out from him that it was June 29th."

Amanda spoke up. "Something like 105 years before you returned from your air mission?"

"One hundred and five years, almost precisely to the day. In researching it when I got home, I learned that it was just two days before the start of the Battle of Gettysburg." Roger nodded in agreement. "When they stopped the wagon, we were at some rear supply area, but it was pretty much empty. Most of troops and equipment must have been already deployed to the south and east in anticipation of the upcoming fight. I saw a field hospital and a makeshift brig— some cages with iron bars—similar to the animal cages that a traveling circus might use. They hadn't even taken them off the wagons yet. It was clear that one was meant for me. They took me inside the field hospital and one of the medics put a clean dressing on my head. A doctor was still looking at the kid when they took me outside and locked me up."

THIRTEEN

Link had been left to himself, so that exploring the bars and floor of his cage for escape possibilities had been easy. Unfortunately, he had found none. An hour earlier, he had been given a dinner of cold beans and hardtack. The beans needed salt, and the two small pieces of fat back pork they had been cooked with smelled old. He wasn't particularly hungry and ate almost none of it.

It was now an hour before sunset and Lincoln Hayes was sitting on the floor of the cell, leaning his back against the iron bars. He had nearly dozed off when he suddenly felt two hands around his neck, reaching in from outside the bars. After a few moments of struggle, he was able to free himself. He rushed to the other side of the cage to get beyond the man's reach. Holding his throat, he turned to face his assailant.

It was Corporal Cooper, the sentry who had accompanied them from the command post, brother of the injured soldier. "You black bastard. Doc says my brother will mos' likely be dead by sunup. If he dies, I'm gonna put a bullet in your head!"

Link thought quickly about how he might defuse this situation. He knew that he could use an ally far more than another enemy if he was ever to get out of this place. "Hold on a minute, Corporal. I can help your brother."

"How's that?"

"You were outside the Captain's tent when we were talking. You had to hear what I was telling him."

"I heer'd you. Sounded like bullshit to me."

"Trust me. It wasn't bullshit. You need to believe it. If you can, you gotta believe that there are people out there looking for me. People who are smart enough to help your brother and save his life."

The corporal was almost crying now. "But he's gut shot. Doc says he won't make it."

"You're talking about 1860s medicine, man. Doctors in my time can cure pneumonia. They operate on hearts and lungs. They are learning how to transplant kidneys and other organs from one person to another. You don't think they can fix a simple stomach wound?"

The corporal stared at Link through the bars for a minute. "I'll help you if you think you can save him, but if you're lyin', I swear I'll kill you."

"I'm not lying, honest. Now listen. The people out there looking for me don't know where I am. I need my radio, that black thing that your Sergeant was holding, so I can talk with them. Kind of like a wireless telegraph. Find it and bring it back here. Bring back the whole survival bag that the Sergeant was holding in the wagon."

It was ten minutes before the Corporal returned. The sun had fallen behind some hills in the distance to the west, but the sky was still a bright blue. Corporal Cooper had the survival pack with him as well as a three-foot long iron bar.

"All right. Now, give me that piece of iron so I can get out of here." Link was reaching for the bar that the Corporal was holding.

"Not so fast Lieutenant. Let's see if yer' friends show up first." The Corporal threw the iron bar under the wagon, then handed the survival bag through the bars to Link. Hayes opened it and pulled out the emergency radio.

"Did you press any buttons on this thing? It's been on."

"That's how I found it. It was next to the bag. I didn't press nothin'. I just put it in the bag and brought it here, jus' like you said to."

Aside from the radio, the bag was empty. Food, water and medicine packs were missing. No pen flares. Worst of all, the spare batteries for the emergency radio were gone. He had no idea how long the radio had been on or how much power was left. It would be pure luck if a friendly aircraft in the vicinity happened to detect the beacon signal coming from the radio during the time it had been activated.

Link switched on the radio transmitter to place a call. "This is Apple Two Bravo, over." The 'Bravo' added to the aircraft call sign would indicate to any friendlies that might be monitoring that it was the Intruder's Bombardier/Navigator placing the emergency call. A pilot making the call would use 'Alpha' instead. Switching to receive mode, Link could hear only static from the small radio speaker. After a few seconds, he repeated the call. This time, he got a garbled response in English mixed with the static.

"Did you hear that? They are close, Corporal. Give me that iron bar." Link pointed to an abandoned camp fire about thirty yards away. "Then go get your brother and meet me over by that fire."

By the time that the Corporal had reached the field hospital tent, Link had already broken open the door of the cage that had held him captive. He was on the ground, headed toward the campfire and in communication with the aircrew of the rescue helicopter, when he first heard the muffled beat of the gas turbine engine and pulsing of the chopper blades. Link picked up a burning branch from the fire and waved it over his head. He couldn't yet see the helicopter, but he could tell the direction from which it was coming. Behind him, Link could now see the Corporal struggling to support his wounded brother as they hobbled slowly toward Link's position.

When they stopped to rest, Link ran back to help.

"He can't walk no more." The wounded man had passed out.

"Then we'll carry him."

"Lieutenant, you gotta promise me. If you can't bring him back here to me, you gotta promise that you'll take care of my brother. You know, he's not very bright. He can't be left to hisself."

When they reached the fire, they placed the wounded man gently on the ground, covering his long john underwear with the army blanket.

"I'll do what I can to get him back to you, but if I can't, I will look after him. I promise. But what about you? They're going to know you helped me escape. You're going to be in big trouble."

"Yeah, I know. I'm gonna have to skedaddle outta here. I've got some relatives up in Canada, so I guess I'll head north."

"Here . . ." Link reached into his survival bag and pulled back the false bottom lining to reveal three one-ounce South African Krugerrands. The gold in the aircrew survival packs was intended as down payment to locals who might be willing to help a downed airman in exchange for fifty ounces of pure gold as promised by the United States Government. Normally, the survival pack contained six half-ounce gold bars, but the Treasury Department had been unable to keep up with the demand from the Department of Defense and had recently begun substituting the more readily available bullion coins that could be purchased from gold dealers. "Take these, they may help you out of a jam some day. I won't need them."

The Jolly Green made one circle over the campfire and proceeded to come down in an area clear of trees about twenty yards away. By now, the noise had attracted the attention of the few personnel remaining at the camp. Fortunately, these people were not armed combatants. Mostly doctors, medics and supply clerks. Several had poked their heads out of tents to see what was going on, but no one approached the landing zone. Despite their curiosity, they seemed content to watch from the relative safety provided by distance. A few men closest to the landing zone bolted out of fear from the noise and blowing dust and wind created by the chopper blades.

The Corporal knelt down and stroked his brother's forehead, then looked up at Link. "Good luck, Lieutenant."

"Good luck to you, Corporal. And thanks for your help." The Corporal helped Link lift the wounded man from the ground and over one of Link's shoulders. The crew of the Jolly Green was gesturing for them to come quickly. In less than a minute, they were at the open side door of the Jolly Green.

Two crewmen had taken the wounded man off Link's shoulder and brought him inside the craft. Another had seen the bloodstained bandage on the man's torso and reached for an IV bottle.

As Link scrambled into the helicopter, one of the crewmen shouted into Link's ear. "Is this your pilot, Commander?"

Link shook his head and shouted back. "No. He's still out there. We've got to find him."

"Who is he and what the hell is this place?"

"His name is Junius." Lincoln Hayes did not answer the second question. As the chopper began to lift off, Link noticed that the door gunner had redirected his fifty-caliber machine gun in the direction of a half-dozen Confederate soldiers, now about 50 yards away, running directly toward the Jolly Green with muskets raised. The men had apparently just arrived to the rear encampment area.

Link tapped on the gunner's shoulder and shouted, "They're friendlies, but they don't know who we are." The gunner gave Link a thumbs-up signal, then aimed his gun at a small stand of pine trees just ahead and slightly to the right of the advancing soldiers. The ten-second burst from the 750 round per minute GAU-15 turned the trees into a hail of toothpicks. Hardly without breaking stride, the Confederate soldiers turned on their heel and beat feet in the opposite direction. By the time they stopped running, the helicopter was nearly out of sight.

Junius was awake again. Eyes flashing wildly, he was clearly frightened by the foreign surroundings, the motion and sound of the helicopter, and the men in the strangely colored uniforms and helmets around him. Link reached out and held his hand and smiled. After a minute, the wounded soldier seemed calmer, looked into Link's eyes and smiled weakly back at him.

FOURTEEN

PROFESSOR ATWOOD ROSE from his chair and walked to the window. "That's Junius?"

"Yes, it is. If you ask, he'll tell you he was born in '44. Just don't ask him what century. Junius is the only living Civil War veteran and the oldest—ever."

"How did you get him here? And how did you manage to keep this all quiet?"

"Don't be so impatient, Roger." Amanda was insistent. "Let the Commander tell his story!"

"It turned out that the Jolly Green crew wasn't even looking for us." Commander Hayes continued, putting off Roger's questions. "They were returning to base from an unsuccessful search and rescue when they encountered the same blinding white light and loss of power that Nat and I flew into. They didn't know I was there until they got my radio call."

"What about Nat, your pilot?"

"They wouldn't even look for him. Without receiving an emergency beacon signal and being low on fuel, they said they would try again the next morning. The chopper pilot headed back in the same direction they came after hearing my call. We flew out in the same way they flew in, white light and all. But we never found Nat. His official status is still 'Missing in Action, Presumed Dead'. I heard that when the chopper crew headed back to the same area the next day, they never returned."

"What about Junius?"

"The surgeons at the Air Force Base in Thailand worked on him immediately. He was conscious the next day, but was pretty overwhelmed by his surroundings. They tried to debrief him to find out how he had gotten separated from his unit—they assumed he was Army—but they didn't learn much. He kept on insisting he was part of the 26th North Carolina Regiment." Reflecting on the image in his head of Junius being debriefed, Link began to smile. "Plenty of Army and Marine units had MIAs unaccounted for, but no Americans with the name Junius Cooper had ever been in-country Vietnam. They didn't diagnose his retardation—just assumed that he was suffering from Posttraumatic Stress Disorder. I think they suspected he was a deserter and that Junius was a made-up name, but that the PTSD was real. After three weeks, he was shipped off to the mental ward at the Salem VA Medical Center, here in Virginia."

"And when you were debriefed, you told your story like you're telling us now?"

"I started to, but the looks I was getting from the medical staff suggested that they were about to pack me off to a psychiatric hospital. At that point, I decided to shut up, which was probably a good decision. When the chopper crew didn't return from their next day's mission, the only one who could corroborate any part of my story was Junius. Except for the bullet."

"You mean the bullet that hit Junius?"

"Correct. It was a Minie ball. The surgeon who operated on Junius knew it wasn't from a VC weapon and asked me about it, but nothing more came of it. At the time, I figured it wasn't unreasonable to tell the military folks that I simply couldn't remember anything that happened from the time I ejected from the Intruder until we were over Thailand in the Jolly Green. I had suffered a pretty severe concussion from the head wound. I decided to keep quiet at least until someone else or some event could verify my story." He stuffed both hands into his trouser pockets and stared blankly at the floor for a few seconds. "That didn't happen until today."

"I was back on the *Enterprise* before they shipped Junius stateside, but I never flew another mission. We headed home a few days later." Commander Hayes interrupted himself. "I'm sorry. I didn't realize that I had been rattling on for so long. Would you like some coffee? I still have the habit from the Navy—I drink it all day long."

"I'd love some," Amanda replied. They rose and followed Link into the kitchen. Commander Hayes continued his story as he opened the cabinet door above the coffee maker and took down three cups.

"I didn't stay in the Navy after my tour was over—they promoted me to Lieutenant Commander but I got out anyway. Junius had been at the VA for six months before I could visit him for the first time. I signed in as his cousin. You know, they actually believed me. After a few weeks they let me bring him home on weekends. Eventually, I applied for full time guardianship and they discharged him into my care. That was a long time ago."

Amanda stretched her arm towards Link and touched him on the shoulder. "You made quite a commitment—to take in Junius."

"Well, hell, you know his brother saved my butt, and I made a promise. Besides, look how he keeps this place up for me."

Roger sat down again next to Amanda. "And you never told anyone this story before today?"

"Just my wife, Sarah." Link looked through the doorway to the dining room picture on the far wall. "She passed away four years ago. We never had any kids. When I got back to the States after Nam I went to see Nat's parents. They were living here in Richmond. But I didn't get a chance to say much; Nat's father was difficult to deal with. The family was pretty broken up about Nat being missing in action. I never tried to see them again. Guess I convinced myself that there wasn't much I could tell them that would be of any help in coping with their grief."

Roger and Amanda followed Link back to the dining room and seated themselves at the table. Link continued, "I had a friend that I went to school with. He's worked in the Physics Department at Princeton for the last twenty years. So, I asked him once, in general terms, how something like this might happen—how someone might wake up one day and find himself in another time and place. He told me that it would probably never be possible to travel to some specific selected point in time at will—you know—like in *The Time Machine*. But a lot of scientists believe that two different locations and times could in theory collapse on one another, occupying the same space-time coordinates for a few seconds, or maybe even longer—hours or a few days. Most likely these are totally random occurrences and not predictable in advance. He called them 'convergence events' and that they actually may be fairly common. A typical case might be something like a location in the Atlantic Ocean in the present day converging with a small area of the Pacific from 80,000 years ago. So in most cases, it wouldn't be particularly noteworthy. He explained it as two event horizons folding back upon one another, resulting in the convergence event."

Link continued, "I've taken a fair amount of science and mathematics in my day, but this stuff was way over my head. My friend claimed that these convergence events might explain why we sometimes find fossils of plants and animals where we know they couldn't have existed. Or why there are documented cases of people who speak in extinct dialects or who have a sense of being part of an ancient culture or past historical event. They could be simply recalling a past time that they will actually experience some time in their future."

Link Hayes paused for a few seconds. "I don't even understand what the hell I just said." He smiled briefly before his expression turned serious once again. "I've put all of this behind me for a lot of years. I guess my only real regret is not knowing what happened to Nat Booth."

FIFTEEN

IT WAS TWO WEEKS since the meeting at the home of Lincoln Hayes. Roger Atwood leaned closer to the bathroom mirror, hands gripping both sides of the sink rim. He felt terrible. He tried to recall how many times in the past he had disproved that urban legend—the one about how you could avoid a hangover as long as you stuck to one kind of alcohol. This was only the second or third time as Roger wasn't much of a drinker. Johnnie Walker on the rocks with plain water was all he had consumed the night before. Just too much of it, now it was clear. He felt as down as he had the night before, but this morning the slightest movement of his head increased the intensity of the throbbing inside his skull, contributing to the depression he felt in his gut.

Roger was not unfamiliar with bouts of depression. He had suffered through at least one short spell nearly every year since he had turned thirty. They usually occurred on a predictable schedule—around the Christmas holidays. After the first episode, the clinical psychologist suggested that the cause was some repressed disappointment over a bike or some Christmas toy he never got as a kid. This immediately dismissed as crap and Roger didn't go back after the third session. He continued taking the prescribed antidepressant medication for a couple of months, but eventually threw the pills away because they dulled his brain. He would lose his concentration during lectures; often forgetting some point he was trying to make. Fortunately, the episodes never lasted more than a few weeks and he could more or less count on being free of the problem for the next several months, until the next December.

After the fourth or fifth year of this cycle, Roger had diagnosed his own ailment: Seasonal Affective Disorder. He was relatively successful in combating it each year by leaving Pennsylvania as soon as possible after the end of Fall Semester and spending two weeks in Florida, or the Bahamas, or Mexico or one of a number of other locations where he could count on spending several hours each day undergoing self-prescribed solar therapy.

So this bout of depression that started two days earlier in the middle of June had blind-sided him. It caused him to have doubts about the accuracy of the self-diagnosis in which he had come to take some comfort over the last several years. True, he was lonely since Amanda had left town a week ago, but she was expected back today. The only other thing he could put his finger on was a pervasive unsettled feeling concerning the unusual—no, incredible—events surrounding Lincoln Hayes. It was a simple problem. If he were an independent third party hearing of the discovery of Link's helmet at Gettysburg, even seeing the actual helmet and then listening to Hayes relate his story; there would be no question in his mind that he was being subjected to a hoax. An elaborate one, yes, but a hoax nonetheless. No other explanation made any sense until he reminded himself that it was Amanda and the man with the bloodshot eyes staring back from the mirror who had unearthed the airman's helmet at the excavation site. It was no hoax; it was an irreconcilable truth.

Added to the mix was the guilt he was feeling over his handling of the discovery he and Amanda had made at the Park. Following the ranger's instructions, he delivered the footlocker to the park office on the Monday morning following the discovery. His guilt feelings were due to the fact that he had neglected to mention to anyone that he had found anything significant *inside* the footlocker. At the time, he justified his decision on the grounds that an airman's helmet was not a Civil War artifact. Now it sounded like a lame excuse and he wondered how it would all play out when and if this remarkable story ever became public. Clearly, it would be tough to explain. It might even hurt his career. Roger frowned at the face in the mirror.

He splashed some cold water into his eyes and shuffled to the kitchen. As the Starbucks coffee beans were being pulverized in the grinder, Roger thought about Amanda and smiled. Today, he would feel better.

By the time Roger had returned from the driveway with the Sunday paper, the phone was ringing. It was Lincoln Hayes.

"Roger, five minutes ago I got a call from Nat's mother. Christ, I thought she was dead—she's gotta be almost ninety."

"And . . . ?"

"And—she said she has some information about Nat and asked me if I knew anyone who could do some historical research for her. I told her about you and Amanda. She asked if we could come over for lunch tomorrow."

"Just a minute, Link." Roger put down the phone. He hadn't heard Amanda come in the house and didn't expect her back this early. He put his arms around her. "I missed you."

"Me, too. And I think I may have found Nat Booth."

"You what?"

"I'll tell you in a minute. Is that Link on the phone?"

"Yes. He wants us to meet with Nat's mother tomorrow. Can you make it?"

"Of course."

Roger retrieved the phone and spoke to Link. "Sorry for the interruption. Amanda just got back in town. We can pick you up. How about eleven?"

"See you at eleven then."

Roger hung up the phone. "Sit down and tell me. Where did you find out about Nat?"

"In Elmira. My parent's new house in Millport is just off Highway 14 north of the town, near what was once the federal prison camp. It's long gone, but all of the records from the camp were transferred to Woodlawn National Cemetery nearby. I stopped there yesterday and checked out the archives. They have a ton of records and I learned that most of the Confederate prisoners captured at Gettysburg were sent to a camp at Point Lookout, Maryland. Later, they were transferred to the Federal Prison at Elmira. They had a roster of prisoners. Let me show you what I found."

Amanda removed a folded piece of paper from her purse. It was a photocopy of a page from the roster, containing perhaps twenty-five names showing the rank, unit and occasional notes. About a fourth of names had a notation that the prisoner had died while incarcerated with the date of death. Near the bottom of the list, Roger saw the name he was looking for:

BOOTH, CPL. NATHANIEL W.
2ND VIRGINIA INFANTRY
ESCAPED APRIL 11, 1865

"Can we be sure that this is him? What about the middle initial?"

"I guess we'll find out tomorrow," Amanda offered while Roger continued to stare at the paper.

"What are you thinking, Roger?"

"Something bothers me about this notation. The war was essentially over on April 9th, the day General Lee surrendered. Surely the news would have reached the prison camp within a day or two. Why would a prisoner risk getting shot by attempting to escape on April 11th when he could have counted on being released within maybe a few more weeks?"

SIXTEEN

THE TEMPORARY STOCKADE built near the railhead at Gettysburg was nearly empty by the end of summer 1863. The prisoner train had made a dozen round trips beginning in August, transporting Confederate prisoners from the Gettysburg battle to their new home: the Point Lookout Prisoner of War Camp in Maryland, also known as Camp Hoffman. Among the remaining 200 prisoners who would be herded into boxcars and open flat cars when the train arrived at noon was a young man in a Confederate Corporal's uniform, Nathaniel W. Booth. Another group— maybe a hundred men, more or less—was not scheduled to make the trip. They were too weak, injured or sick and would probably languish in the filthy stockade infirmary until they died.

Nat sat on the dirt in the open area of the stockade. The guards posted outside the fence line carried Whitworth rifles with instructions to kill any prisoner who ventured into the forbidden zone near the stockade fence. A Union cook stood with one foot on an empty powder barrel with a five-string banjo, picking out a rendition of *Rally 'Round the Flag*. He had been working on the tune almost continuously during the last week whenever his mess duties permitted and now had it down pretty well.

Nat had stopped asking about Lincoln Hayes. One of the prisoners who had been in the first group sent to Point Lookout was among the soldiers present when Link was captured, but he could offer no additional information. No one else Nat encountered knew anything about a tall black man in strange clothes who fell out of the sky on the day before the battle began. For the hundredth time, Nat recalled to himself the sequence of events that led him to his present remarkable situation: He was a prisoner of war, held captive by the government of the very same country that would send him off to battle a hundred years from now.

Nat had ejected from the aircraft only seconds before the Intruder exploded. After struggling to get out of the marshy pond into which he landed, he tried to raise Link with his emergency radio, but with no success. The radio was operating intermittently for a few minutes after Nat got out of the water, but then died completely. Looking for the best close cover, he disappeared into a large wooded area on some higher ground nearby and watched as the search team dispatched by Captain Wilson scoured the area around the creek. The soldiers had to walk past the pond. Fortunately, they didn't notice the footprints that Nat had left in the mud.

The search team stopped frequently to examine pieces of the aircraft, but most of what they found were small sections of the aluminum skin. Nat couldn't see any large pieces of the Intruder. The debris pattern on both sides of the creek suggested that the engines and tail assembly, if they were still intact, were probably under water. Nat watched as the search team hotfooted out of the area upon seeing the Union patrol approach their position. The patrol moved into the same location investigated by their Confederate counterparts. But after a few minutes, they too left the area, disappearing behind a ridge to the east.

Nat felt secure within his protective thicket inside the dense woods. He remarked to himself how these surroundings seemed far more comforting than a Vietnam jungle would under otherwise similar circumstances. A gray squirrel on an overhanging oak limb above his position scolded loudly, but Nat was unconcerned as the only visible human activity was the military encampment in the distance to the west. The woods behind him appeared at least a hundred yards deep. The sense of security he felt, albeit relative, allowed Nat to clear his mind and evaluate his predicament and options.

On the plus side, he was uninjured. He had food and water in his survival kit and a safe place to hide. For negatives, he didn't know where Link was or what might have happened to him after ejecting from the aircraft. With no radio, he had only a few pen flares with which to signal a rescue team. That is, if there was to be a rescue. Worst of all, he had no idea where he was. His only option was to try to locate and hook up with Link. He would wait until dark and then head west.

SEVENTEEN

NAT WAS EXHAUSTED from the stress of the overnight events, but could not sleep at all that morning. He ate some of his survival rations in the early afternoon and was finally able to doze off afterwards. He awoke at dusk and, satisfied that there was still no one nearby, he closed his eyes to rest and wait for darkness to surround him.

An hour later, the full moon poked above the eastern horizon, driving out the pitch blackness. Seeing it brought the impact of what had happened to the forefront of his mind once again. Only yesterday the moon had been in crescent phase, setting shortly after the sun as he and Link waited aboard the *Enterprise* for the start of their bombing mission into Laos. Clearly, there had been a giant disconnect in his time line that he could not explain. Nat gathered up his survival gear and headed west toward the military encampment that he had over flown earlier that morning.

Despite his concern over the full moon illuminating the landscape, he was able to move quickly toward the site of the encampment, taking full advantage of the security afforded by the trees and tall brush. In less than an hour, he was at the perimeter of the camp. He waited and watched from a stand of old oaks. After a few minutes it became clear that the camp was nearly, if not totally, abandoned. No sentries posted and not a sign of the artillery pieces that had engaged his aircraft earlier that day. He could see a few dilapidated tents, but no human activity whatsoever. The entire camp had packed up and left while he was sleeping in his thicket.

Nat searched the grounds of the camp quickly, looking for any sign of Link. The canvas fabric of the few tents that remained was badly rotted and shredded, which explained why they were left behind. In one of them, Nat came upon a pile of discarded Confederate uniforms. He found a corporal's uniform very nearly his size and in relatively good condition and changed out of his Navy flight suit. He removed all of the items from his survival pack and placed everything in one of the gray backpacks that had been left behind.

The last tent that Nat entered was completely empty. Finding nothing, he passed through to the open back of it, and failed to see the footlocker in his path until he fell over it, landing on his face. He was rubbing the shinbone of his right leg to ease the pain when he noticed the white fabric that had partially spilled out of the footlocker when he knocked it over. Nat crawled back to the metal box and righted it. The fabric was unmistakably from a white nylon parachute, but it was clear that most of the parachute material was missing. Wrapped inside the piece of fabric about the size of a tablecloth he found Link's helmet. He was dismayed to see that a jagged section of the plastic was missing. The residue of dried blood on his fingers must have come from the torn lining of the helmet. Nat wondered for a minute if Link was dead or alive. It didn't look good. He rewrapped the helmet and returned it to the metal box.

Nat came upon a dirt road east of the encampment that showed fresh scarring; undoubtedly from the iron-rimmed wheels of the heavy artillery caissons. It was clear that at least the artillery brigade had relocated somewhere to the northeast. Nat Booth grabbed the backpack and headed off along the moonlit road in search of his friend.

EIGHTEEN

THE SUN HAD now moved from the zenith so that the large umbrella over the garden table no longer provided complete shade to the elderly woman and her three guests.

"What are you trying to tell me, Professor Atwood?"

Mrs. Rose Booth was old but elegant and articulate. The surprisingly low square cut neckline of her black dress emphasized the string of expensive pearls that were only slightly lighter in color than her pale skin. A multiple-carat diamond on her left hand flickered blue-white in the sun as she drummed steadily with her raspberry-red fingernails against the glass top of the table. Robert, the butler, was removing the mostly-consumed entree of chicken picatta and steamed fresh vegetables served on white china. The last course of the luncheon menu, which Rose Booth had personally planned, was over.

"We believe, Mrs. Booth, that your son, Nathaniel, was not lost in Vietnam in 1968. The evidence that Ms. Marshall and I uncovered accidentally at Gettysburg Park, plus the testimony of Commander Hayes here and the records that Amanda discovered at Elmira are compelling. We believe that through some freak cosmic event, your son and the Commander were thrust through time and space to Gettysburg in the year 1863."

Rose Booth's steel-blue eyes flashed at Lincoln Hayes. "Although I reserve judgment on the veracity of this claim, can you explain to me, Commander, why you waited over 30 years to tell me what you believed to be the truth concerning my son?"

Lincoln Hayes looked straight into her eyes. "I won't apologize, Mrs. Booth. When I first arrived home, I convinced myself that there was no way you would have believed my story. I might as well have told you that men from Mars had kidnapped Nat. But after a few weeks, I made the decision to tell your family everything that I knew. You definitely had a right to know. But you weren't home on the day I stopped unannounced at your door. Mr. Booth immediately made it clear that he had no interest in learning what I had to say. It took only a brief exchange of words for me to understand that your husband was a product of the old racist south—not untypical for those times. My guess is that he probably never even told you of my visit." Rose nodded in reluctant acknowledgement. "I just turned and walked away from your husband. At that point, I was determined to keep what I knew about Nat to myself."

Rose considered Link's explanation for several seconds before responding. "I'm sorry about my husband, Commander. I found myself apologizing for his behavior on more than one occasion, as you can imagine. And I didn't intend to sound angry with you. In fact, I find myself relishing the notion that Nathaniel may not have died at the young age of twenty-four as I had come to accept; that he may indeed have had a good and full life. For the first time in many years the pain in my heart is almost gone." Rose Booth dabbed at her tears with a lace handkerchief. Amanda used her linen napkin to do the same.

"Robert, we'll be taking coffee in the library." The butler nodded in acknowledgement and assisted Mrs. Booth with her chair as she rose from the table. The three guests followed Rose from the lush garden to the inside of the old and stately Richmond mansion.

The library was large and dark with heavy drapes nearly covering the windows on the one outside wall. The walnut paneling and matching parquet on the floor completely absorbed any vestige of stray light that happened to impinge upon them. Roger Atwood was immediately attracted to the large glass display cases containing Civil War artifacts. One case held copies of *The New York Times* and *The Richmond Whig* headlining General Lee's surrender and the Lincoln Assassination. While coffee was being poured, Roger examined some letters and personal effects belonging to President Lincoln's notorious assassin, John Wilkes Booth. He looked toward Rose with a quizzical expression. "You are related to—"

"To John Booth? Is that what you are asking, Professor?" Atwood nodded. "By marriage, only. My late husband, Wendell, was the Grandson of Edwin Booth, the brother of John Wilkes. As you can see, my Wendell was quite a history buff."

"You have some priceless items here, Mrs. Booth."

"Thank you, Professor. The curator of the Museum of the Confederacy calls upon me frequently. He periodically checks on my state of health as the Museum is named prominently in my will. Come and sit. The coffee is getting cold."

The four sat at an antique carved mahogany card table while Rose continued. "I called Commander Hayes a few days ago because of something that came to light recently concerning Nathaniel. Let me first explain a few things. As you know, Commander, when you last came to visit in 1968 after Nat's disappearance, my husband and I were living in a modest home on the south side of town. We were by no means wealthy. Many of the items in this room were stored in cardboard boxes in our garage. The finances that provided this house, the servants and gardeners, all the comfort that surrounds me now came upon us totally out of the blue a year after Nat's disappearance. One day in July 1969, an Asian man in a gray suit appeared at our door. He carried a briefcase filled with bearer bonds and blue chip stock certificates. He spread them out on our kitchen table and explained that they were from an anonymous benefactor and that they belonged to us. High-grade bonds and thousands of shares of companies like IBM and General Motors; even restricted shares of a little startup company called Intel Corporation covered the table. The total value was over two million dollars. My husband and I were utterly speechless. And for the most part, so was our visitor. He could not, or would not, tell us anything about our benefactor. He wouldn't even tell us his own name. The only clue as to the possible source of our windfall was a transfer stamp appearing on some of the stock certificates with the name 'Khronos Trust Services'. We made a few inquiries at the time, but could find nothing about this organization."

Robert refilled the coffee cups and brought a plate of sliced lemon cake. Rose dropped a single cube of sugar into her cup and continued as she stirred.

"My husband died 15 years ago. I was never able to learn anything more of the source of our good fortune until one week ago when I received this." Rose passed a one-page letter to Commander Hayes, seated on her left. The letterhead displayed the logo of the Bank of New York. "If you would read it aloud, Commander—" Link removed a pair of reading glasses from his shirt pocket and commenced to read the letter aloud for the benefit of Roger and Amanda:

DEAR MRS. BOOTH

WE HAVE BEEN ASSIGNED BY THE SECRETARY OF STATE OF NEW YORK TO ASSIST IN THE FINAL DISPOSITION OF ASSETS HELD IN TRUST BY THE ABANDONED CORPORATE ENTITY, KHRONOS TRUST SERVICES, INC.

A REVIEW OF THE BOOKS OF ACCOUNT OF THAT ENTITY INDICATES THAT THE SECURITIES HELD IN TRUST ON YOUR BEHALF WERE DELIVERED TO YOU AND MR. BOOTH IN JULY OF 1969, AND THAT NO FURTHER ASSETS REMAIN TO BE DISTRIBUTED. HOWEVER, AN ANNOTATION ON THE INSTRUCTIONS FOR THE 1969 DISTRIBUTION WAS APPARENTLY OVERLOOKED. ENCLOSED HEREWITH YOU WILL FIND ONE GOLD PIN TO BE FORWARDED TO YOU EXACTLY TEN YEARS AFTER THE ASSET DISTRIBUTION. WHILE WE CLEARLY HAVE NO RESPONSIBILITY FOR THIS OVERSIGHT, WE DEEPLY REGRET ANY INCONVENIENCE THAT THE DELAY IN DELIVERY MAY HAVE CAUSED YOU.

VERY TRULY YOURS,
S/ MAI TRAN
FOR JAMES L. STAFFORD
VICE PRESIDENT
TRUST DIVISION
THE BANK OF NEW YORK

The palm of Rose Booth's left hand had been closed tightly as Lincoln Hayes read the letter aloud. When he finished reading, Rose opened her hand to reveal a gold pin as worn by U.S. Navy pilots. Link took the pin from her outstretched hand, held it close to read the inscription on the back. It read "N.L. Booth — VA-35."

"When I received this in the mail, it became clear that Nathaniel was somehow connected to the gift of stocks and bonds that we received. From what you have told me today, I understand now how this may have happened."

Rose paused for a moment and then continued. "I am at an age where insurance actuaries count life expectancy in weeks and months rather than years. My single wish at this point in my life— before I pass on—is to learn as much as I possibly can about Nathaniel after the date he went missing. My personal attorney is spending the summer on the Italian Riviera—clearly I am paying him too much—so I called Commander Hayes to inform him of the letter and pin in the hope that he might know of someone interested enough to help. The information you all have provided today has been a great comfort to me, but it is very likely that there is much more that might be learned about my Nathaniel. I believe that you, Professor, are precisely the person I am looking for. If your schedule permits, would you be willing to take on this research project on my behalf? Perhaps with Ms. Marshall's assistance? If you agree, I will fully underwrite the cost of your investigation."

Professor Atwood turned toward Amanda, who returned a smile and a nod, then looked straight at Rose Booth. "I've made a commitment for a lecture series this summer, but it's only six class sessions and it's near New York City. That's where we would start trying to pick up Nathaniel's trail anyway. And I've got nearly two months before fall term at the college, so my answer is 'Yes', and I believe Amanda concurs. We'll do it!"

"Excellent. I have prepared a package of biographical material and photos of Nathaniel from 1968, which should be of help to you."

Amanda took the package offered by Rose. "Would you say, Mrs. Booth, that your son was as much of a student of history as Mr. Booth?"

"My Nathaniel was always interested in the Civil War and our family history since age nine or ten. I recall the day he came home crying in the fifth grade. Some boy in the class was spreading the story that Nathaniel's grandfather had killed President Lincoln. The child had his facts somewhat twisted, but it wasn't far from the truth. My husband sat Nathaniel down that day and told him all about the dark side of the Booth family tree. Nathaniel was certainly no admirer of John Wilkes, but he was proud of his Southern heritage and studied continuously. History was his major in college. You couldn't tell Nathaniel much about the Civil War that he didn't already know."

NINETEEN

IT WAS IN THE AFTERNOON of the second day that Nat first caught sight of the rear elements of the Confederate regimental unit that he believed was holding Link. He needed to get ahead of the column. His thinking was that if he could find a hiding place close to the road from which he could observe, he might be able to locate Link as they passed by. Once he knew how and where they were holding his B/N, he could formulate a plan to infiltrate the unit and hopefully set him free. Finally, he saw his chance: the main road was about to skirt some higher terrain up ahead. Nat came upon a trail that split from the main road and appeared to go up and over the high country—a chance to get ahead of the regiment without being observed. After three hours slogging along the path through the brush, Nat could see that the trail was about to rejoin the main road and that he was well ahead of the regiment. He quickly located a hiding place near the junction from which he could observe. He could hear the sound of horse hooves and wagons approaching from the leading element of the column just as the sun began to set.

Curiously, the officer in charge ordered a halt to the advance just as he was about to pass Nat's position. At first, Nat feared that he had been discovered and that momentarily a squad of riflemen would be sent in his direction in order to flush him out, but soon it became clear that the object of the officer's attention was above him—in the sky. The oblate disk of the sun had fallen completely below the horizon, but still distinctly illuminated a set of vapor trails high in the sky nearly directly overhead. Clearly, to Nat, it represented the obvious: an aircraft—probably military—on a mission flying very high—nothing out of the ordinary. But at the same time it was apparent that the men he was watching from his hiding place—the men on horseback and those in wagons and on foot—had no such understanding. As the officers looked up and pointed and then gathered to confer with one another, Nat confirmed at once that they were without a clue as to what they were witnessing.

After several minutes, the officer in charge gave the order to march. The procession of soldiers began once again to move along the road, passing Nat's position, unaware that they were being watched. After fifteen minutes, the entire regiment had passed. Admittedly, the closing darkness made it difficult for Nat to see, but nothing he observed seemed to suggest that Link or anyone else was being held prisoner by the soldiers. Nat leaned back and closed his eyes for a minute. He was weary. "Link," he thought to himself, "How in God's name am I going to find you in this place?" The long day and disappointing revelation had sapped his strength and soon he was asleep. It was barely light when he awoke hours later.

NAT CAME UP BEHIND the Confederate gun crew about an hour after sunrise. "How about giving us a hand, soldier?" The artillery piece was stuck up to its axle in the mud of a narrow streambed. The Sergeant was coaxing the exhausted horses in front of the caisson to pull harder, but with little success. A corporal was pushing on one of the tall wheels. Nat removed his backpack and immediately joined in the effort, pushing against the spoke wheel on the other side of the gun. After five minutes of rocking the gun forward and back accompanied by a steady stream of curse words from the Sergeant, the caisson was finally free. The horses were able to pull the canon across the shallow stream to the dry road on the other side.

"What are you doing way back here, soldier? Where's your unit?" Now that his artillery piece was no longer stuck in the mud, the Sergeant's focus was upon Nat. What was he doing out here by himself? Most likely he was a deserter.

Nat had expected the question and was prepared with a semi-plausible answer. "I had to tend to a bad blister on my foot. When I went to catch up with my company, I came to that fork in the road about three klicks back and took the wrong fork. Took me this long to get back on the right road."

"What did you say? Three 'clicks'? What the hell is a 'click'?" Now the Sergeant was really interested, and Nat regretted his choice of words.

"You know, kilometers."

"Yeah, I guess I've heard of them. Are you from France, or somewhere like that?"

More regret. "No, Sergeant. I was born in Richmond."

"So you're with our unit, the 2nd Virginia Infantry?"

"Yes, sir. Just joined up recently, though."

"You'd best stick with us. We're supposed to meet up with them, probably five miles up ahead, just north of the Seminary. I'll speak to the Cap'n personal so you won't be in trouble. I'll explain how you helped us out of a fix."

"Thank you, Sergeant. You know, I kinda lost track of time. What day is today, anyway?"

"Today, son, is July 1st and my guess is that we'll be in for it with the Blue Bellies before this day is up or maybe tomorrow."

Nat flashed a broad smile. He knew his history well. The date and reference to the seminary could mean only one thing: Like it or not, he was about to become a participant in the Battle of Gettysburg. Seminary Ridge was the staging point for the Confederate assault against Union positions on the third day of the battle, on July 3, 1863. And although he couldn't remember the exact details, Nat knew that the first engagement of the battle had already begun.

He was right. Earlier that morning, a Confederate division under the command of General Henry Heth was dispatched from Cashtown, eight miles west of Gettysburg, with orders to occupy the town. Around 5 AM, only three miles from Gettysburg, they encountered a detachment of the 8th Illinois Cavalry. The Union soldiers were driven back until reinforcements under the command of General John Reynolds arrived with sufficient men to counter the Confederate offensive. By the time Nat and his fellow travelers approached the engagement area, fighting had erupted at several new locations. McPherson's Farm, Oak Ridge, Barlow's Knoll—all places that Nat had read about lay before him. Nat had no idea of the exact role of the 2nd Virginia Infantry in the fighting, but he was about to find out.

Nat was reluctant to join in the battle as a foot soldier, but he also understood that he couldn't simply stand around and observe the fighting. When asked by the Sergeant if he would temporarily fill the vacancy on the gun crew, Nat eagerly accepted.

TWENTY

ROGER AND AMANDA arrived at the Bank of New York, Trust Division Offices, on Barclay Street in New York City at 4:15 PM for their four-thirty appointment with James Stafford. They were greeted by Stafford's secretary, Julia Gray, who asked them to take a seat. As they waited, they paid scant attention to another bank employee, an attractive Asian woman in her late 20s, watching from the open door of her office, adjacent to the Vice President's. After ten minutes, the secretary escorted them into Stafford's office. The Vice President rose from his chair to shake hands with his visitors.

"I'm so glad to meet you both after my conversation with Mrs. Booth last week. I'm sorry I was unable to speak with you, Professor, earlier when you called. Please sit down." Roger and Amanda eased themselves into the pair of stuffed mahogany-colored leather armchairs facing the desk.

"Not a problem, Mr. Stafford. I am pleased that Mrs. Booth was able to convince you of the seriousness of her interest in the corporation, Khronos Trust Services. We are simply here at her behest."

"Well, yes, indeed. And how can I be of assistance?"

Amanda spoke up. "We are interested in learning anything you can tell us about the corporation and how your bank came to be involved with it."

James Stafford reached for a notepad on the corner of his desk. "I made some notes in advance of your visit. Unfortunately, there isn't a great deal of information available. This is all we have been able to ascertain from the documents provided to us by the State of New York and from our own work." Stafford cleared his throat before continuing. "The first historical reference that we could find indicates that a business entity named "Khronos Trust Services" was incorporated in New York State in 1873. We don't know much about its business activities. As near as we can determine, Khronos performed the usual trust-related activities for wealthy clients and also provided investment advice via subscription to brokerages and individuals."

Roger interrupted. "Any information on corporate officers?"

"Again, not much. Corporate registration histories are pretty much incomplete before about 1905. The earliest available record reads like a family business: President, N. Khronos; Vice President, R. Khronos; Secretary-Treasurer, W. Khronos. But I don't think you can rely on those names. Nineteenth century corporations tended to play pretty fast and loose with state regulations. It was a fairly common practice to use pseudonyms in public records; an internal document would typically show who the true owners were. We simply wouldn't have that information. The last corporate registration was dated August 1977. Here is a copy." Stafford passed the copy of the registration certificate to Roger. "It was recorded by a Mr. Derrick Luu." Roger and Amanda glanced at each other as Stafford continued. The name didn't register. "A renewal registration would have been required again five years later, in 1982. As far as the State of New York is concerned, the corporation was considered abandoned seven years after that date, in 1989, simply because the registration was never renewed; the requisite corporate registration fees were never paid again after 1977."

Now it was Amanda's turn. "How did the Bank of New York get involved? And why after all these years?" Before Stafford could answer, his telephone signaled an incoming intercom call.

"Pardon the interruption. Let me take care of this, if you don't mind." Stafford picked up the phone. "Yes, what is it?" He pauses to listen. "Can't we do this later? My visitors are still here." Another pause. "Very well, but let's make it quick." Stafford hung up the phone and turned to his visitors. "I apologize. Apparently, I missed one of the signature lines on a document that needs to go in the overnight. My assistant is bringing it in. I hope you won't mind the interruption."

"Not a problem," replied Amanda. Two short knocks on the office door preceded the entrance of Stafford's administrative assistant, Mai Tran. She walked around Stafford's desk and placed a thick document—opened to a page near the end—in front of Stafford and held out a pen.

Mai Tran smiled at Roger and Amanda as she waited for Stafford to peruse the open page of the document. "I'm sorry to interrupt. You know, I've spoken with Mrs. Booth by telephone. She seems like a sweet and special lady."

"Yes, she is," replied Amanda. Stafford scrawled his signature on the document.

"Thank you, Mr. Stafford." Mai Tran gathered the document and exited the office.

Stafford now turned his attention back to Roger and Amanda. "Where were we?" Pause. "I know. I was about to explain how the Bank got involved. About two years ago, the Secretary of State embarked on a housekeeping mission. The State found that more than half of the corporations listed in the state records had lapsed registrations. In some cases, these entities had been inactive for more than fifty years.

Before clearing the records and allowing new registrants to use those corporate names, it was decided to give the owners one last chance to reclaim them. The corporate names were published in a legal notice in *The Wall Street Journal*, together with the last known address for legal service. One more mailing to that address was also undertaken. A handful of the companies actually restored their corporate status, but most, including the Khronos Trust Services, did not. The State of New York contracted with our bank to conduct an asset search for the defunct companies. Where the true owner of a corporate asset could be determined, we were instructed to contact the owner and advise him or her of their good fortune. Assets for which an owner could not be determined would escheat to the State of New York. Our bank was to earn a small percentage of all the assets found."

"Frankly, it was a lot of work for our bank with very little reward. In the case of Khronos, we obtained a court order to enter their closed offices."

Roger could not help but interrupt again. "There is actually a corporate location for Khronos Trust Services? Where is it?"

"Well, there was up until two months ago. It's in the Flatiron Building—that's on 5th Avenue, if you don't know—16th floor, I believe. But when our people were there, the rumor was that the office was being taken over by a publishing company—a tenant that already occupied a lot of space in the building."

"From the trust records, our people were able to find the owners of a few securities that were assigned to Khronos Trust Services and held in street name at brokerages in town. Plus a few minor items like the gold pin that we forwarded to Mrs. Booth. That is about all I can tell you for now, but just in case we uncover additional information, how might I reach you?"

"Here is my card," offered Roger. "And you can always reach us by contacting Mrs. Booth."

"And what about while you are here in New York?"

"We're staying at the St. Regis, but I'm not sure for how long."

"Please don't hesitate to contact me if there is anything else I can do to help you or Mrs. Booth." Stafford looked at his watch. "If you decide to check out the former Khronos Trust offices, I'd suggest that you at least wait until morning. Traffic getting over there is pretty brutal this time of day. I doubt you'd find anyone to help you by the time you could get there this evening."

Amanda and Roger rose to leave. "Thank you for being so helpful, Mr. Stafford."

"It has been my pleasure, and please be sure to give my regards to Mrs. Booth."

When Amanda and Roger were in the elevator, Roger remarked, "Amazing isn't it? How cooperative Mr. Stafford was today after Rose purchased that million dollar certificate of deposit from the bank?"

Amanda smiled. She looked down at the copy of the corporate registration that James Stafford had given her. "Who do you suppose this 'Derrick Luu' is? Roger simply shrugged his shoulders.

Before Amanda and Roger exited the building, Mai Tran had entered James Stafford's office through the adjoining door to her own. She sat down.

Stafford began. "You need to keep close tabs on them over the next few days. They're staying at the St. Regis. I expect them to get over to the Flatiron Building sometime tomorrow."

"Why did you have to tell them about the Khronos offices?"

"The likelihood is that they would have found out for themselves. If you hadn't sent that goddamn pin to Rose

Booth, we wouldn't be in this fix. Now if they find out I've been holding back information, it will only make them more suspicious. Those two act like they've been commissioned by the Pope to find the Holy Grail. Very tenacious—-especially that Marshall bitch. Anyway, you got a good look at them, right?"

"Of course!"

TWENTY-ONE

GENERAL ROBERT E. LEE was in overall command of the Confederate forces at Gettysburg. When fighting on the first day of the battle subsided after 9 PM, General Lee was in his headquarters tent near the Lutheran Seminary contemplating the day's action and his plans for the second day of the battle. This location was selected because of the battlefield view afforded by the rooftop observatory of the Seminary. Lee's forces had succeeded in capturing the town and driving back the Union army, but only at a tremendous cost in men and matériel. His plans for the second day would depend upon whether he had sufficient remaining forces to mount the massive assault that would be necessary to drive General Meade's men from their positions near Cemetery Ridge and Culp's Hill.

The final decision to attack was not made until the next morning. General Lee believed that the left side of the Union line was the most vulnerable and he selected General James Longstreet to command the assault. But soon enough it would become clear that the gains made by the Confederate forces earlier in the battle would be only temporary. In the end, the Union soldiers would be able to retake most of the ground they had given up early on the second day of the battle.

Nat Booth had been fortunate enough to miss most of the action during the first two days of fighting. The artillery battery to which he had assigned himself was close enough to the Union lines for only two brief periods during the preceding days. He had loaded the gun maybe ten times. It had been fired at maximum range at suspected Union positions with unknown results. Late in the afternoon of the second day, a contingent of men from the 2nd Virginia Infantry approached the gun line. The Captain in charge announced that the artillery brigade was to be temporarily disbanded. The men were needed to fill now vacant infantry positions for a planned assault on the Union lines later that evening.

Nat understood full well the reason for the vacancies and swallowed hard as he caught the musket and powder bag that were thrown at him. He had no idea how to use this weapon and felt with his right hand for the Smith and Wesson 38 hidden in his waistband.

HENRY CULP WAS THE OWNER of a parcel of land southeast of Gettysburg which included the high ground position on the right flank of the Union line facing the Confederates. It would come to be known as "Culp's Hill." Holding the position since July 1, the Union troops under the command of Brigadier General George Greene had fortified it well by felling large trees and deploying them with a packing of earth to create a barricade called a "breastworks". Firing from behind the barricade, they hoped to be able to stop any advancing infantry from overtaking their position. The Union troops waited in the darkness as the Confederate soldiers and Nat Booth crossed Rock Creek and proceeded toward the summit of Culp's Hill.

"I SHOULD BE the last person here to stumble and fall on my ass—I know this place like the back of my hand." Private Wesley Culp had tripped on a tree root in the darkness and Nathaniel Booth offered an outstretched hand to help him to his feet.

"What do you mean, Private?"

"This is my uncle's land, believe it or don't. I used to play in these hills when I was a kid. Three days back I was visitin' my sisters, not more'n two miles from here."

The comment registered a spark of recollection in Nat's brain—something vaguely familiar about a young Confederate soldier fighting the North on his uncle's land.

"What's your uncle's name?"

"Henry Culp."

The sound of that name struck an immediate chord. "Are you John Wesley Culp?" Nat asked the young man with a tone of conviction that suggested that that he already knew the answer to be true.

"That's right, but how d'you know my name?"

"I heard a story once about you and Jack Skelly and Jennie Wade." Nat now remembered the Civil War love story that he had read and written about in high school, and here he was in the very presence of one of the main characters.

Much to Wesley Culp's amazement, Nat related the essence of the story as he remembered it. Where Nat's memory wavered, Wesley filled in the details. As the story went, Jack Skelly and Wesley were boyhood friends in Gettysburg. In the 1850s, Wesley moved to Shepherdstown in what is now West Virginia and took a job in a carriage shop. When the war broke out, Wesley decided to forsake his northern roots and joined the Confederate Army. He became part of the famous Stonewall Brigade of the 2nd Virginia Infantry. At about the same time, Jack Skelly and Wesley's brother joined the Union army with the 2nd Pennsylvania Infantry. According to Nat, before Jack left Gettysburg in

April 1861, he became engaged to a local girl, Jennie Wade. Jennie was not quite 18 years old at that time.

In June 1863, near Winchester, Virginia, Wesley's unit found itself in a pitched battle against the 2nd Pennsylvania Infantry. This was just one of many instances in which brother fought against brother during the Civil War, which was why Nat had studied it. According to the story as Nat remembered, Jack was severely wounded during the fighting. Wesley found his friend on the battlefield and promised to deliver a message to Jack's fiancée, Jennie.

Nat did not tell Wesley Culp the rest of the story he had read about years before. He would not try to explain to Private Culp that history recorded that he, Wesley, would die during the assault that was about to take place on his uncle's land. He would not tell Wesley that a stray bullet would kill Jennie Wade tomorrow while she baked bread for some Union soldiers. Finally, Nat also would not explain that Jack Skelly would succumb a few days later to the wounds he suffered at Winchester and that both Jack and Jennie would be buried in the Evergreen Cemetery at Gettysburg. Nat simply could not bear to relate the events that he knew were about to unfold upon the young soldier walking beside him as they made their way toward the summit of Culp's Hill.

"But where'd you hear 'bout Jack Skelly getting' shot at Winchester?" Wesley asked. "Haven't seen nor heard of him since '61. Never saw my brother, neither, but I suppose they were both there, shootin' back at us. And I've got no message for Jennie Wade. You know, I almost choked when I heard that Jack was engaged to marry that little trollop."

Nat could hardly believe his ears! The beautiful and tragic love story that he had read and written about and retold many times was apparently a product of revisionist history. How sad, he thought. Well, maybe he could make a further revision to the historical record: Maybe he could help keep

Wesley Culp safe; so that he wouldn't be killed today on his uncle's land.

"You stick close to me, Private, and we'll get through this just fine." Nat continued to offer encouragement to Private Culp as they approached the Union positions, but it was Nat Booth who clearly was in need of encouragement.

When General Greene believed that the advancing enemy was close enough, now only one hundred feet away, the order was given for the Union troops to stand in the darkness and pour volley after volley of musket fire down in the direction from which the rebels were advancing. The barrage was so heavy, in fact, that the Confederate General Edward Johnson presumed that a far larger contingent of Yankees was holding the hill. By midnight, he determined that reinforcements would be needed to continue the assault and the fighting temporarily subsided.

But reinforcements never arrived. The Union counter offensive began about 4 AM with an intense artillery barrage from the Baltimore Pike, followed by an infantry charge. The order was given for Johnson's men to fall back and Nat and Wesley started to move toward lower ground. Nat heard the round that struck Wesley Culp in the back. When he turned, Wesley was on his face in the dirt. Nat pulled the .38 from his waistband and scanned the direction from which the shot was fired, but there was no one to be seen.

"Wesley—don't die on me now." The bullet had passed through Wesley Culp's back and shattered the stock of the rifle he was carrying. Nat struggled to lift the mortally wounded soldier on to his own back and proceeded further down the mountain.

"Hold it right there, soldier. And drop your gun." Nat Booth looked up to find four infantrymen and a lieutenant in blue uniforms, less than ten feet away, with rifles pointed in his direction. Nat dropped his Smith & Wesson and slowly lowered Wesley to the ground and then stood up straight, facing his captors. One of the soldiers bent down to examine Wesley's body.

"This one's dead, sir."

"Let's get moving."

The Union patrol that had captured Nat had been sent into the flank of the retreating Southerners. Nat turned toward Wesley's still body, and then covered his eyes and turned away. He felt only frustration at not being able to protect the young man from his fate.

"Hands together in front of you, Corporal." The order was barked at Nat and he obeyed. One of the infantrymen tied Nat's wrists together and all proceeded in column formation along the side of the hill in the direction deeper into the flank of the retreating Southerners.

Nathaniel Booth was a veteran of two-and-a-half days of fighting. He was glad that his Civil War tour of duty had come to an end and that he was still alive.

History would record that when the fighting at Gettysburg was over, John Wesley Culp's sisters would recover his body and bury him in the basement of the family farmhouse. For the rest of the men in gray and blue in the environs of Gettysburg, Pennsylvania, the third and last day of fighting was just getting underway. Ninety-five thousand Union and seventy-five thousand Confederate troops had been aligned against each other before the fighting started. When the three days were over, each side had lost nearly 25,000 men, killed, wounded, or captured.

TWENTY-TWO

THE TRAIN RIDE from the railhead at the Gettysburg stockade to the prisoner of war camp at Pt. Lookout, Maryland, had been a surprisingly pleasant one for Nat. The flat car in which he was riding provided an inspiring view of the Pennsylvania and Virginia countryside while the train was between—and not within—the dirty towns along the route.

Nat spent a lot of time thinking about his situation. It was understood that he was facing nearly two years incarceration in a prisoner of war camp. He was only somewhat familiar with the history associated with the northern camps, but remembered that they were not much better than their Confederate counterparts. Disease, death and deprivation were common attendants of the camps on both sides. Nat also thought about Wesley Culp and whether or not his life could have been saved. History records that Wesley Culp was shot dead on the morning of July 3, 1863. What would have happened if Nat's intervention had prevented Wesley from being killed that day? Would the course of history have changed in a major or even minor way if Wesley Culp had survived the Battle of Gettysburg? Nat also thought about Link Hayes and whether or not he would ever see him again. But mostly, Nat wondered if this excursion back to the nineteenth century would be a permanent one or would he see 1968 again someday. Something within him, a voice of sorts that had been growing stronger each day, was telling Nat that this was his new life now and that he should get used to it. And as each day passed since his capture, Nat was feeling better about it all. He began to recognize that there could be advantages to being a twentieth century man in a nineteenth century world—that one-eyed man that the Dutch humanist Erasmus spoke of when he wrote that "In the land of the blind, the one-eyed man is king."

TWENTY-THREE

THE FLATIRON BUILDING in midtown New York got its name from the unique triangular shape in which it was constructed. The footprint of the building matches the lot outline formed by the diagonal intersection of Broadway and Fifth Avenue. When completed in 1902, the building had its own electric generator for heating and lighting and stood twenty-two stories high.

It was late morning when Amanda and Roger entered the building from the Fifth Avenue side and proceeded to the bank of elevators. Roger pushed the call button, and in less than one minute they were ascending. Two young men entered at Floor 3 and got off at twelve and the elevator continued higher. Amanda and Roger stepped out at the 16th floor and stopped to look in both directions. Not much difference either way: a corridor with several banks of office suites to the left and a similar corridor with offices that ran off to the right. Directly across from the open elevator was a directory for that floor, but among the few listings—mainly publishing firms—the name 'Khronos Trust Services' did not appear. All of the office numbers except one were listed with a business name next to the number.

"Let's try 1640." Roger nodded in agreement and they headed off to the right. The corridor consisted of three legs, covering the 16th floor in the shape of a large triangle, with office suites on each side. When they reached the end of the first leg, the corridor made a sharp turn to the left. Up ahead, they could see two painters with paint buckets and paint rollers on extension sticks. The floor was covered with drop cloths. When they reached the work area, it was clear that the painters were working in the hallway just outside Office Suite 1640. The suite itself occupied the area between the corridor and the exterior wall of the building along 5th Avenue. At the open doorway, Amanda and Roger looked in and noticed two more workers engaged in renovating the office suite itself. Right before them, a man was using a razor blade to remove the gold leaf name from the glass door of what must have been the main entrance to the suite. The only remaining legible portion consisted of the letters "KHRON" and what appeared to be a stylized sundial, part of the company logo. When the workman saw that Amanda and Roger were not moving down the hallway, but had stopped and were looking in, he suspended his work.

"Can I help you folks?"

Roger answered. "We were curious about the company that was in this suite. Do you mind if we go in?"

"Sorry, sir, but only workmen are allowed. You might want to talk to the building manager."

Roger and Amanda thanked the workman and moved further down the corridor. Roger pressed the call button at the bank of elevators. As the door opened and the couple entered, they failed to notice a figure walking past the elevator door; glancing in at them just as the door closed.

TWENTY-FOUR

"**Y**OUR ARM LOOKS one helluva lot better, but you gotta keep the wound clean. And don't call me 'Doc'. I'm no doctor." Nat Booth was changing the dressing on Private Addison's arm. The young man had been shot a month earlier, on the last day of fighting at Gettysburg. The wound was largely superficial, but an infection set in after a week and for a while it looked like the young Addison might lose his arm to it. Nat started tending the wound and dispensing some penicillin tablets, which were effectively fighting off the infection. "I have medicine for you for only three more days. After that, your body will have to fight that infection on its own. If we don't keep the wound clean, you're gonna lose that arm." The young soldier nodded. Only a few penicillin tabs remained from the medicines in Nat's survival pack. He had used up the morphine on a few hurting soldiers on the train, even before he arrived at Point Lookout.

He was lucky to have any medicine at all. The soldiers who searched Nat when he was first captured were looking only for weapons, maps and papers and ignored most of the survival items that he carried in his backpack and on his

person, except for the money, of course. The gold coins were
confiscated immediately and the fifty-dollar bill that Nat
carried for good luck attracted a lot of attention and laughs
from the Union soldiers. With the picture of President
Ulysses S. Grant, they assumed it was some southern printer's
practical joke. Before most of his possessions were
confiscated at the temporary stockade at Gettysburg, Nat had
managed to hide the morphine and penicillin within his
Corporal's uniform.

Nat and Private Addison bunked together with fifteen
other captives in one of the hundreds of worn out Sibley
tents that had been discarded by the Union army and
collected for use by the Prison Camp at Point Lookout,
Maryland. The tents were named for Henry Hopkins Sibley,
who was granted a patent for the design of the tent in 1856.
They were conical in shape, 18 feet in diameter and twelve
feet high, supported by a central wooden pole.

The Point Lookout Prisoner of War Camp covered
about 30 acres of land in St. Mary's County, Maryland. The
land, which was formerly a seaside resort, was taken over by
the U.S. Government in 1862 for use as a military hospital for
Union wounded, but was converted to a POW camp in
August 1863 because of the need to house the large number
of Confederate soldiers captured at Gettysburg. In the
following two years of camp operation, 52,000 prisoners
would enter the camp and more than 14,000 would die while
incarcerated. The usual causes included typhoid fever, malaria
and small pox, compounded by the deplorable living
conditions. The site was selected because the Potomac River
and the Chesapeake Bay bound it on three sides, and the
Federal ship, *Minnesota*, stood offshore just in case anyone
would be foolish enough to attempt an escape by water.
Fourteen-foot high wooden walls surrounded the prisoner
area. Anyone daring to venture within ten feet of the walls

was shot without warning. Black soldiers were given the guard duty, with orders coming from white officers.

Upon arriving at the camp, Nat was surprised to learn that among the prisoners was a contingent of Maryland citizens—men, women and children—whom the government had deemed to be Confederate sympathizers. They were housed in similar tents, and in some cases small out buildings, near one end of the compound, somewhat segregated from the military prisoners. Nat's group was adjacent to the civilian area.

"I'd sure like to get me some of that." A soldier was at the back of Nat's tent, peering through a hole in the fabric. Upon hearing the remark, two prisoners jumped to their feet and ran back to where the soldier was standing, pushing him aside so that they could see. The object of their attention was a young girl, barely fourteen years old, who could be seen washing herself inside one of the wooden barracks about twenty feet away. She kept a steady eye on the open window, making sure that no one was passing by, unaware today as twice before this month of the voyeurs inside the nearby tent.

"That's my Mary", one of the soldiers remarked, "washin' away the cares of the day."

Nat cautioned the men. "You boys best get away from that peephole or you'll end up like that poor Harris fellow!" Nat was referring to Robert Harris, a sergeant from the other end of the compound who had tried to force himself on Mary Watson the week before. Her screams drew the attention of several men who came to her aid, including her father. George Watson was twice as old as Mary's assailant, but was nonetheless able to beat him into unconsciousness with a few well-directed blows from his large fists. After the carnage was over, George Watson was heard to announce loudly, "Most of you men are young enough to be my sons, and I will strive to treat you as such. I only insist that you consider my daughter, Mary, as you would your very own sister." George

Watson and his family had been arrested several weeks before Nat's arrival after two neighbors reported to the authorities that he had supplied food and ammunition to rebels that were believed to be hiding in the area. The charges were never proven, but the Watson family was escorted to Point Lookout without so much as a hearing before a judge. The order was signed by the local army commandant.

As Nat finished tending the wound, the Private remarked, "Seems like there were more than the usual amount of shooting again last night. What do you think, Doc?"

"I think that prisoners of war have always been treated poorly in the past, and I don't expect that will change much for the next hundred years or more."

"But you know those damn coloreds just can't wait to put us in their gun sights after curfew." Addison was referring to the orders given to the guards to shoot any prisoner seen outside after 8 o'clock at night. Many had been shot while in the course of relieving themselves, for sanitary reasons, away from tents that they occupied. "And what about the relief packages? I heard just yesterday that there were warehouses full of food and clothing for us that the Yankees were just holding and sitting on."

"It's just a matter of payback. In the Southern camps for Union soldiers—like Andersonville—our men are probably treated just as bad. Beatings and killings go on everywhere. Few prisoner exchanges. Not even simple comforts are provided. We don't give them any tobacco; they don't give us any coffee or tea."

With the arrival of autumn, the weather at least began to provide a little comfort to the prisoners at Point Lookout. The sweltering heat and dripping humidity, ideal conditions for breeding mosquitoes and the diseases that thrived on poor sanitation, had finally given way to temperate days and cooler nights. But save for this accommodation of nature, camp conditions and the treatment meted out to the prisoners had become worse. Rations were reduced, and then reduced again. The total lack of fresh vegetables and fruit resulted in hundreds of cases of scurvy among the prison population. Prisoners supplemented their meager rations by cooking rats and eating raw fish or an occasional seagull. The Provost Marshall, Major Brady, and General Benjamin 'the Beast' Butler would often review the camp. The General took particular pleasure in galloping through the throng of prisoners, striking them as he rode by. Random shootings by the guards would occur at all hours of the day or night, and fire would often be directed specifically at a prisoner who might cry out in pain from sickness or a prior injury.

Nat spent most mornings conducting his own daily review of the camp. He would offer words of encouragement, trying to lift the spirits of depressed prisoners, knowing that their ultimate survival depended to a large degree on their state of mind. He helped many of the dying with a last letter to loved ones, holding the letters for a time when they might be safely smuggled out of the camp. Despite the lack of medicine and any formal training, he still was able to help some medical conditions, relying on twentieth century common sense concerning cleanliness and disease. Overall, however, Nat was under no illusion that his efforts would ever save more than a few of his fellow prisoners who would have perished without his intervention. He dreaded the thought that the current winter would be only the first of two that would have to be endured before the end of the war would make their release possible. He had only limited confidence in even his own ability to survive the long months ahead.

A state of boredom was an ever-present condition of the prisoners at Point Lookout, responsible for numerous arguments and fistfights among the men. By the end of that first winter, Nat's efforts to improve morale in the camp included storytelling. From his own rich knowledge of American history, he would relate the human side of events with which many of the prisoners were familiar. At first, participants included only the men in his tent, but after several gatherings, many of his neighbors, including George Watson and his family participated. The eager listeners would usually gather after the distribution of evening rations, and Nat would speak for an hour or so, or until curfew.

He retold the stories that most had heard when they were school children: about Christopher Columbus and the King and Queen of Spain, of the heroes of the American Revolution like Nathan Hale and George Washington, about Dolly Madison saving the original Declaration of Independence when the British burned the White House during the War of 1812. The men were encouraged to ask questions, and often Nat would have one or another relate a story from their own experiences. Everyone looked forward to the talks, and morale among the participants, including Nat, improved considerably.

One day in early April 1864, the prisoner's spirits fell to a new low as rumors spread in the camp that the Federal government had declined, once again, to consider any sort of prisoner exchange and that the war, and their incarceration, might continue for another ten years or more. That evening when the group gathered, Nat could see the discouragement on the faces of everyone present as he began to speak.

"Tonight I'm going to tell you the story of two Generals. Both very competent and proud men, but in most other ways they were very different. The older general was tall and handsome and came from a military background, while the other was of average height and appearance. His father had been a tanner. Both were trained as army officers and, despite their age differences, they had actually met one another years before while fighting on the same side for their country against a common enemy."

"Nearly twenty years later, they found themselves on opposite sides of a struggle that would be remembered forever in human history. That war eventually cost the lives of more than a half million men. It tore families apart and threatened the very existence of a nation. The forces led by the younger general were far stronger and better equipped, but the other side believed in their cause and fought hard and long. In the beginning, it was thought that the army commanded by the older general would prevail, but after two years, the tide began to turn. Finally, almost two more years later, both generals could see the writing on the wall: For the older, his men were tired and discouraged. Food, weapons and the other necessities of war had become scarce. It was clear to the younger general that he had the advantage. He had occupied the capital city of the opposing side and knew now that it was only a matter of time before the enemy would be totally vanquished. But rather than continue the fight, which would cause needless additional death and suffering on both sides, one day in April, he sent a letter to the older general. In it, he suggested to the older man that the fighting should end and that they should meet together to discuss terms of surrender which would finally end the long war."

"After a further exchange of notes, they met together, and while their aides waited outside, the two men sat and talked alone. The older general was dressed in his finest uniform, buttoned all the way up to his chin, with polished boots and his dress sword with a beautifully jeweled hilt at his side. In contrast, the younger man wore a soiled field uniform. They spoke for a few minutes about their brief encounter years before, when both had fought on the same side. The young man then spelled out his terms of surrender. There would be no retribution against the defeated army. The older general asked that his men be allowed to keep their horses so that they could put in their crops when they returned to their farms. To this, the younger general agreed and even allowed the officers of his foe to keep their side arms. The aides were called in and the terms of surrender were written out and signed by both men. Plenty of tears were shed by men from both sides as the defeated army marched to an open field and stacked their weapons, then turned away to return to their homes."

"Fighting still continued for a few weeks in other parts of the land, but finally it all came to an end. The older General's side had fought valiantly for their cause, but in the end the stronger force prevailed. The two sides became one, and after a period of healing, what emerged became the greatest nation on the face of the earth." Nat paused briefly and surveyed his audience.

"I tell you this story because, we, too, are engaged in a struggle of sorts—a struggle to survive. And just as sure as I am standing before you, we will survive. This war will end soon; of this I am certain."

Mary Watson had been sitting in the front of the group as Nat spoke. She, as most others within earshot, had sat spellbound as Nat told the story of the two generals. She was the first to break the silence that had fallen on the gathering from the time that Nat first began to tell his story.

"Is this the month, Mr. Booth? Is this the month that General Lee will surrender, and we can go home?" Not even a breath could be heard from the gathering as Nat knelt down in front of Mary Watson. He stroked her head gently with his hand.

"One more year, Mary. Just one more year and you can all go home. I promise."

TWENTY-FIVE

WHEN AMANDA AND ROGER were still outside the manager's office door at the Flatiron Building, they could hear someone shouting inside. But they couldn't see who was making all the noise because of the obscure glass in the door. Waiting a minute or more for the verbal confrontation to come to an end, to no avail, they finally opened the door to find a heavy-set mid-thirties-aged man at the second of two desks in the large room still yelling into the telephone.

"I don't give a good goddamn. She knows the rent check must be in by the fifth of each month. If it is even one day later, the late payment penalty applies." As he paused to listen to the response, he gestured for Amanda and Roger to come towards him and be seated at the vinyl sofa near the desk. "Yes, I know. . . . Your client has been a good tenant, but in the last six months that has all changed. . . . I don't care what her problem is. I've got two book publishers in the building that would take over that office space tomorrow. . . . Okay. Thank you. I appreciate it." He hung up the phone and looked at Amanda. "Hi. I'm Lester Rathburn. What can I do for you in the next—" He looked at his watch. "—ten minutes. It's almost lunch time."

Since Lester's attention was clearly directed at Amanda, Roger kept quiet and let Amanda take the lead.

"I'm pleased to meet you, Mr. Rathburn. My name is Amanda Marshall and my colleague is Roger Atwood. We have been engaged by a client of one of your recent past tenants to try to find some information regarding that tenant."

"And what tenant would that be?"

Amanda answered without hesitation. "Khronos Trust Services, Incorporated."

Lester Rathburn began to laugh. "Good Luck!"

Roger interjected, "We were hoping you might be able to provide some information. Why is that so funny?"

"Khronos Trust Services is like the invisible man. You believe he is there, but you can never see him."

"What do you mean, exactly?"

"I've been manager here for twelve years." While pointing toward the vacant desk behind them, he continues. "The receptionist, who is sick today, has been here even longer. In that time, neither of us have met or spoken with a live person from Khronos."

"Would you be willing to answer a few questions anyway?" Amanda asked.

"If I can. Sure, go ahead. What do you want to know?"

"We were up on the 16th floor and noticed some work was being done in the offices. It appears that someone else is moving in."

"That's right. The Khronos lease finally expired. We really didn't expect anyone to come forward to renew it. About six months ago, we were presented with a court order to open their offices by attorneys for the Bank of New York. I unlocked the door myself and it looked as if no one had been there for years. The bankers searched the place, took out a couple of accounting books and some file folders and left."

"Anything else?"

"A few things. I made them give me a receipt for everything they took out. I think I've got it here in the file cabinet." Lester Rathburn opened the top drawer of the file cabinet nearest his desk and took out a manila folder marked 'Bank of NY'. He handed the receipt to Roger. There were only ten items on the list: The first two were trust account books, then an entry showing a box of file folders followed by six entries for each of six rolls of uncirculated silver half dollars, one each dated from 1958 to 1963, all assigned to the same account number. The last item on the list was 'Navy Pilot Gold Pin', with a different account number written next to it.

"Could we get a copy of this?" Roger asked.

"Can't see how it would hurt. Oh crap. I shut down the copier ten minutes ago. I swear it takes so long to warm up. That's O.K. This will work just as well." Lester Rathburn fed the page into the fax machine and pushed the 'copy' button. When the machine was done, he handed the copy to Roger.

"What about a contact person? Someone had to be paying the rent." The office manager seemed distracted and ignored Roger's question.

"Excuse me a minute, would you?" Rathburn walked to the office exit door, opened it, and looked out into the hallway to his right. He called out, "Are you looking for someone in particular?"

Roger and Amanda could here the reply of the woman coming from outside, down the hall. "No, it's O.K. I can come back tomorrow, thank you." Rathburn closed the office door and returned to where Roger and Amanda were standing.

"Sorry. I kept seeing someone pass by the door. I thought maybe she was lost. About the rent: Khronos had a thirty year lease with the owners of the building—very unusual—and it expired three months ago. Khronos made a single payment at the beginning of the lease period. Got a sweet deal, too. For the last ten years, their effective rental cost has been about one-third the going rate for office space in this building. Of course, if no one is using the space, maybe it's not a great deal after all."

"So what can you tell us about the remodeling and the new tenant?"

"That started about three weeks ago. We gave Khronos sixty days after their lease expired, but no one stepped forward. A book publisher has now leased the space. They will be moving in on the first of next month." The manager looked at his watch again. "I'd love to continue this chat, but I'm out of here. If you like, you may come back after lunch." Rathburn was now standing behind his chair.

Roger looked directly at the building manager. "You know, we would really like to get into those offices and look around."

"I'm sorry, but there is just no way. Besides, I don't think you would find much of anything. Even the office furniture is gone now. The bank gave us authorization to dispose of all of it. But I can assure you that there was nothing significant. Just the usual office stuff: a few desks, an old copy machine, a conference table and chairs. Nothing special."

Roger slipped his hand into the front pocket of his trousers and pulled out a hundred-dollar bill. He folded the bill lengthwise and held it between the first two fingers of his right hand and extended it toward the building manager. "I just feel that there may be something in those offices that may prove useful to us."

The building manager reached out and snatched the money from Roger's hand and stuffed it in his own pocket. He opened the bottom right hand desk drawer. Locating a large key ring, he began to search through it. He removed a tarnished brass key from the ring and presented it to Roger. "The crew is going to be working late in those offices this afternoon. They will be coming back in the morning to finish up. If you return this evening about 7 PM, there shouldn't be anybody around. When you're done, just come back down here and slip the key under the door."

"Thank you." Amanda smiled at Rathburn as he led them out of his office and locked the office door.

"Have a good evening, folks and I hope you find what you are looking for."

TWENTY-SIX

NAT BOOTH WAS as unprepared for the news as the rest of the prisoners at Point Lookout when he first heard the rumor that the entire camp was to be packed up and moved to the Federal detention center at Elmira, New York. Nat had read about the facility in his history studies, but he didn't remember that among the initial group of prisoners at Elmira were transfers from Point Lookout.

The rumor became reality in July of 1864 when the first contingent of 400 prisoners made the trip. Nat was part of a second group of about 1,200 to make the journey. Unlike the first contingent of men transported by rail, Nat's group would travel by sea because of security issues associated with the first transfer. Several prisoners in the first group attempted to escape from the train, and at least one succeeded when he knocked two guards through the open door of a boxcar and then jumped out after, making his escape. In seeking a more secure mode of transportation, prison officials made the decision to transfer the prisoners first by sea to New York harbor and then overland to Elmira. Nat was appalled when he and fellow prisoners were herded on to the vessel in which they were to be transported. It was an old cattle boat, with inadequate quarters for even half the prisoners that were being packed into it. Nat was thankful, at least, that the civilian prisoners, including Mary Watson and her family, had been released from Point Lookout the previous week and would not be forced to endure the journey.

The little ship with its human cargo had hardly reached the open seas when a group of prisoners began to consider the possibility of overpowering the guards and crew, taking over the ship and sailing it to the nearest Southern port. Escape from Point Lookout itself was never a rational consideration due to the layout of the camp and the local geography, but a ship at sea was an entirely different matter. Besides, word of the earlier successful escape from the train had emboldened the transferees. The band of conspirators were debating over who should be included in the group that would initiate the action against the guards when word was passed below that another Federal ship, the warship *Ohio Valley*, had appeared a few hundred yards off the starboard beam. *Ohio Valley* would be escorting the prisoner ship to New York, it was learned, and the talk of escape was stopped cold—for now.

After a few days, the stench within the hold of the ship became unbearable. Worse yet, because the guard force was understaffed, only a few prisoners at a time were allowed on deck to get a few breaths of fresh air. There was little room to stand, let alone ever sleep, and the rations were predictably poor: pork fat, stale bread and very little water. It took several days to complete the voyage to New York. Nearly all of the prisoners suffered severe seasickness and a half-dozen of the men did not survive the trip.

When the ship finally entered New York harbor, there was a perceptible stirring within the prisoners once again. Nat could tell that the excitement that animated the escape conspirators earlier, however briefly, was in the air once again. He believed that the prisoners' desire to escape their long confinement could not be contained indefinitely. Sooner or later, perhaps after resettlement in New York, another escape plan would be hatched. Nat was certain of that.

TWENTY-SEVEN

"**N**OT EXACTLY. Let me explain again." The Assistant Librarian at the Central West Library just off Broadway was trying her best not to sound impatient with Roger Atwood's questions. Roger and Amanda had a few hours to kill before 7 PM when they could get into the Khronos Trust Services office. "We have nearly all issues of *The Wall Journal* after 1950, but in different formats." She further elaborated. "Hard copies of the last twelve months are available here in the annex to the reading room. Earlier material, but after 1989 is in Adobe PDF format, accessible from any workstation in the library. If you need to see issues before then, you will have to use the microfiche archives in this room."

"With the Acrobat files, can we do indexed searches? Can we look for a company name, for example?"

The librarian pushed her eyeglasses back on to the bridge of her nose. "Yes, you can. But remember, you won't find any pages containing stock and bond quotes for any of the exchanges—just the sections of the paper containing articles and advertisements. We have several historical databases containing stock and bond price data, so it was left out to save space and expense. If you need old stock price data, we have Standard and—"

Roger interrupted her in mid-sentence. "No, thank you. We don't need stock data. We're looking for a privately held company that may be the subject of a column or article, probably from the 1970s or 80s."

"There are some indexes for the microfiche for that period, but they aren't very detailed. You may go blind before you find what you are looking for. Why don't you follow me? I think I have something that will be easier to use."

With Roger and Amanda close behind, the librarian walked to an adjoining room and sat down at a PC workstation. She logged into the Windows 2000 system as 'administrator' and keyed in the masked password. "We have just subscribed to this service, and access is pretty restricted. It is supposed to be limited to researchers and educators, but—"

Roger fumbled for his wallet, pulling out his Gettysburg College staff ID. "I'm sorry. I should have told you. I—I'm a history professor at Gettysburg College. Here—look." Roger handed the card to the librarian.

"Well, Professor Atwood. I think this will be of help to you." The monitor displayed the ProQuest login screen. Moving the keyboard aside momentarily, she examined an index card taped to the desk and looked up the requisite password, printed there with passwords for several other services. After entry, the monitor displayed hyperlinks to a long list of periodicals and newspapers. She clicked on 'WSJ 1889-1985' and then rose from the chair. "You should start here. If you need further assistance, do not hesitate to ask."

TWENTY-EIGHT

THE THREE-HUNDRED-MILE rail trip from New York—actually, from Jersey City—to Elmira on the Erie Railroad was largely uneventful. Mostly, the Confederate prisoners as well as the guards were thankful to no longer be confined to that damnable vessel.

The prison camp at Elmira covered more than thirty acres of land adjacent to the Chemung River. On arrival, Nat was assigned to one of thirty-five buildings in Barracks No. 3. Each building was about sixteen by 100 feet in size and could hold over 100 men. They were constructed on raised post-and-beam platforms about three feet high due to frequent flooding from the river. Inside, Nat picked out what he believed to be a vacant sleeping cot and sat down.

"Hey, soldier! That's my bunk." Nat turned around to see who was speaking. A big man with black hair and gray eyes was staring at him, another smaller man standing nearby stuffed his hands in his pockets, waiting to see if the tension in the air was about to escalate.

"Sorry." Nat was trying to sound sincere. "Our group just got here from Point Lookout and the guard told us to pick out an empty bunk."

"Problem is that the one your sittin' on ain't empty. But this one here is." The big man was pointing to a bunk near where he was standing. The mattress was thin and lumpy. Nat rose and walked toward the two men.

"Thanks, I'll take it. My name is Nat Booth." Nat extended his right hand toward the big man. When he flashed a grin, Nat could see that the man had several teeth missing on the right side of his mouth.

"Pleasure. Name's John King, 24th Virginia Infantry. Yankees caught me at The Wilderness. This here is Washington Traweek; they got him at Spotsylvania." Nat turned toward the other man and shook his hand also.

"You can call me 'Wash'. I was in the Jeff Davis Artillery. Lot's of us here. What unit were you in?"

Unlike Nat, the aviator, downed in a strange environment nearly fourteen months earlier, Nat, the Confederate POW, had in the interim developed a consistent story delivered so many times that he could almost believe it himself.

"2nd Virginia Infantry. I'm from Richmond, originally. They got me at Gettysburg."

"Then you were at Point Lookout for one helluva long time. We wuz there only about a month."

Nat nodded. "Yes, over a year, and it was no picnic. Does it look like it will be any better here?"

"Well the mosquitoes ain't as bad, but the food's about the same. I reckon the winter will be colder, though." John King was looking sympathetically at Wash.

Washington Traweek added, "Yeah, but at least you two will be a little more comfortable in here. I'm assigned to one of them rags that the Yankees call a tent." The Elmira camp was filling up fast and many of the inmates were assigned to temporary tent quarters while additional barracks were under construction. However, it was clear that construction was way behind schedule and a few thousand prisoners would probably be spending the upcoming winter sheltered only by some thin canvas.

Captain Mungery was the assistant to the Camp Provost Marshall, one Major Colt, and acted as liaison to Big Joe Smith, the contractor responsible for feeding the prisoners. It was a lucrative contract, as the camp at one time held as many as thirty thousand men, each earning a few cents per day for the contractor. Only a small fraction of the money actually went to pay for food; most of it ended up in Big Joe's pockets. Big Joe gave explicit orders to his buyers to always look for the least expensive, poorest quality vegetables and tainted meat to serve to the hapless prisoners. Nat, who had been assigned work in one of the food preparation buildings, often heard Captain Mungery and Big Joe engaged in a back room shouting match over the poor quality and insufficient quantity of rations being served to the prisoners. On one occasion, in late November 1864, Nat was sorting through a bushel of onions nearly completely spoiled, and intended for the evening meal of beef stew being prepared for the first serving of about one thousand prisoners. Clay Newton, the kitchen supervisor newly hired by the contractor noticed that Nat was picking only the few unspoiled bulbs from the bushel for use in the stew.

"What are you doing there, prisoner, playing paddy cake with them onions?" The other kitchen workers listened intently, but none dared look up.

"No sir, just pulling out the good ones to add to the stew meat."

The supervisor was visibly irritated. "And who told you to do that? This ain't the kitchen at Buckingham Palace—cut up all them onions and throw 'em in the pots."

Nat objected, "But most are rotten, sir. It'll make the men sick." Now Supervisor Newton was really angry. He walked over to where Nat was seated on a stool and punched him in the ear with his fist, knocking Nat to the floor.

"Do as I say, goddamnit!"

Nat jumped up and grabbed the front of Newton's shirt with one hand and forced the man's back against a post. He continued to hold the man with one hand as he raised his right fist in front of Newton's face, ready to strike, then hesitated.

"You best let go of me now, Booth, or you'll be wearin' a barrel shirt for the next week." Newton was referring to a particularly humiliating form of punishment inflicted upon camp prisoners who violated the rules: a heavy oak barrel with the bottom removed and hole in the top would be placed over the prisoner's head. He would be forced to wear it for hours or days, often with a sign indicating his particular offense, like "I am a thief" or "Dog Eater".

Captain Mungery heard the ruckus from an adjoining room and stormed in. "Stop." Nat released the Supervisor. "What's the commotion about in here?" Mungery looked first at Nat, who was clearly in pain, holding his left ear, then directly at the kitchen supervisor. "What's the story here, Newton?"

"I struck the prisoner, sir. He was being insolent. Said he didn't want these onions in the stew."

The Captain picked up a few of the bulbs, then tossed them back into the bushel and reached for a kitchen towel to wipe the slime from his hands. "You mean these sorry things? I don't blame him—I wouldn't want anyone to eat 'em."

The Captain continued, "Now I'm going to tell you this just once, so listen up. Mr. Newton, you are not to strike the prisoners. If any discipline is required, it will be meted out by military personnel only. And, for Mr. Booth and the rest of you prisoners, you need to know that the Union is hard pressed to provide you rebels with food of any kind and we can ill afford to waste any of it. That means, you may discard the worst of the worst, but most of those onions need to go into that stew—virtually everything you are provided to serve must be used—lest some of your fellow prisoners go hungry. Is that understood?"

The two men nodded affirmatively and everyone answered in near unison with a 'Yessir.'

Before leaving the room, Captain Mungery looked directly at Nat Booth. "After the evening rations have been disbursed and you have eaten, report to my office, Mr. Booth."

TWENTY-NINE

C APTAIN MUNGERY'S OFFICE was at the back of the kitchen building in which Nat Booth worked. When Nat entered the office, Mungery motioned for him to be seated.

"I trust you had enough to eat."

"No, sir. But as you know, the prisoners rarely have enough to eat."

"Unfortunately, that is true, but you work in the kitchen—certainly you have more access to provisions than the average prisoner here at Elmira."

"Yes, and I'm ashamed to say that I sometimes take advantage of that position to the detriment of my fellow prisoners."

The Captain smiled, then selected an apple from the basket on his desk and tossed it toward Nat. He caught it. "Well, I'm glad to hear that you are not totally beyond corruption."

"Unfortunately, sir, that is true."

"You are a strange sort of fellow, Booth. You are aware, I'm sure, that you have acquired a reputation here at the camp for being quite the leader. The prisoners look up to you. I hear stories that they often seek your counsel. Fact is, I've gotten complaints from the Chaplain. He says you're trying to do his job."

"I try to help the prisoners survive here, sir, but I leave their spiritual needs to others." Nat had no idea where this conversation was going.

"My point is this: You have leadership qualities and are obviously an educated man. Frankly, Mr. Booth, I do not believe you were a lowly Corporal in the Confederate Army. Why the charade? To what purpose?"

"I'm just trying to get through this holocaust, like the rest of us. Fortunately, it will all be over in a few more months." The last sentence had scarcely left his lips before Nat regretted uttering it.

Captain Mungery leaned forward in his chair. "You Southern boys never give up, do you? You still think you have a chance to win this war?"

"Not at all sir and I didn't mean to suggest as much. I know—that is—I believe that General Lee will surrender soon and the rest of our scattered forces will follow his lead. The war is over; we just don't know it yet. Believe or not, I have long term confidence in the United States as a great and unified nation. But as a student of history, I regret the terrible cost of a war that wasn't really necessary—a half million dead, thousands more maimed, terrible destruction to property and a huge waste of the country's resources. It will require years to recover, and repercussions from this war will extend through the next century and beyond."

"You have an interesting opinion for a loyal member of the secessionist South! If you had not left the Union, there would have been no war."

"If the U.S. Congress, with a majority of Northern states, had not treated the South like a foreign enemy, there would have been no secession."

"And if the South had long ago forsaken the abomination of slavery—"

"Please, sir." Nat interrupted the Captain in mid-sentence, raising his open right hand with a gesture of 'Stop'. "Pardon the interruption, but this debate will be repeated for years to come, without reaching a common consensus. There is no way we can ever settle it today."

Captain Mungery folded his hands and rested them on his desk. "I must agree, and to be honest, I too, share your optimism for the future. I believe that President Lincoln will move quickly once the war is over to heal the nation. Despite some factions in Washington calling for retribution against the vanquished rebel states, I don't believe it will happen. President Lincoln simply won't allow it." Nat shuddered at the Captain's statement, and offered no response to it. After a polite exchange of closing words, Nat was dismissed from the Captain's office.

On his way back to Barracks No. 3, Nat consumed the entire apple that Captain Mungery had given him; including the core, seeds and stem. As he lay in his bunk, he thought about his conversation with the Captain. There was no shortage of cruel guards and overseers at the camp, but Nat knew Captain Mungery to be a fair and caring officer who had tried to improve camp conditions where he could. For this alone, Nat had great respect for the Captain. He also found that Mungery's remarks about the need to heal the nation after the fighting was over to be particularly prescient. In his college studies, Nat had read extensively about the extreme divergence of opinion in the North as to how the South should be treated after the hostilities were over. For many in the North, the South had become so hated that they demanded that the former secessionist states be taxed to pay for the entire cost of the war. After General Lee surrendered on April 9, 1865, some demanded that he be tried and hung. General Grant was so inflamed against this proposed action that he threatened to resign if any charges were brought against Lee.

Surprisingly, the opinion that the South should be treated with compassion was also held by General William Sherman, who is known to this day for wreaking merciless wartime devastation on southern cities and towns, including civilian homes and farms. Yet, when the war was over, he was just as aggressive in demanding that the Federal Government assist the South in returning to normalcy and refrain from imposing reparations.

But the key individual who would set the tone for the fate of the Southern states after the close of the war was President Abraham Lincoln. And it was generally known that the President's considered position, almost from the very beginning of the war, was to extend compassion to the South at war's end. Indeed, when Lincoln spoke at Gettysburg in November 1863 on the battlefield where his forces achieved victory, his message, the Gettysburg Address, was clearly one of consolation, national sorrow, humility and hope for the future. It was not the triumphant speech of the victor over the vanquished.

Nat recalled reading that President Lincoln frequently agonized over the events of the Civil War. Four years had worn heavily on the President, who was known to have experienced fits of deep depression throughout the duration. Even as a young schoolboy, Nat had felt that Lincoln had been cheated at the end of his life. Only five days after Lee surrendered, effectively ending the war, the President was shot in the back of the head while attending a play. What course might history have taken if Lincoln had not gone to Ford's Theater that fateful night? What impact would there have been on Southern reconstruction had John Wilkes Booth been persuaded not to take the President's life? How differently would the second century of American history played out had Lincoln survived to see the beginning of it?

Nathaniel Booth had often pondered these questions as a student of history. It was an interesting speculation, but that is all it was. That is, until now. Nat was beginning to consider that maybe, with a little intervention on his part, there might be a chance for Abraham Lincoln to have the full measure of impact on history that Nat had felt this president always deserved.

THIRTY

THE PROQUEST BROWSER on the library workstation offered some advanced search options, but Roger ignored them and instead entered the single word "Khronos" into the local search engine textbox. He looked up at Amanda who was standing at the left side of his chair, smiled weakly, then clicked on the button marked 'Search'.

Within seconds, a results form appeared and almost immediately a half-dozen relevant result summaries were displayed. When the search was over ten seconds later, two additional entries had been added making a total of eight. Roger clicked on the first entry dated Monday, August 25, 1873. The word 'Khronos' was highlighted in yellow on the new page that appeared. The word was inside a paragraph in the classified advertising section of the paper and read as follows:

> ASSET PROTECTION AND WEALTH PRESERVATION. IT IS NOT TOO LATE. OUR PROFESSIONAL STAFF CAN HELP GUIDE YOU THROUGH THE PERILOUS FINANCIAL WATERS AHEAD AND THE EVENTUAL RETURN TO PROSPERITY. REASONABLE FEES. CONTACT N. BOOTH OR T. LUU AT KHRONOS TRUST SERVICES, 90 BROAD STREET.

"Here, you sit down. I'll get another chair." Roger rose and pulled lightly on Amanda's arm until she was seated in the chair which he had been occupying."

"This is great." Amanda was excited. "We have been able to place Nathaniel at Gettysburg in July 1863. Then probably at the prisoner of war camp in Maryland after that. We don't know when he was transferred to Elmira, New York, but we know he escaped on April 11, 1865. Now this shows he was in New York City in August 1873. He must have hooked up with this 'Luu' guy sometime before then."

"Right." Roger replied. "And do you know what is significant about 1873?"

"Dammit, Roger, I'm not in class right now. Just tell me, for crying out loud!"

"O.K. It turns out that a financial panic—an economic depression—started in September of that year. It was known as the 'Panic of 1873'."

"I've heard of that," she replied.

"And I'm sure Nathaniel Booth knew about it as well. Of course, he had the advantage of knowing about it before it occurred! By placing this ad in August, I believe he was putting Khronos on record as having some kind of financial crystal ball. Let's print a copy of this—better print two copies so that we can send one to Rose Booth—and then check out the other references."

Amanda clicked on the browser printer icon twice, then the back button where she selected the next reference in the results summary list; this one dated September 8, 1873. A new page of classifieds appeared, containing the Khronos ad with identical wording as before. Without waiting for a comment from Roger, Amanda went back to the result list and selected the third item, dated October 6, 1873. Again, another ad with the same wording, but this one contained one additional sentence: "See our *Wall Street Journal* notices published August 25th and September 8th." Amanda printed this page and then found that the next three entries were identical to the third one, except each was dated on the first Monday of the subsequent months: November and December 1873 and January 1874.

"Nothing new here." Amanda remarked. After selecting the next entry, dated July 11, 1898, Amanda read the text aloud.

> KHRONOS TRUST SERVICES EXECUTIVE, NATHANIEL BOOTH OF NEW YORK CITY, AGE 59, HAS RECENTLY STEPPED DOWN FROM THE POSITION AS PRESIDENT OF THE CORPORATION. MR. BOOTH WILL BE SUCCEEDED BY MR. TRUNG LUU, AGE 49, ALSO OF NEW YORK CITY AND FORMER CORPORATE TREASURER. IT IS WIDELY REPORTED THAT KHRONOS TRUST SERVICES WAS SUCCESSFUL IN PREDICTING IN ADVANCE THE PANICS OF 1873 AND 1893, AFFORDING SIGNIFICANT FINANCIAL ADVANTAGE TO THOSE WHO HEEDED THE RECOMMENDATIONS MADE BEFORE THE ONSET OF THE FINANCIAL CRISES. MR. LUU STATED THAT MR. BOOTH AND HIS WIFE LILY, ALSO A FORMER PARTNER IN THE CORPORATION, ARE ENJOYING AN EXTENDED VACATION IN CALIFORNIA. MR. BOOTH WILL CONTINUE TO HOLD A POSITION ON THE BOARD OF DIRECTORS.

"Remarkable." Roger was excited. "I guess it makes sense. It's true that he would have been about fifty-nine years old in 1898."

"And he was apparently married by then."

"And apparently pretty wealthy." Roger added. Amanda pressed the print button twice again, and then moved on to the last Khronos hyperlink reference. This one was dated May 19, 1978:

SPOKESPERSON LYDIA MCCABE OF KHRONOS TRUST SERVICES, INCORPORATED, CONFIRMED TODAY THAT PRESIDENT AND CHIEF OPERATING OFFICER, MR. DERRICK LUU, AGE 39, WAS KILLED IN A PRIVATE PLANE CRASH IN THE FLORIDA EVERGLADES SEVERAL DAYS AGO. MR. LUU'S TWIN ENGINE BEECHCRAFT LEFT REPUBLIC AIRPORT IN EAST FARMINGDALE ON MAY 12 AND WAS SCHEDULED TO ARRIVE IN MIAMI NOT LATER THAN MAY 14. A SEARCH FOR THE MISSING AIRPLANE WAS MOUNTED THE NEXT DAY. WRECKAGE FROM THE PLANE WAS DISCOVERED TWO DAYS LATER, ON MAY 17. PASSENGERS INCLUDED BRENDA LUU, AGE 35, SPOUSE, AND CHILDREN AMBER, AGE NINE AND DERRICK JR, AGE FOUR. THERE WERE NO SURVIVORS.

MISS MCCABE ACKNOWLEDGED THAT THE CRASH REPRESENTED A TERRIBLE LOSS FOR THE CORPORATION WHICH HAS DONE BUSINESS IN THE STATE OF NEW YORK SINCE 1873, BUT WANTED TO ASSURE CLIENTS AND SUBSCRIBERS THAT "THE CORPORATION WOULD CONTINUE TO OFFER THE HIGH QUALITY OF SERVICES THAT OUR CLIENTELE HAS COME TO EXPECT FROM KHRONOS TRUST SERVICES". WHEN ASKED, SHE STATED THAT "IT HAD NOT YET BEEN DETERMINED WHO WOULD TAKE OVER THE CORPORATE

DIRECTORSHIP NOW VACANT DUE TO THE
TRAGIC PASSING OF MR. LUU." FUNERAL
ARRANGEMENTS ARE STILL PENDING.

The article included a photograph of Derrick Luu. As Amanda began to print, she looked at Roger. "Do you think that Rose will recognize this man? Do you think that he is the guy that brought the stocks and bonds?"

"Could be. You know, it's sad to hear about this sort of thing—especially the kids, but it's amazing information at the same time. We need to overnight a copy of this to Rose."

Amanda was trying to figure dates and ages in her head. "If Derrick Luu was 39 in 1978, that means he was born in 1939. The other Luu, what's his name? Trung—yes, this Trung would have been too old to be Derrick's father. There must be another Luu in there somewhere between 1900 and 1940."

"Probably, but let's first see if we can find any specific references to Nat in these WSJ archives". Amanda selected 'Advanced Search' this time and entered various combinations of Nathaniel and Nat Booth, both with and without the middle initial 'N'. The only reference returned was the same one that they had seen previously that announced Nat's retirement from Khronos Trust Services. "What about a general web search?"

"We already did that. Remember the genealogy listings that we got? One Nathaniel Booth was a Revolutionary War soldier and another was born in England and became a butcher or something."

She looked up at him again. "Yeah, I forgot."

"But don't be discouraged. I repeat, this is really great stuff! And now we have a new name connected to Khronos."

"I agree. But there are some holes in the time line. We have Nat Booth placed up to almost age sixty, but what about Khronos? We have a major gap between 1898 and 1978."

"That's true, but I think that Mrs. Booth would be most interested in personal details of Nat's life, rather than Khronos Trust Services."

"Yes," Amanda added. "But I know that *you* are interested in Khronos. As far as Rose is concerned, it is possible that we may eventually find that Nathaniel Booth died before his mother was born."

"I've thought of that, and it's going to be a tough thing to tell her. She believed for years that he died in 1968. It would be like telling her he died twice."

"So, what now, Roger?"

"Well, I'm hungry. Let's get a bite to eat before we go back to the Khronos offices, then maybe tomorrow we try to find Lydia McCabe."

THIRTY-ONE

ALTHOUGH NAT HAD HEARD various escape rumors almost from the beginning of his incarceration at Elmira, none of them seemed credible until John King told him of the tunneling work that had just begun under Wash Traweek's tent. John made Nat swear an oath that he would not reveal the escape plan to anyone else, to which Nat agreed.

It was March 1st and Nat understood that the work would need to proceed rapidly if he was to make his escape in time to get to Washington before April 14th, the day that Lincoln was to be assassinated. It wouldn't be easy. The entire escape team consisted of only eight people: Nat, John King, plus Wash Traweek and the other five occupants of his tent. They estimated that they needed to tunnel about eighty feet to get a safe ten feet beyond the fence line. When Nat made his first visit to the tent and the escape tunnel, he found that the heating stove had been temporarily set aside and the work crew had begun digging a vertical shaft where it had previously rested. One of the men was stationed as a sentry so that if a guard or uncleared prisoner came near, the shaft could be covered quickly by repositioning the stove.

For Nat, it was a particularly curious case of déjà vu. As a teenager, one of his favorite television sitcoms was *Hogan's Heroes*. In the TV series, the allied POWs were perpetually engaged in one or more tunneling projects in order to escape the camp. And here in Wash's tent, the stove, just as in the TV series, had been concealing the entrance to the tunnel.

"This is going to take forever," Nat thought to himself. He could see that Wash was working at the base of the shaft using a cook's spoon as a shovel. The hole was about six feet deep and two and one-half feet in diameter. Every few minutes Wash would pass a stocking full of dirt up to one of the escape crew workers, trading it for an empty stocking. Each sock had a band of fabric that had been stitched to it at the toe. When a worker had two socks full of dirt he would tie the open end of each with a long draw string, then roll up his pant legs and use the fabric band to secure one of the dirt-filled stockings to each calf just below the knee. He would then pass the draw strings up his pant legs to his waist and roll down his pants, hiding completely the dirt payload he was carrying.

The procedure was tedious and slow, but no one could come up with a better idea for concealing their work: they needed some way to get rid of the dirt from the tunnel. With two socks full of dirt hidden in the legs of his trousers, the 'mule' would walk inconspicuously from the tent to one of several construction sites around the camp and, when no one was looking, pull on the drawstrings releasing the dirt. Using a work crew of two or three digging and carrying away dirt continuously during daylight hours, the small band of determined workers could move nearly a cubic yard of earth each day. Nat wasn't certain, but he thought he recalled a similar technique depicted in the film, *The Great Escape*, starring Steve McQueen.

After the vertical shaft was about six feet deep, the men started digging horizontally and were able to advance the tunnel about three feet per day. Nat became more optimistic with their progress. At this rate, they would be done and could make their escape well before April 14th, giving him several days or more to get to Washington and interdict the assassination plot.

But by mid-March, their progress had begun to slow. The men were getting tired, and as the digging advanced further from the tent, it took longer to move the dirt out for disposal. A third hindrance was rocks. They were encountering larger ones—some that couldn't be carried away in the stocking bags. The crew had to waste valuable time by digging short tunnel extensions perpendicular to the main tunnel as a place to stow the larger rocks. To deal with the ever-increasing distance that the dirt had to be carried in the tunnel, one of the men fashioned a flat wooden box, a sort of sled, with a long rope tied to each end. When the box was full, the digger would tug lightly on the rear rope to signal a man in the shaft below the tent floor to pull the sled back and empty it. The digger would then use the other rope to pull the box back to his location where it could be filled up again. Meanwhile, the worker at the shaft-end of the tunnel would fill stockings with the last sled full of dirt and pass them up to the men in the tent for the usual disposal. The sled invention had helped the men regain their former rate of progress, but it wouldn't be long before other problems began to surface.

Less than an hour after work had started one morning, the men in the tent were surprised to see a digging tool fly up out of the hole with John King raising himself out after it. He was disgusted. The tool, the last of the cook spoons that Nat had procured from the kitchen, was worn to a nub.

"I can't work with that piece-of-shit spoon. We need a real shovel."

"Great idea," Nat offered, "but how do you suggest we get one?"

"I got some money," Corporal Cooper offered. "I think I can bribe one of the guards over where they're buildin' on the new barracks."

Washington Traweek stated sarcastically, "I don't think the guards will be much interested in Confederate paper dollars!"

"No. I mean that I have some real money—gold." The Corporal reached into his pocket and pulled out two gold pieces, each slightly smaller but a little thicker that a U.S. twenty dollar gold piece. "I had three of 'em, but I bought me a coat and shoes and some extra food last month. I was savin' these for after we got out." Everyone looked at the two coins in Cooper's outstretched palm. Forty dollars in gold was a lot of money to men who seldom had more than a few dimes and pennies, or on rare occasion, a silver dollar.

"Let me see one of those." Nat reached for one of the coins. It was shiny and showed practically no wear. "Where did you get these, Cooper?"

"Why? They're real gold—says so right on 'em—'one oh-zee fine gold'."

John King jumped in, "That's 'one ounce', you idiot!"

Then it was Nat's turn. "I know they're real, Cooper, but did you notice the date on the coins? They're dated '1967'." Nat grabbed Cooper by the shirt. "Tell me where you got these. Who gave 'em to you?"

As the other men pulled Nat off of him, the Corporal cried out. "All right. I'll tell you. I took 'em off a Yankee soldier we captured. A real strange one he wuz. But he helped my lil' brother, Junius who wuz shot jus' before the fightin' started at Gettysburg."

"And was this Yankee soldier by any chance a black man?" Nat was calmer now.

"Yes, he was. How'd you know?"

"And can you tell me—" Nat was now speaking very deliberately to Corporal Cooper who was sprawled on the ground. "—what happened to the black soldier?"

Cooper smiled momentarily, looked around at the other men, then looked down at the ground and spoke very softly. He was embarrassed by what he was about to say. "He flew away."

"What?" Everyone else in the tent except for Nat Booth murmured in protest. A round of catcalls began, directed at Corporal Cooper.

"Yes, dammit. We wuz takin' the prisoner back to the rear supply camp along with my poor gut-shot brother, when all of a sudden this noisy metal machine comes outta the sky. It wuz nearly as long as a railroad boxcar and blowin' a fierce wind down on us. It had three or four men and a couple real big guns inside. We had no choice but to give up the black Yankee to them. They took Junius, too. Said they could fix him up. That wuz all right with me, 'cuz our doc said that Junius was gonna die. The Negro climbed in with my brother an' they flew away, makin' one hellacious noise." After this exposition, the uproar rose again from the men in the tent.

"Quiet down. You'll bring the guards in here." Nat pleaded with the men to hold down the noise. "He's telling the truth. The man's name is Lincoln Hayes." The men fell silent. Those closest to Nat stepped back. "I know what you're thinking. But I'm no Yankee spy."

John King spoke up first. "I don't suppose you are a spy, or you would mos' likely have turned us in long ago. Maybe you and Coop here are just a little bit crazy."

Cooper protested, "I'm tellin' you the truth. It' just like I—"

Nat cut him off. "What else can you tell me, Cooper? Did you talk to him? Was he hurt?"

"One of the boys shot and grazed his head before he wuz captured, but he weren't hurt bad. But I didn't see it happen. He and I talked about Junius, but that's about all."

"And you're sure you saw the black man fly away?"

"Sure as you're standing here, I saw it."

Nat was elated. Lincoln Hayes had been rescued. He had no reason to doubt Cooper. The man was obviously describing a helicopter rescue. There is no way he could have made that up.

"I hope your brother is okay, Coop. Now I suggest you take one of those gold coins and see if you can arrange to get us a real shovel."

The tunnel conspirators agreed that they would suspend further work that day until a decent shovel could be obtained. That evening at dusk, Cooper walked to the other side of the camp where a construction team was just finishing up work for the day. Two additional barracks buildings were about to be erected. The perimeters had been staked out at the four corners. Twine had been strung between the stakes as a guide for the prisoners who had been digging postholes for the raised post-and-beam platform that would support the building itself. An armed guard watched closely as the prisoners threw their tools into the bed of a wagon and were marched back to their quarters. The chestnut gelding hitched to the wagon stroked the dirt with one hoof and turned toward the guard as if to say, "What's the holdup? Let's get going."

"Hi, Sarge." Cooper walked toward the guard.

"What's up, Cooper?"

"Jus' thought I'd come by to see how the work was goin' on my new quarters—I'll sure be happy to move outta that tent."

"I wouldn't be movin' your stuff just yet. Word is that we 'bout have Richmond surrounded. My bet is that you Southern boys are almost ready to give it up. You'll probably be sleepin' in your own bed at home before the Fourth of July!"

Cooper was just trying to make small talk, but was caught off guard by the Sergeant's comment. "If that's so, then why be buildin' more prisoner shacks?"

The Sergeant was shaking his head. "Beats the hell outta me. It's just a damn waste of money."

"Sarge," Cooper was getting to the point, "you know the river has been real high for the last few days and it's goin' to be floodin' out the low spots by the latrines. Some of the boys would like to dig out a channel back towards the river to keep the latrines dry. Otherwise, there will be one helluva mess there."

"So . . ."

"So, I was wonderin' if we might borrow one of them trenching shovels to do the work. We can't dig with our bare hands."

"Not a chance. You know the major told us just last week to keep our ears open. Seems some of you boys may be trying to dig escape tunnels out of this place."

"C'mon, Sarge. You just told me the war will be over soon. You'd have to be a fool to try an' escape now. And it's real important to the boys. You know, we'd be willin' to pay the cost—so the fed'ral gov'ment wouldn't be out any money." Cooper reached into his pocket and pulled out one of the gold Krugerrands.

The Sergeant glanced around quickly to make sure no one was watching. "Let me see that." Then he took the coin from Cooper's hand and held it close to examine it in the failing light. "What kind of joke are you tryin' to pull? I've never seen any money like this. And what about the date? It says '1967'!"

Cooper shrugged his shoulders. "I think it might be French, or sumpthin'. That date is 'jus a misstrike. But you can tell it's real gold—feel how heavy? An' it sez' so right on it."

"I see that—'one ounce'. That would be worth twenty dollars—an awful lot to pay for a shovel that cost 'bout a dollar." The Sergeant was suspicious.

"Well, we could use two shovels, and I can take the change in silver."

"You can have one shovel, no change, and if you get caught with it, you found it somewhere layin' on the ground. Understood?"

"Yessir. Thank you, Sarge."

The Sergeant took one of the trenching shovels out of the wagon and placed it on the ground, then jumped up into the driver's position. He turned his head back toward Corporal Cooper. "You best get back to your tent right away—the sentries will be passin' this way before long." Then he drove off in the wagon. Cooper picked up the shovel and hid it the best he could under his shirt. He walked at a fast pace back toward his tent and the tunnel, feeling the cold steel of the shovel blade against his breast.

"You're back awfully soon." Washington Traweek greeted Cooper as he entered the tent. "No luck, huh?" Traweek didn't see the prize concealed under Cooper's shirt until the Corporal pulled it out and raised it high in the air for all in the tent to see. "Yes!" Everyone in the tent raised his right fist acknowledging Cooper's prize.

Work resumed in earnest the very next morning. With Cooper working furiously at the end of the tunnel, the "mules" could scarcely keep up. A few members of the team supported the notion of bringing additional prisoners in on the escape, but in the end, none were added to the original eight. Ten days later, on April 2nd, the team had reached their goal. The tunnel was eighty feet long, as verified by Nat Booth measuring exactly twenty lengths of a four-foot long stick. But Nat and Wash had some concerns. After all, no one had actually measured the required distance as eighty feet; it was just a consensus estimate. Measuring the distance above ground would have attracted unwanted attention. Not to mention the fact that any prisoner daring to venture close to the fence line would likely be shot. Finally, the pair persuaded the rest of the team that they needed to make sure that the end of the tunnel was beyond the perimeter fence. Although risky, the plan was simple: Nat, from within the tunnel, would dig upwards until he encountered some plant roots, probably within a foot of the surface. Then, using the point of the measuring stick, he was to push cautiously through the sod. Four of the men were selected to stand about in the prison yard between the tent and the fence, keeping an eye out for the point of Nat's stick. The team decided to assume the further risk of carrying out this plan in broad daylight rather than waiting until dusk when the sentries would be less attentive. After all, if it were too dark, no one would be able to spot Nat's probing stick.

At about 5 PM, Nat entered the tunnel. After twenty minutes, the word was passed that he was ready to push up through the sod and John King, Wash, Cooper and a fourth member of the team were dispatched to their positions outside the tent and Nat was signaled to proceed. Wash was closest to the fence. Every few seconds, he would glance in the direction of the expected exit point. Nothing. After another minute, Wash noticed that John King, some fifteen feet away, was trying to get Wash's attention. John was pointing down at his foot. When Wash looked down, he was shocked to see the tip of the measuring stick not more than two inches from his left shoe. Without thinking, Wash stepped on the end of the stick, forcing it down. John King headed quickly back toward the tent, determined to get the bad news to Nat and rest of the team as quickly as possible.

"What's going on there, prisoner?" A sentry at the fence line had raised his musket, directing it at Wash.

"Nothing, boss."

"Then move along." But Wash didn't dare move, fearful that Nat, inches below him under the sod, would unknowingly push the probe upward again for the sentry to see. In order to stall the guard, Wash knelt on his right knee to retie his left shoe.

"I'll jus' be a minute, boss." The sentry kept his weapon trained on Wash until Traweek rose slowly and made his way toward the tent. He hoped that someone had gotten word to Nat about the screw up.

Inside the tent, the other seven members of the escape conspiracy were waiting for Wash. The interior of the tent had been completely secured, with the stove put in place over the planks covering the open shaft.

"What's the problem, Nat? You can't even get a simple measurement job right?" Washington Traweek was upset.

"The tunnel is eighty feet long. Measure it yourself if you don't believe me." Nat's arms were folded in front of him.

"Then how do you explain that we're almost ten feet *this* side of the fence line?"

"Easy." Nat rose. "Come over here." Nat led Wash to an opening at the back of the tent that provided a view of the fence line and the sentry near where Wash had been standing. "You see the point beyond the fence that we were aimin' at?"

"Yes."

"And you see about where you were standing, there on the right—where I punched up through the sod?"

"Yes." Wash still didn't understand.

"Don't you see, Wash? We dug a tunnel eighty feet long, but we didn't dig straight. The tunnel curves off to the right. The last digging we did is almost parallel to the fence line. My guess is that since most of us are right-handed—except for Coop here—that we just naturally worked with a right hand bias."

"Sum-bitch," offered Wash.

"We got almost twenty more feet to dig."

One of the men spoke up. "Maybe we should just give it up. I heard that General Lee lost another big battle just yesterday. I don't think it will be too long before the fightin' will be over and they'll be sendin' us home anyway."

It was true. On April 1st, General William Sherman attacked Lee's forces at a place called Five Forks and inflicted over 5,000 casualties on the Confederates commanded by Major General George Pickett. And for the Southern command, the bad news was about to get even worse. After Sherman's decisive victory at Five Forks, General Lee telegraphed Jefferson Davis, President of the Confederacy, and advised him to abandon Richmond. Davis immediately moved the government to the relative safety of North Carolina, temporarily out of the path of the advancing Union Army. Petersburg fell on April 3rd, 1865, and Union troops entered the City of Richmond that very same day.

"Maybe he's right. Maybe it ain't worth riskin' a bullet in the back just to get home a month or two early." John King was torn between two emotions. He was happy to hear that the war might soon be over, but the fact that their hard work over the last several weeks had left the tunneling crew short of their intended mark was depressing.

Nat Booth was conflicted as well. While John King was merely speculating about prospects for a final end to the war, Nat had inside information: he knew to a certainty that it would be only a matter of days before General Lee surrendered. He also knew that his secret mission depended upon completing the tunnel and making a successful early escape. Without question, he was willing to risk it for himself, but was it fair to the rest of the escape team? Finally, it was Washington Traweek that would resolve the issue for all of them.

"We've come this far. I say we finish the tunnel," Wash offered. "Then each man can decide for himself. Those who want to stay can stay. Whoever wants to go—well, they can go. I say we vote on it." Wash looked around to see that everyone was nodding in agreement. "Everyone who wants to finish the tunnel, raise your hand." Wash, Nat and Cooper raised their hands immediately. Then, more slowly, four of the others. Finally, John King raised his also. "It's settled then. Let's quit for the day, then get started again first thing in the morning."

THIRTY-TWO

AFTER ONLY A FEW DAYS into the month, it became clear that April 1865 was quickly shaping up to be one of the most significant in American history. After the fall of Richmond, General Lee was faced with his toughest decision of the war. As long as Richmond was the capital of the South, his war strategy was necessarily constrained by the need to assure the defense of the city. But no longer. He now had the freedom to prosecute the war by considering only what made the most sense in terms of military strategy. The fall of Richmond broadened his possibilities and brought to serious consideration the option of continuing a guerilla-style war of attrition against the Union. It certainly made tactical sense: Lee commanded 55,000 men who, despite the lack of provisions, still maintained a high level of morale. As one option, he could move his men 140 miles south and join up with General Joe Johnson; together hoping to mount a successful conventional offensive against Union General William Sherman. Then a guerilla campaign could continue the war for another decade or more and perhaps lead the North to finally give up the notion of preserving the Union. This was the course of action called for by Jefferson Davis, President of the Confederacy. But Robert E. Lee had serious misgivings. He believed that such a military strategy would not only fail to save the South, but would invariably cause a bitter divide in the country that might require the passing of several generations before the country could recover.

There had been some earlier attempts to end the fighting. President Davis had sent a commission to Canada to meet with U.S. representatives, including the famous American journalist, Horace Greeley. But the meeting resulted in no real progress toward ending the conflict. Later, on February 3, 1865, President Lincoln and his Secretary of State William Seward met with Confederate representatives aboard the President's steamer, *River Queen*, at Harper's Ferry, Virginia. Lincoln remained steadfast on three conditions for peace: dissolution of the Confederate armies, preservation of the Union, and freedom for the slaves. When the Confederate representatives expressed a desire for more favorable terms, Lincoln suggested that he would be willing to consider remuneration by the Federal Government to the Southern States for the economic loss that would result from abolition. It was understood, however, that such payments would require the prior approval of Congress. Even this peace initiative came to no satisfactory result. To the President, it became clear that the fighting would continue until the military situation for the South became more desperate.

It is not known exactly when General Lee came to the conclusion that the war must end, but several events of early April 1865 were no doubt significant in his decision: On April 6th, Lee's forces were routed by General Grant at Sayler's Creek, Virginia. The next day, General Lee learned that the long-awaited train of provisions, desperately needed by his men, was at risk of being intercepted by Union forces under General Sheridan. Later that day, Lee received the following history making communication:

FROM: HEADQUARTERS, ARMIES OF THE U.S.
    5 PM, APRIL 7TH, 1865
TO: GENERAL R.E. LEE, COMMANDING C.S.A:

THE RESULT OF THE LAST WEEK MUST CONVINCE YOU OF THE HOPELESSNESS OF FURTHER RESISTANCE ON THE PART OF THE ARMY OF NORTHERN VIRGINIA IN THIS STRUGGLE. I FEEL THAT IT IS SO, AND REGARD IT AS MY DUTY TO SHIFT FROM MYSELF THE RESPONSIBILITY OF ANY FURTHER EFFUSION OF BLOOD, BY ASKING OF YOU THE SURRENDER OF THAT PORTION OF THE CONFEDERATE STATES ARMY KNOWN AS THE ARMY OF NORTHERN VIRGINIA.

U.S. GRANT, LIEUTENANT-GENERAL

Within an hour of receiving the message, General Lee wrote a reply that was received by General Grant after midnight on April 8th:

APRIL 7TH, 1865
TO: LIEUTENANT-GENERAL U.S. GRANT,
    COMMANDING ARMIES OF THE U.S.

GENERAL: I HAVE RECEIVED YOUR NOTE OF THIS DATE. THOUGH NOT ENTERTAINING THE OPINION YOU EXPRESS OF THE HOPELESSNESS OF FURTHER RESISTANCE ON THE PART OF THE ARMY OF NORTHERN VIRGINIA, I RECIPROCATE YOUR DESIRE TO AVOID USELESS EFFUSION OF BLOOD, AND THEREFORE, BEFORE CONSIDERING YOUR PROPOSITION, ASK THE TERMS YOU WILL OFFER ON THE CONDITION OF ITS SURRENDER.

R.E. LEE, GENERAL

Another message from General Grant was passed through the Confederate lines:

APRIL 8TH, 1865

TO: GENERAL R.E. LEE, COMMANDING C.S.A.:

YOUR NOTE OF LAST EVENING IN REPLY TO MINE OF THE SAME DATE, ASKING THE CONDITIONS ON WHICH I WILL ACCEPT THE SURRENDER OF THE ARMY OF NORTHERN VIRGINIA, IS JUST RECEIVED. IN REPLY I WOULD SAY THAT, PEACE BEING MY GREAT DESIRE, THERE IS BUT ONE CONDITION I WOULD INSIST UPON, NAMELY, THAT THE MEN AND OFFICERS SURRENDERED SHALL BE DISQUALIFIED FOR TAKING UP ARMS AGAIN AGAINST THE GOVERNMENT OF THE UNITED STATES UNTIL PROPERLY EXCHANGED.

I WILL MEET YOU, OR WILL DESIGNATE OFFICERS TO MEET ANY OFFICERS YOU MAY NAME FOR THE SAME PURPOSE, AT ANY POINT AGREEABLE TO YOU, FOR THE PURPOSE OF ARRANGING DEFINITELY THE TERMS UPON WHICH THE SURRENDER OF THE ARMY OF NORTHERN VIRGINIA WILL BE RECEIVED.

U.S. GRANT, LIEUTENANT-GENERAL

Some minor skirmishes continued between the two forces as General Grant was determined to block all escape routes that the Confederates might use to break out to the south. After a further exchange of messages, the two generals agreed to meet in the early afternoon of April 9th, 1865, in the small, one-street village known as Appomattox Court House, Virginia.

The generous terms of surrender that General Grant offered Robert E. Lee were consistent with President Lincoln's desire for a conciliatory treatment of the defeated South. This desire was expressed earlier that year in the closing words of Lincoln's inaugural address at the beginning of his second term in office. He said, "With malice toward none, with charity for all, with firmness in the right as God gives us to see the right, let us strive on to finish the work we are in, to bind up the nation's wounds, to care for him who shall have borne the battle and for his widow and his orphan, to do all which may achieve and cherish a just and lasting peace among ourselves and with all nations."

Three days after the generals negotiated the terms of surrender, the officers and men of the Army of Northern Virginia marched to a field outside Appomattox Court House, folded their flags and stacked their weapons. Some, with tears streaming down their faces, ripped cherished battle flags from their stanchions and stuffed them in their shirts. For Lee's Army of Northern Virginia, the war was over.

THIRTY-THREE

NEWS OF GENERAL LEE'S SURRENDER spread quickly through the prisoner of war camp at Elmira. By Monday evening, the day after the Generals' meeting, hardly a soul could be found who hadn't heard the news. The guards and other members of the Union staff uniformly welcomed the news as did most of the inmates. But many of the men who had fought with General Lee could not help but feel sadness out of the deep love and respect they held for their Commander-in-Chief. They knew him well enough to almost sense his disappointment, all the while looking forward to the prospect of returning to their own homes and families.

The small band of escape conspirators had another reason to celebrate. On Tuesday, the tunnel extension was finished and this time successful completion was confirmed. That afternoon, Washington Traweek looked beyond the fence line and saw the tip of the measuring stick that Nat pushed up through the earth ceiling at the end of their narrow, man-made cavern. The escape was planned for that very evening after midnight. What was uncertain was just how many of the other seven conspirators would be joining Nat.

Earlier in the day when Wash and the others first heard about the surrender, the consensus was that the prospect of an early release made an escape attempt now seem rather foolish. But as the day progressed, word began to spread that an early release was unlikely. Outside of the northern states and Virginia, the war was still a fact of life. No one knew how long before it would be completely over. Maybe weeks, maybe months. After some discussion, each man decided for himself. Nat, Wash, Cooper and two of the others would make their escape that evening. The other three, including John King, would wait for a prisoner exchange or the final end of the war, whichever came first.

Camp curfew was 9 PM, when all of the prisoners were expected to be in their assigned quarters. Nat was at a disadvantage because his bunk was in one of the barracks buildings, at least one hundred feet from the tent that housed the others in the escape group. Consequently, it was decided that Nat would wait until one AM before making his way to the escape tunnel. By then, the other four would be long gone. Their escape would not be jeopardized in the event that Nat was stopped by one of the guards.

Nat tried to get some rest in his bunk, but was unable to sleep. On the hour, he could hear the sentries call out as they made their rounds. "Eleven o'clock and all is well." It seemed like hours before he heard the next announcement, "Midnight and all is well." He knew that the other four conspirators were now in the tunnel, with Washington Traweek removing the last of the earth barrier to their freedom above his head in the escape shaft. Nat could picture in his mind Wash poking his face out of tunnel exit and looking around to make sure they wouldn't be seen. Nat strained to listen for anything unusual—any commotion or perhaps a gunshot that would indicate that the escape plot had been foiled. Thankfully, he heard nothing at all.

But Nat was troubled by something else: the extra time that it had taken to complete the tunnel—ten more days—had jeopardized his mission. He had only two days to get to Washington, nearly three hundred miles away. It seemed hopeless. Nonetheless, he was determined to try.

Finally, the sentries completed their one AM rounds. Nat was up in an instant, quietly stuffing some rolled up blankets under his bunk covers to make it appear to a passing guard that he was still sleeping. The morning roll call would be soon enough for the guards to discover that he was gone. He crawled over to John King's bunk. John had been awake all along. As Nat approached, King held out his hand and Nat grasped it firmly.

John whispered to him, "Take this money, Nat. It's twenty dollars I been savin'. You can use it more than me." Nat whispered a 'thank you' and stuffed the bills into his pocket. He was extremely grateful. On his own, he had managed to save less than five dollars in change.

Without another word, Nat gave John King a smile and a wink, then crawled to the nearest open window. Carefully, he looked out. The way was clear and he could hear nothing but the quiet roar of the nearby river and faint chirping of crickets in the night. In a second he was on the ground, then secure in the darkness under the three-foot high platform that supported the barracks building. Slowly but deliberately, he made his way under the platform to the other side where earlier that day he had stowed a bucket of wagon axle grease. Mixing some with the dirt, he spread it on his face and arms, then set out in the darkness in the direction of the tent and the entrance to the escape tunnel.

Inside the tent, the three who would remain behind were waiting for Nat. He quietly greeted each one of them in turn, grasping their hands firmly with both of his. One of the men offered Nat a small loaf of black bread and dried beef wrapped in oiled paper. Nat stuffed the package inside his shirt, then lowered himself into the vertical shaft of the tunnel. As he crawled along he could faintly hear the men he had left behind covering the shaft opening with planks. In a minute, the dried-out pieces of sod would be arranged over the planks followed by the heating stove, concealing once again any outward evidence of the escape plot.

Nat raised his head out of the escape shaft at the end of the tunnel and looked back toward the camp. He could see the faint light of a few lanterns inside some of the staff buildings on the far side of the camp. But what concerned him was much closer: Along the fence line and just inside of it, not more than sixty feet away, a group of three—maybe four—guards were gathered, faces flickering in the reflected light of a camp fire. Nat could barely hear the muffled tones of their conversation above the sound of the nearby Chemung River. Keeping a wary eye on the gathering by the fire, Nat raised himself out of the escape shaft and then slowly crawled on his belly in the direction of the river. It took ten minutes to reach the riverbank. Rolling over the edge of the bank, he was now completely hidden from view and stopped to catch his breath.

THE CHEMUNG RIVER BASIN was carved out by advancing glaciers from the last Ice Age. The river itself, meandering along the Pennsylvania-New York border, was formed by the confluence of two other rivers, the Tioga and the Cohocton. Just across the Pennsylvania border at Sayre, the Chemung joins the Susquehanna River and eventually flows into the Chesapeake Bay. A legend of the Algonquin Indians told of a giant horn found at the edge of the river, now thought to have been a tusk from a mastodon that roamed the area during the Ice Age. The word Chemung means "Big Horn" in the Algonquin language.

Each spring, the runoff from melting snow would cause the river and its tributaries to flood, but Nat was thankful that the river was not yet too deep to cross. With another week or two of warm weather, the river would become a torrent.

But that also meant that the water was extra frigid. By midstream, Nat was nearly neck deep in the icy chill. The cold took his breath away as he held the precious package of provisions above his head and waded slowly to the other side. He scrambled over the rocks on the far bank and began to run as fast as he could, not daring to look back. He was shivering as he ran—as much from the adrenalin coursing through his bloodstream as from the cold air rushing through his wet ragged clothes.

The original plan was that the small band of escapees would meet briefly at an abandoned barn that could be seen across the river from the prison yard. But when Nat got there, Washington Traweek was the only one waiting for him.

"Am I glad to see you!" Without waiting for the question, Wash continued, "The others left almost an hour ago. Coop headed north—said he had some relatives in Canada and would wait out the end of the war up there. The other two headed west along the river. Which way should we go, or d'you think we should split up?"

"Wash, where I'm headed, you don't want to go."

"Where would that be?"

"Washington."

"Washington City? That's the most foolish thing I ever heard pass your lips, Booth. Why in hell would you want to go there?"

"I've got to meet someone, and if I don't get to Washington by Friday, it will be too late."

"Too late for what?" pleaded Wash. "You're not makin' any sense."

"It's better that you don't know."

"But it's nearly 300 miles, as the crow flies. No way can you get there in two days!"

"Yes, I can—thanks to John King. He gave me twenty dollars. We can pick up the rail line south of here and ride together as far as Baltimore, then you can cross into Virginia on foot and through the Confederate lines at the North Carolina border. You'll be home in Alabama in a couple of weeks. I'll go on into Washington."

"You are one crazy sum-bitch, Nat, but I guess I'll tag along. Let's get movin'."

"Great. But first we've got to get some fresh clothes and clean up. We can't get on the train lookin' like this."

With the moon just rising over the hills to the east, the men headed south. The sun would be up in less than four hours, and with it, the prisoners in the camp would be awakened for roll call. Even staying off the roads so as not to be seen, Nat figured they could still be nearly fifteen miles away before the Camp Commander learned of their escape.

THIRTY-FOUR

AFTER TWO HOURS, Nat estimated they had crossed the state line into Pennsylvania. The land was only sparsely populated, essentially a wilderness of virgin forests of oak, chestnut and hickory between scattered small farms. Finally they came upon what they were looking for: tracks of what appeared to be the main rail line running south. They sat on the tracks to rest for a minute and shared the beef and bread that Nat had been given before he left the camp.

The men were coming up upon Columbia Township in Bradford County, Pennsylvania, and the tracks were the main line of the Williamsport and Elmira Railroad. Early township records report that this region of Pennsylvania was first settled about 1795 by a man named Doty and two other men: the Ballards, twin brothers from Burlington, Pennsylvania. But living conditions were harsh. There were no roads—not even footpaths. Only blazed trees kept the earliest travelers from becoming hopelessly lost in the dense forest wilderness. After building a log cabin, Mr. Doty reconsidered his move and left the area. The Ballard twins managed to clear four acres of land for planting, then sold their claim for five dollars and a hog.

But slowly the demand for arable land resulted in more and more pioneer settlement and progress. An early farmer of Columbia Township could trade a bushel of wheat for a yard of calico at the Tioga Point store or carry it for miles to Thomas Barber's grist-mill on Sugar Creek near Troy. By 1810, a public road was opened to East Troy in the south and, by 1814, to the New York State line.

The veil of stars had disappeared and the ink-black sky was turning a majestic blue when Nat and Wash reached the small farm they had seen a quarter-mile east of the railroad tracks. The sun would soon be above the eastern horizon.

"Looks deserted to me, what d'you think?" Wash asked.

"I think you're right. Except for those few scrawny chickens, I don't see any farm animals. And these fields don't look like they've seen a plow in the last year. Seems to me that anyone living here would at least have the ground prepared for planting by now."

"If that well ain't dry, we can at least clean up some. Maybe we can find a change of clothes in the cabin."

When they arrived at the well about twenty feet from the log farm house, Wash looked down to see the surface of the water about eight feet below. He lowered the wooden bucket by its attached rope until it tipped to one side and filled with water. By the time he pulled the bucket back up, nearly half of the water had leaked out. He emptied what was left into a "carrying" bucket nearby, then began to lower the rope for another draw.

"What in hell are you boys doin' on my land?" Nat spun around, first noticing the musket she had trained upon him, and a second one on her right leaning against the doorframe of the cabin. He had little doubt that they both were loaded. The woman looked about fifty-five years old, but Nat quickly reminded himself that pioneer women generally aged poorly and that she was probably still in her thirties or early forties. Her hair was mostly gray and matted, but her face looked washed and the dress she wore was faded but clean. Wash was so startled that he let go of the rope and the bucket splashed into the bottom of the well.

"Pardon us ma'am. We wuz jus' tryin' to get some fresh water. We're awful thirsty."

"You boys look pretty ragged to me. You wouldn't be from the prison camp across the state line, now would you?" She raised the weapon a little higher as Nat and Wash glanced at each other for a moment.

"To tell you the truth, ma'am, you're exactly right." Nat offered, "But you probably haven't heard the news that the war is over. General Lee surrendered two days ago."

"That so?" The musket was still trained upon them.

Wash chimed in, "Yes ma'am, it's true. They set us free last night. We're headed—"

Nat interrupted. "That's not exactly correct, ma'am. They didn't give us a farewell party. We just left on our own."

She lowered the weapon. "Where you boys from?"

"Wash here is from Alabama. I'm from Virginia. Richmond. My name is Nat Booth." Nat took a step toward the woman and extended his right hand.

"That'll be far enough. My name is Rebecca Cantrell and I'd be obliged if one of you'd climb down that well and retrieve my water bucket. I suppose you boys are hungry. Why don't you take some water into the barn? There's some soap and rags in there so's you can clean yourselves up. Meanwhile, I'll fix you sumpthin' to eat."

"Thank you, Missus Cantrell. That's very kind of you, ma'am."

"And don't be gettin' any foolish notions. I'll be keepin' this musket close by, and I'm a pretty good shot."

"Yes, ma'am." Mrs. Cantrell carried the weapons inside the small log cabin and barred the door. Wash retrieved the bucket rope using the foot and hand holds on the rock lining of the old well and drew up enough water to fill the carrying bucket. Then he and Nat headed off to the log barn.

Thirty minutes later, Nat and Wash had nearly consumed the large plates of fried eggs, fat back, potatoes and coarse brown bread that Mrs. Cantrell had prepared on her old iron cook stove.

"Mrs. Cantrell, this is the finest meal I've had in two years," Wash offered after wiping his face with his sleeve.

"Me, too," Nat added. For the first time since they met, Mrs. Cantrell smiled.

"You know, I'm originally from Virginia myself. Came up here when the war started on account of my damn fool daughter married a Yankee officer. She and I wuz livin' here while he was out fightin', but last month he was reassigned to Washington City and she up and left to join him. They are sposed' to be sendin' for me, but haven't heard no word from them yet."

"I'm sure you'll be hearing from them soon, Mrs. Cantrell." Nat tried to sound sympathetic.

"Well, I don't really mind it too much here. I'm not much for city life, but it has been lonely since my daughter left. So, are you boys gonna' walk all the way to Virginia?"

"We've got money for the train, ma'am," said Nat.

"Well that might work if your friend keeps his mouth shut and you do all the talkin'. That Alabama accent is sure to give you away. They'll be packin' you two back to Elmira if you're not careful. Excuse me a minute, boys." Mrs. Cantrell stepped back into the cabin. When she returned to the porch minutes later, she was carrying two sets of clothing that had been carefully folded. "These belong to my son-in-law. I'm sure he won't mind you havin' them, so long as I don't tell him I gave 'em to some Rebs. He's 'bout mid size between you two, so they should mostly fit."

Twenty minutes later Nat and Wash returned from the barn in their new clothes, holding their old rags in front of them. "Give me them old clothes. Fire in the wood stove is still hot," said the woman. Each of the men was wearing a clean white shirt and wool suit. Nat's was black and Wash's was dark blue with a white pin stripe. Wash got the lone hat. "Sorry I can't do much about them worn out shoes, but at least you won't have everyone on the train wonderin' what chain gang you escaped from."

"We can't thank you enough, ma'am," offered Wash.

"You boys are welcome. Now, the station is about three miles south o' here at Columbia Cross Roads. There should be a ten o'clock train headed south this morning."

THIRTY-FIVE

"THIS LINE ends at Williamsport. You'll have to purchase another ticket and change trains there to go on to Baltimore." The ticket agent at the Columbia Cross Roads station replied to Nat's request in a condescending tone that suggested that Nat should have known better than to ask for tickets through to Baltimore. "Two for Williamsport, then?"

"Yessir."

"That'll be two dollars and sixty cents." Nat reached into the right-hand pocket of his trousers and pulled out a handful of silver coins. He counted out the exact amount and slid the coins toward the agent.

"When do we arrive in Williamsport?"

The agent pulled a railroad timepiece out of the watch pocket of his trousers. "We're runnin' almost twenty minutes late, so you should arrive about twelve-twenty-five. The train for Baltimore leaves at one PM, sharp."

Nat and Wash sat on the long wooden bench outside the small station house as a few other travelers purchased tickets for the southbound train. A well-dressed mother in her mid twenties sat at the end of the bench reading a newspaper while her two offspring—a little girl about three and a boy maybe six years old—alternately peeked at Nat from around the corner of the building, then disappeared in a fit of giggles whenever Nat looked in their direction. Every few minutes mother would look up to verify that her children were nearby and that her luggage had not disappeared from the baggage cart twenty feet away on the arrival platform. The scene reminded Nat of a time years ago when he traveled with his own mother by train from Richmond to Philadelphia. The wooden baggage cart with tall, spoke iron wheels wasn't much different from the ones he remembered from 1950. Besides the half-dozen pieces of luggage belonging to the young woman and her children, the cart also held two flat wooden cages of white leghorn chickens. These belonged to a nervous young man about nineteen. Periodically, he would return to the ticket agent, expressing his concern that the train was late.

Minutes later all heard the whistle of the steam locomotive approaching from the north, and the passengers rose and moved on to the railroad platform. The locomotive let out one long loud gasp as the engineer disengaged the throttle and released excess pressure from the boiler, reducing the powerful steam engine to idle speed.

There were no passengers getting off at Columbia Cross Roads today, and the agent, having completed his ticketing duties for this departure, had closed the ticket window and was now boarding the new passengers. He directed the young man and his chickens together with the rest of the baggage to the fifth and last car of the train and then helped the mother and her excited children board car Number Four. Nat and Wash followed. The pair quickly selected seats near the rail car entrance, staying as far as possible from the three Union Army officers that they saw seated at the far end of the car, in the direction of the engine. The train began to chug slowly out of the station even before the young mother and her children were settled in their seats.

The conductor came down the aisle minutes later, punching tickets and announcing the next stop, Troy. And additional stops followed in short order: Granville, Alba, Canton, Ralston, Lycoming, Dubois. At most of the stops, a few more passengers boarded than left the train. The stops were so frequent that Nat noticed that the engineer was often unable to completely accelerate to full speed before having to throttle down again for the next stop. At Trout Run, they began to climb. Their speed slowed considerably as the engine labored to lift the heavy locomotive and string of cars against the relentless force of gravity. As he looked out, Nat was struck by the awesome beauty of the Allegheny Mountain wilderness. He seemed to be the only one on the train to appreciate it.

Crescent, Cogan Valley. Finally, the conductor began his last pass through the cars. "Final stop, Williamsport. Gather your personal belongings. Everyone will be leaving the train at Williamsport. Final stop."

The train had just begun to slow down for the last stop when Nat noticed the Army officers had risen from their seats and were now making their way in his direction to the car exit near where he and Wash were seated. Quickly he grabbed Nat's hat and placed it over his own face, pretending to be asleep.

"What the hell? Give me back my hat, Nat!"

"Shut up, fool. One of those officers is Captain Mungery, from the camp. I've been in his office so many times, he's sure to recognize me!"

"So what am I supposed to do?"

"Look outside, twiddle your thumbs, I don't care. Just don't look at them when they pass by."

The officers were engaged in conversation and smiling as they gathered their belongings and moved down the aisle toward Nat and Wash, then stopped, standing right beside them while waiting for the train to come to a halt. From under his hat, Nat could see the gold trim of Captain Mungery's uniform only inches away. Mercifully, the train finally came to a complete stop after what seemed to Nat to be a very long minute. He could see the uniforms moving past him toward the exit stairs and breathed a sigh of relief. Nat was about to remove the hat when he felt a large hand firmly grip him on the shoulder. Captain Mungery leaned over and whispered loud enough for both of the men to hear, "Now, you boys be careful going home—it's dangerous out there." And then he exited the train car. Neither Nat nor Wash said a word as they watched the Captain run to catch up with his traveling companions.

THIRTY-SIX

HE WILLIAMSPORT STATION was a busy place. As the rest of the passengers left the train that had arrived from Elmira and points north, the steam locomotive on the adjacent tracks of the Northern Central Railroad was being prepared for the run to Maryland. Workers were busy adding water to the boilers and loading the coal that would be used to fuel them.

Ten minutes before the scheduled one o'clock departure, Nat and Wash were comfortably seated near the forward end of the last car. Minutes earlier in the station house, Nat had spent eight dollars on two tickets to Baltimore. Wash used twenty cents of his own money for some cheese sandwiches and spent two cents more for five rolled cigarettes. He hadn't had a good smoke in more than a year. The two men had been up all night and by the time the train crossed the Susquehanna River at Dauphin, they had finished their lunch and fallen asleep.

An hour out of Baltimore they awoke and Wash asked Nat to join him at the rear platform of the car. He wanted to talk freely beyond the prying ears of their fellow travelers. The speeding train was gobbling up track at a ferocious rate and spitting it out from beneath their feet like the wake of a fast ship.

"What's on your mind, Wash?"

"Last night at the barn before Cooper left, he started tellin' me some crazy stuff."

"Like what?"

"He was tellin' me stuff 'bout him and that black Yankee officer—the one that you kept askin' about. Did you know that Coop wasn't captured by the Yankees at Gettysburg like we all thought? He wasn't even in the fight. Said he had to skedaddle before the fightin' started on account of he helped that Negro escape. Some Yankee farmer found Coop sleepin' in his barn and turned him in."

"I guess that is all possible."

"Yeah, but what's crazy is that Coop thinks that black man was from the future—from a hundred years from now. His name was 'Hayes' and Coop said he fell out of some flyin' machine after our boys hit it with a canon shot. And Coop overheard the black man talkin' about all manner of future things—told the Cap'n that our boys would be beat good at Gettysburg and that General Lee would give it up at Appomattox. Coop swears he heard all this on the day before the fightin' started."

"Give me one of those cigarettes, Wash." Nat stepped away from the back of the platform to light the cigarette out of the wind. "You're wondering what the connection is between me and that black man, Lincoln Hayes." Washington Traweek nodded. "I knew him personally; as well as I know you. The two of us were in that flying machine together when we got shot down. That was the last time I saw him. He must have got himself captured by Cooper's people. The Union Army caught me three days later."

"So you think Coop was tellin' the truth?"

"Well, it's a different story than he told us the first time. But I can't really blame him for not wanting to say that he skipped out just before the Gettysburg fighting and deserted. Coop was no coward, but it sure would have sounded like he was."

"And the part about the black man bein' from the future?"

"Don't ask me about that, Wash."

"What about you goin' to Washington City?"

Nat looked away and then began to shake his head. "I still can't tell you. I'm sorry, Wash, but if I fail at what I need to do there, it will be terribly dangerous for anyone who knew anything about it in advance. I can tell you that Friday is the big day. If it doesn't work out, you will know all about it by Saturday morning—it's that important."

Nat and Wash were back in their seats when the conductor came through to announce the stop for Baltimore.

"Wash, I'm going to ride this train on into Washington, but I think it's best if you get off here like we planned. It will be pretty risky anywhere near the Capitol."

"I guess your right." Wash was feeling bad because he and his friend would soon be parting, most likely never to see each other again. But most of all, he was disappointed that his friend had been unwilling to trust him with his secret.

THIRTY-SEVEN

ROGER ATWOOD LOOKED UP and down the hall on the sixteenth floor of the Flatiron Building before unlocking the door to the former offices of Khronos Trust Services. With a smile of hopeful expectation, he ushered Amanda Marshall through the door ahead of him.

"Rathburn wasn't kidding. Not much here," Roger remarked after switching on the lights and scanning the room. He was no longer smiling. The empty main office was large enough for a receptionist area and maybe three additional desks. The floor, some nondescript asphalt or vinyl tile, was covered haphazardly with stained painting tarps. The Navajo white walls were completely dry, but had that damp look characteristic of very fresh flat finish paint. A few ceiling tiles were missing; probably some damaged ones removed by the workmen and awaiting eventual replacement. There were three doors at the back of the room. The center one was partially open revealing a bathroom. The doors on the left and right of the bathroom were closed. Overall, the office appeared largely utilitarian and not particularly impressive.

With arms folded in front of her, Amanda leaned against the wall next to the door from which they had entered the office. Her eyes followed Roger as he walked slowly around the perimeter of the room. She was sensitive to Roger's realization that this room, at least, was not about to yield any useful information concerning Khronos Trust Services.

"Let's check the back offices," Roger announced. Amanda followed as Roger approached the door on the left side of the back wall and opened it. Roger did not switch on the lights, but there was sufficient illumination coming from the lighting in main room to show that this had been a private office. Roger could feel the plush and musty smelling carpet under his feet as he walked to the large window at the back wall, a thick layer of dust on the sill. The view across 5th Avenue and the partial New York skyline at dusk was impressive, even from only the sixteenth floor, but Amanda understood that it was disappointment, and not the view, that was the cause of Roger's silence. The room was absolutely empty. Amanda's arms encircled Roger's waist from behind. She rested her chin on his shoulder as they both looked out on 5th Avenue.

"I'm sorry." She spoke softly.

"Sorry about what?" Roger snapped back. Without waiting for an answer, he exclaimed, "There's one more room."

The room on the right next to the restroom had probably been a conference room, but it, too, was empty. Roger switched on the lights and walked over to the wet bar on the left side. The spout of the decorator style faucet dripped at about a once-per-ten-seconds rate and the stainless steel sink was dull with lime deposits—the result of months or perhaps years of the slowly dripping water. Roger dragged his hand over the dusty black surface of the bar, stopping to look inside the empty cabinets above it. The drawers in the matching base cabinet also proved to be empty. Roger turned around, back against the bar, half propping up his upper body with outstretched arms and the palms of his hands face down on the edge of the counter top. His chin was on his chest.

"I'm sorry." He spoke softly.

"I'm listening," was Amanda's reply.

"I'm *very* sorry." No reply. "I'm sorry for acting like an ass over this Khronos thing and for taking my frustration out on you. We were on such a roll this afternoon at the library; I guess I was disappointed to find nothing here."

"Apology accepted." As she spoke the words, she noticed something on the floor just outside the doorway. Walking over to it, she bent over and picked up a business card and called out to Roger, "At least we know where the furniture went—Saul's New and Used Office Furnishings and Pawn."

"This is kind of odd." Roger was speaking to no one in particular. Then he called out, "Amanda—come back in here and look at this, would you?" Roger was standing in front of the bookcase adjacent to the bar. Amanda came over immediately. "What do you notice about these shelves?"

"They're dusty."

"Yes, but look closely at the two lower ones." Pause. "The top shelf has been empty for a long time, but all the dust on these two shelves is only along the front edge. My point is, there were books on these two shelves that have been removed recently. Where are they?"

"Well, Roger. There were books listed on the receipt of items that the Bank of New York took out of—"

Roger didn't wait for her to finish. "Only a couple of accounting ledger books. Not two full shelves full!"

"O.K. So what are you thinking?"

"I think that tomorrow we need to find Lydia McCabe, and then go see Mr. What's-his-name."

"Saul."

"Right—Saul. We should find out if maybe Mr. Saul has the missing books. First thing in the morning. And I'm thinking that right now we should get some dinner—"

"Roger that!

"And then we should go back to the hotel."

"Roger that!"

Before they had opened the door to the hallway and left the office, the woman who had been listening outside the door, unseen, had scurried down the hallway, around the corner beyond elevator.

THIRTY-EIGHT

ROM THE CAPITOL BUILDING, Nat had an awe-inspiring view of the historic city. Since the last time he was here, it seemed as if someone had simply reached down and removed block after block of twentieth century structures, leaving only the historic buildings. The wide avenues and streets were all there, but the surfaces were dirt and gravel, scarred by the iron wheels of carriages. The White House was prominently visible down Pennsylvania Avenue. Directly south of the Executive Mansion stood the unfinished Washington Monument. Work had been suspended in 1854 at the 150-foot level and it would be twenty-five years before it would start again. Nat could also see a small portion of the facade of the National Hotel, six blocks away at the corner of Sixth Street and Pennsylvania Avenue.

He had spent the night sleeping on a bench in the train station. It was Thursday, April 13th and Nat was well aware that without his personal intervention, President Lincoln would be shot dead tomorrow evening. For the last several weeks, Nat had considered how best to stop the assassination plot. Now he was here and it was time to put his plans into action. Because time was short, he felt that it was important to warn the President—or at least those charged with protecting him—that a plot on the President's life was planned for Friday evening and that, above all, the President must stay away from Ford's Theater. But Nat was also aware that John Wilkes Booth was obsessive in his conspiracy, having embarked on two previous initiatives to kidnap the President. What would be gained if the President's life were saved on April 14th, only to be taken a week or a month later by the same assassin? Nat knew that he would need to deal directly with Mr. Booth as well.

John Wilkes Booth was born in 1838, and from an early age had two important goals in life. The first was to become a more famous actor than his father and the second, to do what ever he could to assure the preeminence of the white race in America. Booth was from a family of actors and played his first serious role when he was only seventeen. In 1858 he became a member of the Richmond Theater and his career began to advance rapidly. John Wilkes Booth was considered to be a handsome man, with particularly striking facial features. He attracted admiring audiences and was rarely without an abundance of female companionship.

It is not known when the seeds of racism first began to stir in Booth's psyche, but as his success as an actor grew, so did his hatred for anyone or anything that might further the notion of equality for the black race in America. When John Brown was hanged in 1859 for his role in attempting to foment a slave insurrection at Harper's Ferry, Booth was determined to be present. He obtained a militia uniform and stood near the scaffold during the execution. Booth's intolerance extended to virtually everyone that was not naturally American. For a time, he had been a member of the "Know Nothing" political party, whose platform centered on the restriction of immigration and immigrant voting rights.

After the war started, Booth continued to pursue his acting career, playing to Yankee audiences in city after city, while secretly working as a part-time Confederate agent. Coded letters and a diary found after his death confirmed his association with a band of smugglers and spies known as the Knights of the Golden Circle. The underground activities of this group included carrying quinine and other medicines from Canada to needy Confederate forces in Virginia.

But as the outcome of the war began to turn decidedly against the South, Booth realized that his greatest fear would very likely become a reality. That is, black slaves everywhere would become free citizens, eventually to acquire the same rights as whites. He expressed his deep anti-black sentiments in an 1864 letter to his brother-in-law. He wrote, "This country was formed for the white not the black man. And looking upon African slavery from the standpoint, as held by those noble framers of our Constitution, I for one, have ever considered it, one of the greatest blessings (both for themselves and us) that God ever bestowed upon a favoured nation."

By the autumn of 1864, Booth believed that the war effort could be bolstered if only the large number of Confederate prisoners held in the northern camps could be released to rejoin the Confederate Army, but all initiatives for a prisoner exchange had been turned down by the Union. Clearly, the military establishment in Washington understood that exchange would only further prolong the war. Frustrated, Booth decided to take independent action and gathered a group of like-minded individuals with a plan to kidnap President Lincoln and hold him as ransom for the release of Confederate prisoners of war. Their plan was to snatch the President from the State Box at Ford's theater during a performance on January 18, 1865, but the plan failed to materialize. The President never arrived at the playhouse.

After meeting on March 15, 1865, at a restaurant in Washington, the group of conspirators learned that Lincoln would be traveling to Georgetown two days later to attend a benefit at the U.S. Soldiers Convalescent Home. This time they intended to seize the President from his carriage and spirit him off to Richmond. But this plot also was foiled when the President made a last minute change of plans.

Booth understood that time was running out for the Confederacy, and if he were to do anything to help the southern cause, he would have to do it soon. When he learned that General Lee surrendered the entire Army of Northern Virginia on April 9th, Booth was beside himself with frustration. Two days later, President Lincoln was in the White House, considering how best to implement political initiatives aimed at bringing the former secessionist states back into the Union fold. Clearly, the President and his Cabinet were operating in uncharted waters. How should reunification of the United States best proceed? Although various opinions abounded, no one had a certain answer to that question. Twelve thousand citizens of the State of Louisiana had recently approved a reconstituted state government, pledging their allegiance to the Union. Perhaps Louisiana could serve as a pattern for the other states to follow.

When the President became aware that a crowd had gathered outside the White House, he acknowledged their presence from an upstairs balcony and began to address them, delivering a speech from his notes on the matter of reconstruction. The speech included a call to bestow voter rights on certain groups of black people. But the crowd that gathered outside the White House that day included John Wilkes Booth and two of his fellow conspirators. When Booth heard the President express his thoughts on the matter of black suffrage, he became newly enraged and swore that this speech would be the very last that Lincoln would ever make.

THIRTY-NINE

THE CLERK at the front desk at the National Hotel sounded sincerely apologetic. "I'm sorry sir, but we haven't seen Mr. Booth yet today, and I don't believe he was in his room last evening." The National Hotel was the temporary residence of John Wilkes Booth whenever he spent time in Washington.

"Would you have any idea where he might be? It is very important that I see him." Nat leaned in closer to the clerk's face.

"And your name, sir?"

"Nathaniel Booth."

"You are related, then?"

"Distantly, yes."

"Then I'll assume that your business is of a personal nature. Just a minute, Mr. Booth, I'll see what I can find out." When the clerk disappeared into the back room, Nat turned to survey the lobby of the National Hotel. The room was ornate with ball and claw tables and plush easy chairs with dark brocade upholstery. An elderly gentleman was seated nearby behind a copy of the *Washington Star*, the front page headline read "Stanton: War to End Soon in the West."

"I'm sorry sir. I have no further information, except that we expect Mr. Booth to return sometime later today. Would you care to leave a message?" Nat considered the clerk's offer for a moment.

"Perhaps I'll just wait here a while."

"By all means. Please make yourself comfortable." The clerk gestured toward the lobby seating area.

Nat decided that he could use the time and opportunity to compose a letter warning of the impending assassination attempt. If he were unable to contact the President directly, he could at least leave the letter with someone in authority at the White House. Nat seated himself at a walnut writing desk and, after fumbling for a while with an unfamiliar writing pen and inkwell, proceeded to compose his letter on hotel stationery:

DEAR PRESIDENT LINCOLN,

IN RECENT MONTHS, YOU HAVE NO DOUBT RECEIVED NUMEROUS THREATS UPON YOUR PERSON, NONE OF WHICH, THANKFULLY, HAS BEEN ACTED UPON. THE PURPOSE OF THIS LETTER IS TO WARN YOU THAT THERE IS A NEW AND IMMINENT THREAT TO YOUR LIFE FROM A BAND OF CONSPIRATORS CURRENTLY OPERATING IN THE WASHINGTON AREA. THEY WILL ATTEMPT TO ASSASSINATE YOU AS WELL AS VICE PRESIDENT JOHNSON AND SECRETARY SEWARD THIS FRIDAY EVENING, APRIL 14TH. ALTHOUGH I DO NOT BELIEVE THAT THIS GROUP IS ACTING UNDER THE DIRECTION OR SANCTION OF JEFFERSON DAVIS OR HIS ADMINISTRATION, THEIR MISGUIDED PURPOSE IS TO CREATE A CONDITION OF CHAOS IN THE GOVERNMENT WHICH MIGHT SOMEHOW ENABLE THEIR SIDE

TO SEEK AN END TO THE WAR UNDER TERMS
MORE FAVORABLE TO THE SOUTH.

WHETHER OR NOT YOU TAKE THIS WARNING
SERIOUSLY—AND MY HOPE IS THAT YOU
DO—I IMPLORE YOU TO TAKE SPECIAL STEPS
TO INSURE YOUR SAFETY, AND ABOVE ALL, TO
STAY AWAY FROM FORD'S THEATER, A LIKELY
LOCATION AT WHICH THE CONSPIRATORS MAY
STRIKE.

NATHANIEL BOOTH

Nat wondered about the advisability of signing his real name, but decided it was necessary if the note was to have any credibility. He sealed the letter in an envelope and then moved to an overstuffed chair nearby. While waiting for Wilkes Booth, Nat browsed through issues of *Atlantic Monthly* and other periodicals that had been provided for visitors and guests. The April 8th issue of *Scientific American* contained articles about recent successes growing oranges and lemons in Southern California and a prescription for the cure of drunkenness containing sulfate of iron, magnesia and peppermint water. But after two hours of reading and waiting, Nat decided he could wait no longer.

As Nat approached the exit, the clerk called out, "Shall I tell Mr. Booth that you were looking for him?" Nat stopped and returned to the front desk.

"Yes, that would be fine, thank you."

"And where are you lodging while in Washington City?" Nat had an uneasy feeling about the hotel clerk's interest in who he was and where he was staying. Nat was unsure whether he should pass it off as simply the honest and helpful concern of a hotel staff member on behalf of a valued and prominent guest—as Wilkes Booth certainly was—or if there might be some ulterior motive for the clerk's inquiries.

"Uh—well, I just came to town this morning and haven't yet secured lodging for the evening. I'll be back later today."

"Then have a good day, Mr. Booth." Nat stepped out of the hotel and headed up Pennsylvania Avenue in the direction of the White House. He turned on Tenth Street, walking past Ford's Theater. Three blocks further north were a number of rooming houses where Nat secured a room at Mrs. McGill's Guest House for one dollar and twenty-five cents. The mattress was a little lumpy but the sheets were clean. After listening to Mrs. McGill's list of prohibitions—no tobacco use, alcohol or women were permitted in the guest rooms—Nat put his room key in his pocket and made his way toward the Executive Mansion.

FORTY

OMPANY K of the 150th Pennsylvania Infantry
Regiment had been assigned the responsibility of
protecting President Lincoln and his family at the
White House beginning in 1862. The next year, after
concerns expressed by the Governor of Ohio, security was
stepped up with the addition of a unit of the Ohio Cavalry
known as the "Union Light Guard" which provided escort
protection when Lincoln was traveling. Near the end of the
war, members of the Metropolitan Police were assigned to
provide additional security, guarding the President inside the
White House itself.

"State your business." The guard at the main gate was
abrupt.

"I need to speak with someone in authority concerning
the President's safety. I have credible information regarding a
threat on the President's life."

"Private Lewis." The guard called out to a young soldier
standing nearby. "Search this man for weapons, then take
him to Sergeant Whittaker." Nat stepped inside the gate, then
raised his arms as Private Lewis carefully padded him down.
As the Private escorted him toward an open door at the base

of the Portico, Nat remarked to himself that the Private looked very young—maybe not even sixteen years old.

"How can I help you?" Sergeant Whittaker placed his pen back in the inkwell. Private Lewis stood at attention outside the door.

"I have information concerning a serious threat to the President's life."

"And who is it that is threatening the President today?"

"A man named John Wilkes Booth and some of his associates."

"Do you mean that actor, Booth?" The Sergeant began to smile as he leaned back in his chair.

"Yes, Sergeant."

"Well, I must admit that I haven't heard that one before. Sir, are you aware that we get mail threats on the President's life every day? Since Lee surrendered, we've been getting twice as many as usual. This basket contains threats and warnings received just this week." Nat looked down to see a wire basket full of letters.

"I understand, Sergeant, but I believe that the danger to the President in this case is very real. Is it possible to see him?"

"You are not going to see the President." The Sergeant by this time was clearly irritated with his visitor. "Do you know that most of the people that send us warnings of plots and conspiracies against the President turn out to be crack pots? Are you a crack pot, sir?"

"No, definitely not."

"Well, I think that you are indeed a crack pot. I don't believe that anyone of the stature of John Booth the actor would have designs on the President's life. Private Lewis, would you escort this gentleman off the grounds, immediately." Nat reached into his jacket and pulled out the envelope.

"Sergeant, would you please at least see that the President gets this before tomorrow?"

"I can turn it over to one of the President's body guards. It will be up to him as to whether or not he passes it on to President Lincoln." After Nat and Private Lewis left the Portico area, Sergeant Whittaker looked at the unopened envelope that Nat had given him, then tossed it into the wire basket, adding to the accumulation of threat and warning letters received earlier that week.

It was still too early to check back at the National Hotel for Wilkes Booth, so Nat walked to Lafayette Park nearby. A Marine Band arrived, played for an hour, and then left. As darkness began to fall, Nat set off for the National Hotel.

"I'M SORRY SIR, we haven't seen Mr. Booth today." It was a different clerk at the hotel desk. "You might want to try again in the morning."

"Do you know if he will be staying here this evening?"

"We're not expecting him, no, sir." There was little more he could do before morning, so Nat went back to his room at Mrs. McGill's.

FORTY-ONE

I T WAS FRIDAY, April 14th. At the White House, the guard detail had changed. Sergeant Whittaker's relief had finished gathering the day's hate mail and added it to the growing stack. On Sunday morning, one of Metropolitan Police detectives would be looking at each piece in more detail, the customary precaution. Earlier that morning, the President had breakfast with Mary Todd Lincoln and their sons, Tad and Robert. The President had just concluded a meeting with Speaker of the House Colfax when the head of the residence guards had persuaded the President to make a change of plans.

"I'm sorry sir, but we believe it is far too dangerous for you and Mrs. Lincoln to travel to Baltimore as you had planned. The volume of threats has doubled in the past week. I think it would be prudent for you to stay in Washington City for the next few days. Might I recommend a play? *Our American Cousin* is being performed at Ford's this very evening and I have advised Henry Clay Ford that you and Mrs. Lincoln may be attending. May I send a messenger with a confirmation?"

Carriage and foot traffic along Pennsylvania Avenue was heavy that morning, and Nat failed to notice the handsome man in the horse-drawn taxi that passed him in the opposite direction. Nat was on his way to the National Hotel for a third attempt to meet with Lincoln's would-be assassin, while John Wilkes Booth was headed to Ford's Theater to pick up his mail. The clerk at the hotel recognized Nat from the day before.

"I'm sorry, Mr. Booth, but you just missed him this morning. I explained that you wished to see him. He left as message for you." Nat unfolded the message and read.

M. NATHANIEL BOOTH

I DO NOT BELIEVE THAT I HAVE EVER MADE YOUR ACQUAINTANCE, NOR DO I RECALL A RELATION ON MY FATHER'S SIDE WITH GIVEN NAME 'NATHANIEL', BUT I WOULD BE HAPPY TO MEET WITH YOU IF YOU CAN COME TO DEERY'S TAVERN AT 4 PM TODAY, FRIDAY.

JWB

"Where would Deery's Tavern be?" Nat asked the clerk.

"Deery's is upstairs above Grover's Theater. That's about four blocks west of Ford's on Pennsylvania Avenue."

FORTY-TWO

THERE WERE FIVE L. and Lydia McCabes in the Manhattan telephone book. Roger Atwood considered calling first, but not knowing what reaction someone might have when questioned about events of a quarter-century ago, he decided it was best to try to locate the Lydia McCabe of Khronos Trust Services in person.

Numbers One and Two were black and white women, respectively, in their mid-thirties. Much too young, and only the black lady was a Lydia. After a brief conversation with a daughter who came to the door, Roger learned that Number Three had passed away a month before but had never been associated with Khronos Trust Services. Now it was mid-afternoon. As they walked up to the brownstone residence of Number Four on 12th Avenue, a woman in her early sixties had just locked the door and turned to descend the four steps to the sidewalk.

"Mrs. McCabe?" Amanda called up to the woman who wore a pale green dress and matching shoes with a half-height heel. There was no trace of gray in her short, blonde-colored hair.

"Do I know you?" The woman still held her keys in her right hand and a cream-colored purse in the crook of her left arm. "My name is Amanda Marshall, and this is Roger Atwood. We have been trying to find some information—about people you may have known from years ago?"

"What people?"

"People connected with Khronos Trust Services." In seconds, Lydia McCabe had descended the stairs and was on the sidewalk, virtually sprinting past Roger and Amanda, keys still in hand.

"I'm not familiar with that company. I can't help you." She was abrupt. Roger and Amanda glanced at each other knowingly; this woman was most likely the Lydia McCabe they were seeking.

"Please, Mrs. McCabe, we're just trying to help an old woman learn something about her son who was lost in Vietnam. It would mean a great deal to her. Please—we won't take up much of your time."

"You're not representing the building owner, or some unhappy former client?"

"No, absolutely not."

"Look—it's been twenty-five years." She walked on, with Amanda and Roger following close behind. "Khronos Trust Services is gone. Everyone connected with the company is gone—except for me."

When they reached the coffee bar at the corner, Roger spoke up, gestured toward the open doorway. "Please, Mrs. McCabe. Just give us a few minutes."

Roger ordered three coffees as Amanda and Mrs. McCabe seated themselves at a small table near the rear of the bar.

"Who is this man—the one who was lost in the war?" Lydia asked.

"His name was Nathaniel Booth and his mother's name is Rose. We believe he knew the Luu family that ran Khronos Trust Services.

"The Luu family has——had——been running Khronos for a long time. As I recall, Mrs. Booth and her husband were trust clients——very special ones. I believe that Derrick Luu, the last owner, managed their account personally for several years."

"What about Nathaniel Booth?"

"The company founder was a Nathaniel Booth, but that was a long time ago——1870-something. He couldn't be the man you're asking about." After several seconds of silence, Roger decided to press the issue.

"We think that maybe he could be." Roger looked down at his cup of coffee.

"What are you trying to suggest?" Mrs. McCabe leaned forward. "That the Nathaniel Booth that founded the company in the 1870s is the same person——the Vietnam veteran——that you are asking about? Sorry. It's just not possible."

"From what we have learned, Khronos——in its day——was obviously a very successful operation. Didn't you ever wonder how their investment advice could consistently hit the mark?"

"Of course I wondered, but I didn't ask too many questions. The company delivered sound investment advice, but was poorly managed, in my opinion. Derrick Luu *was* Khronos Trust Services. The rest of us were essentially clerks. When he died, so did the corporation."

"What happened to the company, exactly, after Derrick Luu's death?" asked Roger.

"Nearly all of our clients went elsewhere. I tried to hire new analysts, but they couldn't match Derrick's knack for securities and real estate investment."

"So you just shut the place down?" Amanda asked.

"I was under tremendous pressure, and not very well-equipped to handle it. Eventually, the money dried up. I wrote out some bonus checks—including a substantial one to myself that Mr. Luu had promised me—and then I sent everyone home. On Christmas Eve 1978, I locked the door at Khronos Trust and never went back."

"I understand," said Roger, "that the building manager at your old office claimed he had never seen anyone from Khronos during all the years that he worked there."

"You were there?"

"Yesterday. Your old offices are being refurbished for a new tenant."

"I'm surprised they hadn't rented it before now, even though our lease must have just expired. The building management was very difficult to deal with. I tried to get them to buy back the remainder of our pre-paid lease, but they weren't interested. They wouldn't even let me sublet the office—said I wasn't a principal in the corporation and didn't have the authority to negotiate or approve anything."

"We were told that the State of New York stepped in recently and authorized the building manager to sell off your old office furniture and maybe some other things. When you shut down the office years ago, you must have been in a hurry."

"I guess so. When the business started falling apart, I just wanted out."

Amanda spoke up, "Can you tell us, Mrs. McCabe, any earlier history about Khronos? Anything about Nathaniel Booth? When did Derrick Luu take over, and from whom?"

"How about one question at a time! I understood that Nathaniel Booth arranged to set up the Booth trust. I assumed that it was some kind of generation-skipping investment instrument."

"And Derrick's family?"

"Derrick Luu's father—his name was Loc Luu—ran the business from after World War I until he died about 1960. I'm not sure of the exact year. I wasn't hired until 1966. I believe that Derrick took over right after his father's death. He was only twenty-one, but he was a bright kid. I'm told he graduated from Harvard with honors at nineteen. I really don't know much about the father. The rumor was that he had supported the Vietnamese insurgents in the 1930s and 40s. He may have sent millions of his own money to help overthrow the French colonial government."

"And in the last ten years of the corporation—from 1968—was there any change in operations? Was the investment analysis and advice just as right on as before?"

"I saw no change. We made a lot of money for people right up until the day Derrick Luu died. Now, if you don't have any more questions, I have a doctor's appointment in ten minutes."

In the taxi on the way back to the hotel with Roger, Amanda was thinking out loud. "Mrs. McCabe's answer to my last question was rather odd, don't you think?"

"Because—?"

"Because up until 1968, Derrick Luu could base his investment advice and decisions on historical information passed on by his father—information that Nathaniel Booth no doubt previously shared with Derrick's grandfather, Trung Luu. But Nathaniel wouldn't have any advance knowledge of history after 1968. Derrick would have had to wing it for the next ten years, don't you think?"

"Maybe he was just a sharp analyst."

"Maybe."

Outside the coffee shop that they had just left, Mai Tran, the young Asian woman, was waiting for an available taxi to come by. She spoke emphatically into her cellular telephone. "James, we have to talk. I'm coming back to the office."

FORTY-THREE

NAT ARRIVED AT GROVER'S THEATER a few minutes before 4 PM. The theater itself appeared to be empty, but just inside the entrance was a stairway and a sign on the wall with the word 'Tavern' and an arrow pointing up. Inside the barroom were a half-dozen patrons seated at tables and one standing at the bar. Most were nursing beers and none looked even vaguely similar to the photos of Wilkes Booth that Nat remembered.

"What will you have?" The bartender sported a large handlebar mustache, partially concealing a full set of yellow teeth.

"Beer's fine." The bartender pulled a draught from the barrel, blew off the foam with whoosh of air from his lips and topped off the glass mug.

"That'll be five cents." Nat pulled a handful of change from his pocket and picked out a silver half-dime. It had been a long time since Nat had tasted beer. This one was warm.

"Are you Nathaniel Booth?" It was now nearly 4:30 and the man next to Nat asking the question had just entered the tavern. It was not John Booth.

"Yes, I am."

"My name is Alfred. I'm an associate of Mr. Booth. He would like to speak with you privately. Mr. Booth is downstairs in the theater waiting at this moment." Nat followed the man, who was about his own age, out of the tavern, down the stairs and into the small theater. Alfred seemed rather rough looking, and walked with a limp. Except for a few flickering gaslights near the stage, the room was dark. "He's in one of the dressing rooms. Follow me." The young man led Nat behind the stage curtain and into one of the small rooms at the rear of the building. There was a lantern turned low on the dressing table. Nat caught a glimpse of a water pitcher on a sideboard table with a built-in washbasin, but then darkness quickly enveloped him as if someone had extinguished the light.

When Nat awoke, his face was dripping wet with water and he was bound hand and foot with ropes and propped up against a wall. The back of his head was throbbing. As his eyes came to focus, he could see the young man who had summoned him and another standing next to him with a fancy single-barrel Derringer pointed in his direction. Nat didn't have to ask. It was John Wilkes Booth.

"So, you are Nathaniel Booth. Just who is Nathaniel Booth, may I ask?" Nat winced from the pain as he tried to keep the lump on the back of his head from resting against the wall. "Are you perhaps the bastard son from one of my dear departed father's many harlots?" Nat made no response. "No matter. What is your business with me?"

"I came to stop you from carrying out the plan you have for this evening. Hopefully, to convince you to give it up, but failing that, to stop you any way I can."

"How would you know of my plans for this evening?" Wilkes Booth squinted accusingly at Alfred, then turned his attention back to Nat. "There was no plan until noon today!"

"When you attempt to extract loyalty from your conspiracy friends by paying for it, it's not worth very much."

"And why in God's name should I listen to you?"

"Good question." Nat paused briefly. "I have no doubt, Mr. Booth, that you love the South; just as I do. I spent the last two years in a Yankee prisoner of war camp. But taking your revenge on President Lincoln because the North has won the war will serve only to hurt the South. You know that the President's desire is to unite the country again and has extended a hand of friendship to the southern states. But there are forces within the Federal Government that disagree—they want to extract a heavy price from us—trials for treason and payment of reparations. Without the President's strong leadership, those forces will gain control and the South that we love will pay dearly for your crime."

"But Lincoln will bring ruin to the country. The hand that he extends is to the black race. He won't stop until the niggers have become our equal." Wilkes Booth was now nervously pacing back and forth in the small room. "They will take our women and within a few generations, the United States will become a nation of mongrels—a second-rate country with citizens of inferior intelligence and brutish features."

"Your fear of the black man has possessed you. They didn't ask to come to this country and they only want what every American wants: the right to live in peace and to work hard so that their children can have a better life than they have had. For all their work and forced sacrifice, don't you think that they, too, deserve a piece of the American dream?"

"But this is our country—not theirs. They were brought here to serve—just as an ox tills the soil; that is what God has ordained."

"Slavery is over. Wake up and accept it. It should have been abolished years ago, but at least it is finally over. A hundred years from now, the past injustice of slavery will still stand between the races." Nat paused a few seconds, looking for any spark of revelation in his adversary's eyes. There was none to be found. "But there is another, more personal, reason for you to abandon your plan. You believe that you will become a hero to your cause. In fact, just the opposite is true. Our family name will be reviled for generations. You will be counted among the most hated men in world history, while Lincoln will be revered. Your band of inept conspirators will fail at the grisly tasks you have assigned to them. They will meet their demise at the end of a rope, and you will be tracked down and shot like a mad dog."

"And now you dare to suggest that you possess some clairvoyant powers? After I complete my righteous endeavor, I will make good my escape, but should I be captured and killed, so be it. Could I ask for a better role for my final curtain than to be a martyr for my cause?"

Nat was silent. There would be no convincing this man who was hell-bent on carrying out his plan.

"But now my dear half-brother, if that is what you are, what am I to do with you? I should kill you right now, but I believe I shall spare your life for a few hours until you, too, know that I have succeeded in my task." Wilkes Booth passed a pearl-handled knife to his Alfred. "If he tries to escape or cry out, kill him immediately. Otherwise, wait until eleven o'clock. Well before then, you should hear the good news that Lincoln is dead. Then you can finish the deed and make good your own escape."

FORTY-FOUR

JOHN WILKES BOOTH returned to his room at the National Hotel and prepared for the task before him. He dressed in a black suit and hat and hid a Bowie knife in his left boot. Booth checked the Derringer that he had previously loaded with a single .44-caliber lead ball, then left the hotel for a final meeting with his co-conspirators. George Atzerodt was a German immigrant and ferryboat operator who had been enlisted in one of the earlier kidnapping plots. Lewis Powell had fought at Gettysburg. He had been captured by the Union Army and later escaped and was also involved in the earlier Lincoln kidnap conspiracies. Atzerodt was to kill Vice-President Johnson while Powell's target was Secretary of State William Seward. A third conspirator, David Herold, was to kill Secretary of War Stanton at his home. It was decided that the three assassinations were to be carried out at a quarter past ten PM, precisely coinciding with Booths attack on the President.

Shortly after 8 PM, President Lincoln and Mary Todd left the White House by carriage. On the way to the theater, they stopped to pick up Henry Rathbone and Clara Harris who would be guests of the Lincoln's that evening in the State Box at Ford's Theater. When they arrived at the theater, the play had already started, but as was customary for a Presidential visit, the performance was stayed and the audience stood while the orchestra played *Hail to the Chief*. After the President and his guests were seated, the play resumed.

Back at Grover's theater, Alfred sat in the dressing room with the pearl-handled knife in his right hand. Nat was on the floor, still bound up and leaning against the wall. Curiously, Alfred was the one doing the pleading.

"I'm not going to listen to you. If I don't do exactly as he says, he'll kill me. He's half crazy, you know."

Nat persisted. "I don't believe you want to hurt me, or even want the President dead. How could you have gotten involved with John Booth, anyway?"

"It just sort of happened, slowly over time. I was discharged after being wounded during the Wilderness Campaign and came to Washington City to live with my sister and recuperate. I always liked the playhouses, and got to following Wilkes Booth. You know, he really is a fine actor. Some of us would go to the tavern after the performances and we'd all get pretty drunk and he'd talk about the war and slavery and such. Some didn't want to hear it and left, but a few of us stayed on. It got to be a regular thing. Then he started passing out the cash. After a while, he felt like he could trust us, and he started throwing out some pretty wild ideas. At one point he suggested that the Confederacy could be saved if we could just kidnap the President and hold him for ransom. Lincoln wouldn't be harmed so it didn't seem like such a bad thing. We came pretty close on two occasions, but it didn't work out. I figured he'd forgotten all about it, especially after General Lee surrendered. I hadn't seen nor heard from him. Then, today about noon he finds me and tells me he's going to kill the President tonight. He said that there was a suspicious character asking about him at the hotel and he needed my help. I think at first he thought maybe you were a Federal agent."

"Well, I'm no agent, but I do care about the President. Lincoln is a good man. Why don't you help me stop Wilkes Booth from harming him?"

"Sorry. I can't. I gave my word."

FORTY-FIVE

JOHN BOOTH WAS FAMILIAR with the play, *Our American Cousin*, that was being performed that evening. By his estimation, at about 10:15 the play would be at a specific point early in the third act where only one actor would be on the stage. Booth arrived at Ford's with about forty-five minutes to spare. After hiring a young theater employee to watch his horse—a mare he had rented earlier in the day—Booth went to the tavern next door for a drink.

Shortly after ten o'clock, John Wilkes Booth entered the lobby of Ford's Theater and ascended the stairs to the entrance to the President's box. The third act of the play had already begun. The President's driver, Charles Forbes, was sitting near the outer door to the State Box, but John Parker, the President's bodyguard, had not yet returned from the tavern where he had gone during the last intermission.

Back in the dressing room at Grover's Theater, Nat was desperate as he knew that time was getting short. "Alfred. You've got to listen to me. Please cut me loose. You can get away—I swear I won't turn you in. I don't even know your last name." Alfred was fidgeting and Nat could see beads of sweat on his forehead.

"All right. All right." Alfred bent down and cut the ropes that bound Nat's hands together.

"Thank you. You're doing the right thing. Now—my feet."

"No. I'm sorry but I don't trust you. I'm getting out of here first. I'll leave this knife at the edge of the stage. You're going to have to free yourself."

Alfred bolted out of the dressing room door without another word. With his feet bound together behind him, Nat moved quickly on his hands and knees toward the door. Crawling under the stage curtain, Nat looked about but Alfred was nowhere to be seen. The light was very dim and he used up precious seconds until he found the knife where Alfred had left it.

It was four blocks to Ford's Theater and Nat ran as fast as he could. When he got to 10th Street, a horse and rider galloped by. Nat stopped and turned backwards to look just as the rider did the same. It was John Wilkes Booth. They stared at each other for a few seconds and then the rider turned, buried his spurs in the mare's flanks and dashed away. Nat turned back toward the theater to witness a throng of people exiting the building. There were shouts and screams, "The President's been shot!"

FORTY-SIX

JAMES STAFFORD was leaning back in his desk chair, elbows resting on the arms of the chair and with fingers of his two hands—except for his pinkies—touching each other. He looked up at Mai Tran.

"You don't believe that for a moment, do you? The trust account was obviously set up for the airman before he was declared MIA—probably by the old lady Rose and her husband. The Khronos founder may have been the kid's great-grandfather or something, but so what? He's long gone, and the airman is not coming back from Vietnam." Stafford was trying to get Mai Tran to look at the situation realistically.

"But I distinctly heard them they tell the McCabe woman that Nathaniel Booth, the founder, was Rose's son. They were one in the same person. Why would they say that?"

"Christ! Who knows why? I don't believe for a minute that Atwood and his little friend came here to do historical research on Khronos Trust for a book or something. They were hired by Rose Booth to snoop around in hope of finding out what happened to the trust account."

"And if they keep poking around, they are likely to find out." Mai Tran was now sitting on Stafford's desk.

Stafford stood up. "That's why I've had you following them, remember? If I actually believed that they were going to bring in the authorities—that they uncovered any evidence of wrong doing—then we would need to roll back the transfers to the Cayman account and cover our tracks, but I don't think that will happen."

"I know what you're saying. I get it." Now they were both standing.

"But just in case, you need to continue to keep close tabs on what they are doing as long as they are here in New York. Once they get tired of all this and go back to Rose and Richmond, we'll be in the clear." Mai Tran nodded. "Now, where were they headed when they left you?"

"Back to their hotel. I heard Atwood tell the driver before they got in their cab."

"Then that's where you need to be."

"O.K., but I also overheard our couple inside the Khronos offices talking about some books and office junk that may have been sold to a used office furniture store. I want to check it out before they get there in case there's something we don't want them to find."

"Whatever you think you need to do." He watched as she walked toward the door. "And Mai Tran—"

Turning to face Stafford once again she asked, "Yes, James?"

"Please. No more talk about 150 year old Vietnam MIAs." Without acknowledging the comment, Mai Tran turned back toward the door and left Stafford's office.

FORTY-SEVEN

OCTOBER 1872. It had been more than seven years since the assassination. The frightful sounds and poignant images of that night outside Ford's Theater still found their way into Nat's consciousness from time to time, but they no longer occupied his every waking moment as in the days following that dreadful night. Nat had cried as he watched them carry the mortally wounded President across 10th Street to the Petersen House. He had waited with the sad and silent crowd of onlookers gathered outside until the next morning when the announcement came that President Lincoln had died at 7:22 AM.

Nat often reflected on how he might have been able to stop Wilkes Booth. Instead of attempting to meet and then reason with the would-be assassin, what if he had simply tracked him down before the performance and killed him? Or perhaps he could have mounted the stage at Ford's during the second act intermission and divulged the plot to the entire audience. The fact that he had failed, just as he had failed to save Wesley Culp at Gettysburg, disturbed him greatly. But gradually, he had come to consider and finally accept that creating an alternate history was simply not possible. He now believed that there was no way that he could have saved President Lincoln. The proof was that the President was, indeed, assassinated. It was a fact known to the world as he was growing up. If he had been successful, then the history books written after 1865—the history he learned as a boy—would have confirmed an alternate outcome. He had come to believe that he was simply acting out a script that had been prepared in advance. If someone had preserved the guest register from Mrs. McGill's Guest House and showed it to him in 1968, he firmly believed that he would have found his own name there.

Nat was thirty-three years old and he had gotten on with his life in 19th century Washington DC. Three days after the assassination, nearly penniless, he walked into the editor's office at the *Washington Star* on Broad Street and pleaded for a job as a news reporter. It would be another ten days before Wilkes Booth and David Herold would be tracked down in Virginia, and because of the assault that nearly killed Secretary of State Seward, wild rumors concerning the extent of the conspiracy began to circulate. Nat argued that he had a special interest in the case as a distant relative of the assassin and could bring a useful perspective to the paper's readers. Despite his admitted lack of newspaper experience, Nat convinced the editor to hire him on a conditional basis at a generous starting salary of twenty dollars per week.

In the days and weeks that followed, he assisted a more senior reporter in coverage of the conspiracy trial and was present at the executions of conspirators David Herold, Lewis Powell, George Atzerodt and Mary Surratt. Mrs. Surratt ran a boarding house where the conspirators often stayed, and although the extent of her participation in the conspiracy was probably exaggerated at the military tribunal, she was among the four that were hanged on July 7th, 1865, at the Old Arsenal Penitentiary. Mary Surratt became the first woman in American history to be tried and executed for criminal behavior.

Nat's managing editor often remarked that the junior reporter displayed a unique ability to delve into the possible future ramifications of any significant news event, often successfully predicting the unintended consequences of a law passed by Congress or a change in reconstruction policy proposed by the current administration. He sometimes rankled his readers when he wrote of the deplorable treatment of Indians in the West, or when he supported Seward's purchase of Alaska from the Czar of Russia in 1867 for the unimaginably vast sum of seven million dollars. After three years as a reporter, Nat was promoted to associate editor.

He put in long hours at the paper and when he wasn't working, Nat spent much of his time at Lily's Tavern located across the street from the newspaper building. Lily Fremont was twenty-two and had come from England six years earlier with her father, who had run the business until his death in 1870. Lily was an attractive, petite brunette and despite her common upbringing, usually spoke with a polite version of the Queen's English. Usually, that is, until an inebriated patron became belligerent about a bar tab or dared make a coarse suggestion for an intimate rendezvous. In such instances, Lily's normally pleasant demeanor would be slowly transformed. She would patiently wait as the insolent patron completed his unwelcome remarks before launching into her tirade. Regular customers in the tavern would look away from the pending confrontation, smiling at each other with the certain knowledge of what was about to befall the hapless perpetrator.

Nat and Lily would sit and talk for hours in the tavern— often about local politics or world events, but just as frequently concerning some bit of neighborhood gossip. She loved him, which was obvious to anyone who saw her face all but glow whenever he walked into the tavern. He thought she was too young, and when he first met her five years ago, she definitely was. Nat wouldn't admit the feelings he had for Lily, even to himself.

One evening in late October, Nat sat at his favorite spot in the tavern at the end of the long bar. Lily was bartending and another patron had engaged Nat in his favorite subject for discussion: presidential politics. Election day, November 5th, was a week away. U.S. Grant, the Republican candidate, was seeking his second term in office. The Democrats had selected Horace Greeley to run against the incumbent.

"So, tell me, Nat. Do you think my man Greeley has a chance?" The patron was seeking an expert opinion from the newspaper editor.

"No. The *Alabama* claims matter was the only issue that Grant could be beaten on, and that's going away." Nat was referring to the U.S. Government's war claim against Britain for the damage done to Union shipping during the Civil War. Britain had staunchly proclaimed her neutrality at the onset of hostilities, and should have refrained from assisting either side in the conflict. But British shipyards were put under contract by private southern citizens for the construction of several warships, one of which was the cruiser *Alabama*. This vessel wreaked havoc on Union shipping until she was finally sunk by the *USS Kearsarge* in 1864. The U.S. Government's failure to extract payment for damages from the British had been a criticism of Grant's first administration until the matter was finally resolved.

Nat continued, "Greeley will get a good share of the vote, but I don't think he'll get much support from the state electors." What Nat wanted to say, what he knew to be fact, was that Horace Greeley would die before the electors met and the votes earmarked for him would be split among several Democratic candidates. Grant would take the election—as the saying went—like he took Richmond.

Up until now, Nat had not confided in Lily much about his past. She knew that during the war he had been captured at Gettysburg, and about his time at the Point Lookout and Elmira prisoner of war camps, but little else. When asked about his childhood, he tended to generalize, or change the subject entirely. He knew that Lily felt hurt about his reticence to open up, but Nat was reluctant to divulge the truth because he doubted that she could accept it. Frankly, he was afraid of losing her. But now he believed that the Greeley matter and other events surrounding the election might give him an opportunity to divulge a little more of his own history and at the same time eliminate the reasonable doubts she was certain to harbor upon hearing it.

That evening after the tavern closed, without going into great detail, Nat related the essence of what happened to him between June 1968 and July 1863. When he was finished, she simply stared blankly at him, not knowing what to believe.

"Look, Lily. I know what I told you sounds crazy, and I can't blame you if you are unable to accept it on faith: I'm not asking you to. In fact, I won't bring it up again after this evening, but now I'm going to tell you about some things that will happen next month, so that when they come to pass, you can know that what I've told you is the truth and that I am not mentally deranged." She objected at first, stating that she had no interest in putting his credibility to a test, but he insisted. In the next few minutes, Nat related what he could remember from his history studies about the election of 1872 and Horace Greeley. Predicting Grant's victory did not require a crystal ball as the incumbent president was clearly the frontrunner well before the election, but then Nat explained to Lily that Mary Greeley, the wife of Grant's opponent, would die two days after the election, on November 7th. Moreover, that election day itself would be a landmark in the women's suffrage movement because a woman named Susan B. Anthony would be arrested with several of her followers while attempting to vote in Rochester, New York. Finally, Greeley himself, depressed over the death of his wife and the outcome of the election, would pass away before the end of the month.

The subject was never brought up between them again, but determined that Lily harbor no vestige of doubt concerning his sanity or credibility, Nat collected newspaper clippings reporting the events as they occurred in the sequence he predicted. One by one, as each event unfolded, he left the clippings on the bar where she would be sure to see them.

By December, Lily was tired of the political discourse that had infected her establishment for what had seemed like months. She wanted desperately to change the subject of the day. Resting her elbow on the bar and her palm in her chin, she looked directly at Nat. "Did you know that I hired a new piano player?"

"Another one?" Nat asked.

"You mean that Chink?" offered a patron sitting nearby.

"He's not Chinese—he's from some other country over there. Siam or something, I can't remember. He's kind of old, but he's composed a lot of catchy tunes and plays well. He speaks passable English and he's quite fluent in French, which I thought was rather odd. But I had to give him a chance. Do you think my customers will mind?"

"He's a Chink, isn't he?"

Nat had no opinion. "He'll probably work out great," he said.

FORTY-EIGHT

THE NEXT EVENING, Nat was back at Lily's. His day had been difficult as his reporters, it seemed, were equally uninspired after weeks of repetitive election analysis.

"Hi, Lil."

"Good to see you, Nat."

"Beer?"

"Beer's fine." Lily pulled a draught from the iced-down barrel—an extravagance requested by Nat and made available only to her best customers. At the opposite wall, Van Luu, the new piano player had captivated several of Lily's patrons with his skill at the keyboard of the old upright piano. He played most of the popular tunes of the day and, for good measure, had just completed an emotional rendition of *La Marseillaise*—the French National Anthem since 1795—performed at the request of a French visitor who sang accompaniment. Before the song was over, the Frenchman had tears in his eyes.

"Another tough day?" Lily was sympathetic.

"Just the usual", Nat answered. "Seems that we're always fighting the press deadline. I'm getting tired of this rat race;

I've got to find something else to do." Van Luu played on. Nat noticed that the entire room was particularly taken with Van's instrumental rendition of *Alexander's Ragtime Band*. He followed up with the Irish favorite, *Danny Boy*, for which he sang and played his own accompaniment. The tears began to flow again in the tavern as no one seemed to be bothered by Van's affected Pigeon-Irish brogue.

"He's very good, don't you think? And he's composed most of these songs himself." Lily was clearly pleased with her new employee.

"Really?" Now Nat's interest was piqued.

"He's still a Chink," came the voice from the other end of the bar.

"Oh! Oh!" Lily was excited as Van began his next song. "He wrote this one, too. It's my favorite. Listen." Nat registered a look of surprise on his face as Van belted out the words to *Take Me Out to the Ball Game* to the delight of all gathered around him. Nat wondered why Van would claim these songs as his original work. And although he was by no means an expert on music history, Nat had a vague sense that the last three songs that Van performed were products of the early twentieth century, not the nineteenth.

Van finished his performance with a flourish, then pushed himself away from the keyboard. He had been playing for the agreed upon ninety minutes and was tired, but the audience clapped for more. They were relentless and continued their applause until Van held up one finger. "One more song," he cautioned and began to play again.

When the first few words poured out after the instrumental introduction, Nat had heard enough. "That's it." Now he was certain.

"What's the matter with you, Nat?" asked Lily.

"Don't you hear those words? 'Over There—Over There. The Yanks are coming'? That's not a Union Army fight song he's singing. It's about Americans in France. That song won't be published for forty-five years!"

"Are you out of your bloody mind?"

"Over there, over there. I'm going over there and throttle him until he owns up." Nat started to rise off his barstool.

"You'll do nothing of the kind. Obviously, you are mistaken, but after he's finished, the three of us will sit down and have a calm discussion and resolve the matter." When the applause died down, Lily motioned for Van to come over to a secluded table near the rear exit. She had poured him a beer. "You were excellent tonight, Van." He nodded an acknowledgment. "This is my friend, Nathaniel." Van nodded again. "He has a problem with the last few songs that you performed this evening."

"What problem?"

Nat jumped in. "Lily here tells me that you wrote these songs yourself. Is that correct?"

"Yes, I write them."

"Well, I think that maybe George Cohan and Irving Berlin, the true composers of a couple of those songs might disagree with you." Nat's voice became louder. "They might disagree, that is, if it weren't for the fact that they haven't been born yet!"

Now it was Lily's turn to jump in. "That's ridiculous, Nat. Why would Van lie about such a thing?"

"No, Miss Lily. Your friend is correct. I not write any of those songs. I learn them when I was a young man in Vietnam."

"And when was that, Van? Tell us, won't you." Nat was relentless in his probing.

"In 1930s," Van answered sheepishly. Then he looked directly at Nat. "And what about you, Mr. Nathaniel? From what year you come here?" Nat didn't answer. Just closed his eyes and held his head in his hands. Now Lily was clearly distraught.

"All right, I get it. This is some kind of joke you two have arranged." Nat reached out and took her hand, then Van spoke up.

"Van is sorry that I lie to you, Miss Lily, about the songs. Sorry you mad. Van go home now." Van Luu rose to leave, but Nat stopped him.

"Lily's not mad, and neither am I. Please sit, Van. Let's listen to his story, Lily. I want to hear every detail."

Van sat silently for a moment, collecting his thoughts, then he began. "When Van was twelve years old in Vietnam, I go to Catholic school. That is where I learn to play piano. I like to play American songs, even though I don't understand the words very much."

"Vietnam was under control of French. My uncle, Nguyen Thai Hoc, was fighting for freedom of my country, much like American Revolution, but French army was strong and Hoc's people were few. My uncle was captured and killed in Yen Bay along with many of his friends. They chop his head off. It was a very sad time. My mother and I were sent to work in rubber plantation in the south. No more playing piano. It was hard work, and one night in 1933 we run away. We were on road, walking to village where relatives could maybe help us. A strange storm came, but there was no rain, just white light everywhere. Light so bright that we could not see, and when it passed we were no longer on road in Vietnam. We did not know where we were and my mother and I much frightened. Men came and they talk to us, but we did not talk American and they did not understand us, so I talk in French. Nuns in Catholic school teach me French, too. I talk pretty good French. The men take us to the French Consul in Washington City, and I tell them what happened. But they don't believe. They say it is year 1828, not 1933, and they think Van is crazy. But they find place for us to live. My mother cry a lot. Later, people find work for my mother as gardener and I get clean-up job at French Consul. My mother very unhappy here. She want to return to Vietnam, but it was impossible. She die after about five years. Later I marry and have one son. He is about your age, Mr. Nathaniel. He study business and economics at university." Van paused for a few seconds. "And how you get here, Mr. Nathaniel?"

Over the next several minutes, Nat related the abridged version of how he started out in Vietnam in 1968 and ended up in Civil War America in 1863. Van was most curious about what brought Nat and the U.S. military to Vietnam. "You help us fight against the French?" Van asked.

"No. You guys kicked the French out years before we got there. In 1968, Americans and Vietnamese in the South were fighting the North Vietnamese. Your country was split in two. Sorry, Van." Van looked sad, Lily seemed confused.

When Nat finished, Van stood up to leave. "I must go home now. It is late. Do you want me come back and play piano again, or should I stay home?"

"You're the best piano player I've had here, Van," Lily offered. "Please come back. Same time, tomorrow night."

FORTY-NINE

VAN LUU NEVER SPOKE AGAIN about his strange experience. He played the piano and sang at Lily's for about three months when Lily noticed that he wasn't looking well. After Van missed two days work, Lily received a visitor. It was Van's son, Trung Luu. Van had died in his sleep the night before.

The funeral service for Van Luu at St. Anne's Catholic Church was well attended. There were at least twenty regulars from Lily's Tavern plus Lily, Nat and Trung. Van's pastor gave a heart-warming sermon from the story of Joseph, a man who was a stranger in the land of Egypt who nevertheless was able to overcome adversity. Lily spoke a few words, then Trung thanked everyone who had befriended his father. After the burial at the church cemetery, all returned to Lily's Tavern for the wake. For the first time, Nat and Trung Luu had a chance to speak with one another.

"My father always liked you, Mr. Booth."

"Please call me Nat."

"I remember him telling me about the night you first met. He laughed when he told me how you confronted him about those songs he claimed to write."

"You should have seen the look on his face when he knew he had been found out. He was pretty shocked. I don't blame him, though. Your father was pretty resourceful. You should be proud of him. It had to be a difficult thing for a young man to be suddenly thrust into a strange land, not knowing the language, and with no one around except his mother from the old country."

"Well, that wasn't completely true. Did he ever tell you about my mother?"

"No, he never mentioned her."

"When my father was about twenty-one, he worked for a time for a wealthy landowner. This man had a land grant from before the Revolutionary War—about fifty square miles of land east of Charlottesville along the Chesapeake Bay. A sharecropper family lived on a small plot of his land. The old sharecropper spoke in a Vietnamese dialect, close to my father's language. He lived with an Algonquin Indian woman and they had a daughter about twenty years old. A few weeks after they met, my father married the daughter."

"The old man—my grandfather—said that years before he had been tending a rice crop outside his Vietnamese village when he stopped to rest for a few minutes. He fell asleep, and when he awoke, he was surrounded by a group of Algonquin braves. He believed that if he had been a white man, they would have killed him for sure, but instead, they sort of adopted him. This happened about thirty-five years before my father's similar experience."

Nat had been listening intently. "That makes three such events that I know of, including my own. I wonder how often this happens—this space relocation and time disruption—or whatever you want to call it."

"I've heard of no other cases, anywhere."

"Let's get another drink."

At the bar, Lily asked Nat, "Did Trung tell you that he's going to help me expand the business? We're going to open another Lily's Tavern." Trung looked over at Nat.

"Yes, it's true. My father left me a little money, and I think it would be a good investment." Nat looked concerned. "You don't mind, do you?"

"No, I don't mind at all. I just don't believe now would be a good time to expand. In fact, I think it would be best for Lily to sell this place, while the market is high."

"That's silly, Nat. Why would I want to sell out now? Business has been booming."

"Yes, but it's about to bust. Real estate prices and commodities have been on a tear, but it's going to come tumbling down before the end of the year."

"You know that? For sure?"

"Yes. It will be known as the Panic of 1873. Sorry to burst your bubble, but it's going to burst!" Now he turned to Trung Luu. "Didn't your father tell you about what's coming?"

"He was only fifteen in 1933. He told me a lot about Vietnam in the early 1900s and airplanes and automobiles and about the Great War in 1914. He even told me of Black Friday in 1929 and the collapse of the stock market in New York and the big depression that followed, but he didn't have much to say about this century, unfortunately."

"I guess that's understandable. Fact is, there will be another economic downturn in the 1890s, but there will also be a number of opportunities in the next thirty years to make some money. Right now, though, you should start thinking about liquidating any business investments and turning them into hard currency. I'm talking about gold, and stay away from the banks. Plenty of them are going to fail and people are going to lose a lot of money." Now Lily was concerned.

"How long do we have, Nat?"

"You've got some time—'til the end of the summer, anyway. But then you'd better be ready. It will be about five years before things turn around and improve."

FIFTY

IT STARTED innocently enough. During the first week of September 1873, a bank financial analyst in London was reviewing a request from one of the bank's oldest customers to extend their credit line. It is not known what specific item within the customer's financial statement led the analyst to recommend against any extension, but the bank officers agreed and the request was denied. The account manager at the bank apologized profusely to his client, who passed it off as only a minor irritation and inconvenience. After all, the client had substantial investment assets that could be quickly liquidated to raise the needed cash. An order was placed with his broker in New York to sell his sizable position in the investment banking firm of Jay Cooke & Company. This firm had underwritten most of the U.S. Government's wartime loans and had provided the financial backing for the tremendous expansion of the nation's railroads after the war.

But soon rumors began to spread throughout the New York financial community. Did the British company have inside information concerning Jay Cooke & Company? Was the investment banker overextended? Would the second transcontinental railroad line, the Northern Pacific that

Cooke was promoting, prove unprofitable in the face of existing rail over-capacity? Without waiting for answers to these questions, investors ran for the exits, liquidating bond and stock positions en masse. On September 18th, Jay Cooke & Company declared bankruptcy and hundreds of other banking firms followed. Thus began the financial debacle that would come to be known as the Panic of 1873.

A month earlier, few took notice of the small investment firm that had quietly opened its doors at the end of Wall Street at the very edge of the financial district. The firm was definitely not overcapitalized, but resources were adequate: Lily had sold the tavern in Washington on July 31st for twenty thousand dollars. Before resigning his associate editor position at the *Washington Times* on August 1st, Nat had managed to save about a thousand. Trung Luu still had the eighty-five hundred dollars left by his father. The three were on the train to New York City a week later. By August 15th they had rented office space and filed incorporation papers. It would be another month before Khronos Trust Services, Inc. would be officially recognized as a broker-dealer by the New York Stock Exchange, but the firm already had everything that the State of New York required in 1873 to operate an investment business: an office and a shingle.

But customers were not exactly flocking to the new concern. In the first two weeks, only a handful of potential clients wandered in. And while the men appreciated chatting with Lily, the attractive office manager, and grudgingly admitted that the oriental analyst might have some good ideas, they weren't willing to listen to Nat's pessimistic view of the future economy, especially when investment valuations had never been higher.

Their first client, almost a month after they opened, was a widow who responded to a small ad they had placed in the *Wall Street Journal*. She was concerned about the safety of her life savings, five thousand dollars, currently on deposit with a local bank. After an hour of investment counseling, the woman agreed to place her funds under Khronos trust management, for which the company would earn an annual fee of twenty-five dollars plus two percent of the asset value. When the woman left the office, there were smiles all around: they had signed up their first client!

The next morning, a fancy carriage stopped outside the office and the driver came in and presented a calling card to Lily.

"Mr. James Osterbrook the Third would like to make an appointment for this afternoon to discuss the possibility of placing the management of his extensive holdings with your firm. Would three o'clock be satisfactory?"

"Yes, of course," replied Lily. We would be pleased to meet with Mr. Osterbrook at three."

The carriage drove up at 3:30. The driver opened the door and James Osterbrook III stepped out, stopping for a few seconds to survey the façade of this singularly unimpressive brick building at the end of Wall Street. Inside, Lily was pretending to work at the reception desk while keeping a curious eye on the potential client. Osterbrook was about forty and wore a gray pinstripe suit and a bowler hat. He was clean-shaven and held a lighted cigar in his left hand. Lily rose to meet him at the door of the office as he entered.

"Mr. Osterbrook. Please come in, and welcome to you, sir."

"Thank you, my dear."

"The business manager and our chief analyst are waiting in the conference room. Let me take your hat."

Inside the small room were a table and six chairs. Nat rose and introduced Trung and himself, shaking Osterbrook's hand firmly. When Trung offered his hand, Osterbrook acted as if he had not noticed and quickly seated himself. Lily brought in a large brown glass ashtray for Osterbrook's cigar.

"How can we be of service, Mr. Osterbrook?" Nat asked.

"I've noticed your firm's advertisements," Osterbrook began, "in the *Wall Street Journal*, and they seem to have struck a resonant chord with me. You see, while I am invested in some shipping and mining ventures, most of my assets are tied up in railroad stocks. My shares have appreciated nicely in the past two years, but I am concerned that many of these new rail lines have yet to report a profitable quarter. How long can that go on, before we see valuations tumble?"

Nat clasped his hands together on the table and leaned forward in his chair toward Osterbrook. Then he began to speak. "We share the same concerns, Mr. Osterbrook. This has been an era of speculative excess, and we don't believe that the situation can continue for long. Mr. Luu, here, has been assessing the issue."

"Yes, Mr. Osterbrook." Trung offered. "There are over 350 rail companies in this country—more that twice as many as at the end of the war—all competing for the same level of freight business and with only small growth in passenger traffic. We believe that investors are already becoming impatient. Once they start to withdraw their support, these firms will be in grave financial difficulty."

"That's very interesting." Osterbrook drew on his cigar and exhaled a large billow of smoke in Trung's direction. "But what does one do? One can't simply hide one's money under the bed."

"Let me explain our investment philosophy here at Khronos Trust Services." Nat paused briefly. "In normal times, we believe in investing in the largest and fastest growing businesses in America, with an eye toward those companies and industries that we believe will be at the forefront of progress and new invention. But these are not normal times. We believe them to be particularly perilous times, a time when investors should think first in terms of capital preservation. When valuations fall—and we believe that a fall is virtually certain—we will be able to scoop up securities at bargain prices; maybe for as little as twenty-five cents on the dollar."

"You mean you would advise individuals to liquidate everything at this time?"

"Not necessarily. There are always special situations that present themselves, so that one can make money even in hard times, but for most of your portfolio, capital preservation should be the watchword for now. But I do not mean to sound pessimistic. The economic downturn that we believe is imminent won't last forever. I have faith in the long-term growth and progress of this country. We shall come out of it, and when we do, opportunities will abound."

"And you have substantial client assets under management at his time?"

"Considerable."

Osterbrook leaned back in his chair, thoughtfully considering Nat's words and filling the room with more blue-gray smoke from his cigar. After a minute, he extinguished the cigar in the ashtray and looked directly at Nat. "Would it be possible, Mr. Booth, for you and I to speak privately?"

"I'm not sure what you mean, Mr. Osterbrook. Mr. Luu, here, is our chief investment analyst. You may be assured that anything you say will be held in strictest confidence."

Trung rose from his chair, "It's not a problem, Nat. I have some errands to attend to. I'll leave you and Mr. Osterbrook to yourselves." Trung Luu quickly exited the conference room and closed the door behind him.

"What is it that you wanted to tell me, Mr. Osterbrook?"

"You'll be happy to learn, Mr. Booth, that based upon our discussion today, I have tentatively decided to turn the management of my investments over to your firm, but—"

"But?"

"But I am concerned with your sense of business acumen as it pertains to the selection of your staff."

"You're referring to Mr. Luu?"

"Yes, Booth. We have a problem in this country with social and economic inroads being made by outsiders, particularly the Negro and the Chinese. I think it reflects poorly on your firm that you would hire such an individual as anything other than a courier or janitor." As Osterbrook spoke, Nat could feel the tension building in his own face. He was angry.

"I have three things to say Mr. Osterbrook. First, Mr. Luu is *not* Chinese. He is an American, born in Washington. Further, he is not an employee, but a trusted principal in this firm." Nat was standing now. "Finally, Mr. Osterbrook, if there is anything that will prevent this country from achieving its destiny for greatness, it is people with attitudes such as yours. Khronos Trust Services does not need your business." Nat opened the conference room door and gestured toward the doorway.

"You're making a big mistake, Booth. I was ready to place a million dollars in assets under management with your firm. Good day." Osterbrook walked out of the conference room, into the front office where Lily was standing at attention holding Osterbrook's bowler. He grabbed the hat as he strode swiftly past her, eyes fixed on the exit. Trung, returning from his errands, squeezed past Osterbrook in the doorway.

"What's the matter with Mr. Osterbrook?"

"He thought our fees were too high," Nat offered.

FIFTY-ONE

THE COLLAPSE of Jay Cooke & Company set off an economic chain reaction that could not be stopped. At the New York Stock Exchange, anxious investors tried to liquidate securities, but buyers could not be found. To prevent a total collapse of prices, the exchange was closed for ten days. Over the next two years, twenty thousand U.S. businesses would fail and the unemployment rate would reach fourteen percent.

By the time the stock exchange reopened on September 30th, Khronos had signed up two dozen clients, with more coming in every day. Security prices followed a downward sloping saw-tooth pattern. Prices would stabilize briefly, even increase somewhat before succumbing to another wave of selling. A week later, Khronos had a repeat visitor.

"Mr. Osterbrook! Welcome back." Lily greeted the man warmly. Osterbrook was nervous, clutching his bowler.

"I was wondering if I might speak with Mr. Booth."

"Let me see if he is available." Lily entered Nat's private office to advise him of their visitor. Nat met Mr. Osterbrook in the front office.

"Thank you for seeing me, Booth. I've had a chance to think about our last meeting, and I realize that I acted rather boorishly. I wish to apologize to you and to Mr. Luu. You were right; in this country, no one should be denied opportunity because of prejudices we may harbor."

"That's quite a turn around, Mr. Osterbrook. To your credit, I guess we all have prejudices we must deal with."

"I believe that anyone can overcome those prejudices, in time." Osterbrook was fidgeting with his hat again. "I was hoping that you might reconsider and agree to handle my investments."

"How much have you lost since the crash?"

"Over two hundred thousand dollars!" Osterbrook answered in low tones while mopping the beads of sweat from his forehead with a handkerchief.

"We'll see if we can help reverse that," Nat offered. "Lily, please check with Mr. Luu and see if he is available to meet with Mr. Osterbrook and set up an account."

OVER THE NEXT YEAR, Khronos Trust Services enjoyed quite a reputation for not only maintaining client portfolio value in the face of difficult times, but of achieving modest growth for their clients. Their approach was to first divest new clients of the riskiest investments of the day, notably railroad stocks, and moving them temporarily into the safety of gold. Then they selectively reentered the securities market. Particular successes included investment in The Consolidated Virginia Mining Company, which subsequently discovered large silver deposits in Nevada, later known as the Comstock Lode. Other successful enterprises included the newly formed Bethlehem Steel Works as well as the Remington Fire Arms Company, which diversified into the manufacture of typewriters in late 1873. A client from San Francisco persuaded Trung Luu that the first cable car company in the city promised good returns. By February 1876, Trung was recommending U.S. Government Bonds to Khronos' more conservative investors. Many bonds, having lost fifty percent of their face value since their issue date, were now yielding an attractive ten percent interest rate.

By this time, the firm was not taking any new clients. Despite Nat's "crystal ball", the stress of direct management of fifty million in client assets was enormous. It was Lily's idea to offer an investment newsletter by subscription to interested parties. The annual subscription rate was three thousand dollars per year for investment firms and three hundred for individuals. The newsletter was mailed out monthly. The trio's personal lives had also prospered. Trung had met and married the half-Vietnamese daughter of a French rubber plantation owner. Nat and Lily became officially engaged and set a wedding date for June 1876.

Most of the invited guests were from New York and the Washington DC area, but in March, Nat had sent inquiries and eventually located John King in San Francisco and Washington Traweek in Alabama. King would be unable to attend. They had also invited Vital Jarrot, an associate of Lily's father from East St. Louis who had been a successful businessman and financier. Mr. Jarrot had served in the Governor's office in Illinois and in earlier years had been an associate of Abraham Lincoln in the Illinois General Assembly. Jarrot was heavily invested in the railroad industry prior to the economic debacle in 1873 and Lily had pleaded with him to sell his holdings, but to no avail. Jarrot was wiped out. Despite the fact that the wedding invitation included round trip rail tickets from St. Louis and a bank draft for expenses, Jarrot wrote back expressing his regrets. He wished the couple well, but would unable to attend the ceremony. His letter, returning the tickets and bank draft, was mailed from the Dakota Territory.

Although Lily knew that Vital Jarrot was very proud and obviously devastated by his reversal of fortune, she believed that the real reason he declined to attend was more of a personal nature. Before the Eads Railroad Bridge in Missouri was completed in 1874, it wasn't exactly true that the transcontinental railroad completely connected east and west. There was a major break in the line at the Mississippi River at St. Louis. The heavy steam engines remained on one side of the river or the other while freight and passenger cars were ferried across the mile-wide river by massive barges owned by the Wiggins Ferry Company and other smaller transport firms. The going rate was one dollar per car, but in a joint venture funded by J.P. Morgan and Khronos Trust Services, the Wiggins Company bought out the competition. Now with a monopoly on the rail car ferry service, Wiggins immediately raised the rate to five dollars per car, further squeezing profits from the financially strapped railroads. In a letter to Lily, Vital Jarrot had complained bitterly that the effects of the monopoly particularly savaged the rail firms in which he was invested. Lily believed that this was the real reason why Jarrot didn't come to their wedding.

The guest list was not particularly large, but the wedding was nonetheless a grand event. The ceremony was performed by the Reverend A.P. Dutton of the South Manhattan Episcopal Church. Trung was best man, while two of Lily's cousins visiting from England and Trung's wife, Kim, were maids and matron of honor, respectively. A number of members of the New York financial community were in attendance, but what people remembered most about the ceremony were the flowers: hundreds of white lilies decorated the church in Lily's honor.

The reception was held at the posh Stork Club on the waterfront. More lilies and a sumptuous buffet of St. Louis prime rib, lobster and magnums of the best French champagne. After a week-long search, Nat had managed to find a baker who was willing to experiment and finally create a delicious multi-level chocolate wedding cake with vanilla butter cream frosting. It was Nat's favorite and something totally unheard of in 1876 New York City. The orchestra played late into the night as the guests waltzed.

At Lily's insistence, Nat was able to spend some time in private conversation with his old friend, Washington Traweek.

"When I heard that President Lincoln had been shot, I wuz still in Virginia, headin' south," Wash explained. "They said the assassin was a man named Booth, and at first I thought, 'My God, Nat, what have you done?' Then I remembered what you said; that if I had heard of some huge event takin' place, that I would know that you had failed at what you were goin' to do. That's when I knew fer' sure that you had tried to stop it."

"You know, Wash, that I didn't keep it from you because I didn't trust you. I was just trying to protect you."

"I know, Nat."

When it was over, Nat and Lily retired to their room at the Waldorf Astoria. On the following Monday, they boarded the steamship *Everhorn*, together with Lily's cousins, for an extended honeymoon in England and France.

FIFTY-TWO

AUL'S NEW AND USED OFFICE FURNISHINGS & PAWN
was about eight blocks north of the now closed
Khronos Trust Services office. The painted store
window promised passers-by file cabinets from $19, office
chairs from $29, and desks from $39. But when Amanda and
Roger entered the store, what they saw mainly were the
desks—a sea of used gray metal and occasional wooden ones.
They were arranged back-to-back in double rows like tightly
packed starter homes in the blocks of a blue-collar
subdivision. Access paths between the rows were only a few
inches wide. A single line of used file cabinets extended the
full length of one wall to the rear of the store. After a minute,
a smiling young man in a white shirt and tie, obviously not
Saul, walked rapidly toward them down the single wide
middle aisle from the back of the store.

"Hi folks, can I help you find something?"

"We're looking for some items that came from an office
in the Flatiron Building, maybe ten days ago. There would
have been desks and file cabinets, but we were interested in
some old books that would have been included in the load."

"I think I remember taking delivery. Those items are still
in the back room, but I don't remember any books. Why

don't you follow me?" The young man led Amanda and Roger to what appeared to be a warehouse area at the back of the store building. The steel rollup door, leading to a loading dock, was open. Several pieces of office furniture were pushed up against one wall: four ordinary office desks and one expensive-looking wooden one, a conference table and chairs, plus several file cabinets. "This is all of it. I didn't think I remembered seeing any books."

"Do you mind if we open up the drawers and look inside?" asked Roger.

"Be my guest." Amanda and Roger inspected every drawer and cabinet, but they were all empty.

"Do you remember who brought these items in?"

"A couple of guys. The boss was a big man—said he was the building manager and he had a helper—a skinny black kid. You know, I think the big guy may have been in the week before with a couple of IBM Selectrics. I remember because those are hard to find nowadays, if they're in good condition. These looked brand new. There might have been some books, too. I'm not sure because Saul was handling it."

"Where would that stuff be?" asked Roger.

"Upstairs, in the pawn department. That is, if it's still around. Saul's up there. Why don't we ask him?" The young man led Amanda and Roger back into the showroom and up the stairs. Saul was reading a magazine inside a U-shaped arrangement of mismatched glass display cases containing the store's smaller, high-value items including hundreds of watches, rings, necklaces, cameras and collector coins. Scattered throughout the large room were tables displaying used office machines, telephones, musical instruments, and assorted scattered boxes of books and miscellaneous office items. "Hey, Saul," the young man began. "These folks were interested in the stuff that the manager from the Flatiron Building brought in."

"It's still by the loading dock." Saul looked up from his magazine.

"No, Saul. I'm talking about the stuff he brought in the week before. You know, when you were dealing with him."

"Yeah, I remember now. He didn't say he was the building manager until he brought in the second load. The stuff from the previous week is on the last table over there. Most of it, anyway. I sold one of the typewriters to some kid a couple of days ago and a woman bought one of the books, just this morning. There was a set of three, but she only wanted one of them."

Amanda and Roger looked through the box of books— mainly investment titles covering subjects such as stock charting and market timing, plus some law books on trusts and tax law. There were also two identically bound volumes, marked I and II, in brown cloth that were not in English. Roger guessed they were Vietnamese. He held up the two volumes to show Saul. "Was the other volume just like these two?"

"Yeah. It wasn't printed in English, but she was oriental—maybe Cambodian. She must have been able to read it."

The cover of Volume One was printed with the words "Lịch Sử Cận đạI 1900 - 1945." Roger opened the first volume and noticed a name scrawled in ink at the top of the inside front cover. It looked like 'Loc Luu,' followed by the year, '1933'. Flipping through the pages, he was unable to understand the words, but from the photos, it was clearly a history textbook. The second volume was similar, but covered the years 1946 to 2000. But what startled Roger was on the title page of the first and, he quickly verified, the second volume. Near the bottom of the page was the international copyright symbol and a year, "© 2035." Without saying a word, he pointed out his discovery to Amanda, who let out a faint gasp.

Roger tossed the two volumes back into the box with the other books. "How much, for the entire lot?" he asked Saul.

"How about a hundred?"

As Roger pulled a hundred dollar bill from his wallet, Amanda asked, "The lady who bought the book—was she a regular? Did you know her?"

"Never saw her before, but I won't forget her. She was a real knockout!"

Amanda ignored the editorial comment. "Did she maybe pay by check, or credit card?"

"We only take cash up here."

FIFTY-THREE

THE YEAR 1897 initiated a new wave of prosperity in America. The second post-Civil War economic depression which began four years earlier was over. It would be another year before the battleship *Maine* would explode in Havana harbor, touching off the Spanish American War. Telephone service and electricity were in wide use in the cities and automobiles had begun to make their appearance. The Wright Brothers, Orville and Wilbur, were still running their bicycle shop in Ohio, but were experimenting secretly with manned gliders. In Paris, a Brazilian named Santos-Dumont had already flown his gasoline-powered dirigible around the Eiffel Tower. And in New York City, the investment management and economic advisory firm known as Khronos Trust Services, Incorporated continued to prosper.

Trung Luu and his wife, Kim, had three children. The two oldest, boy and girl twins, were studying in France. The daughter hoped to marry a French diplomat, while Trung's son was drawn to the arts, particularly classical music. Neither showed much interest or aptitude for the family business. Trung had come to accept the idea that the twins would probably be content to live off the proceeds of the sizable trust funds he had established for them. His sense of regret was mild, however, because his youngest son, Loc, now fourteen years old showed great interest in his father's and Nat's business. Like his own father before him, Trung was determined as well to pass on the old country language and culture to his youngest son.

Lily and Nat were childless; a condition that greatly disappointed Lily. She had for the most part ceased her formerly active participation in Khronos and contented herself with social and charitable endeavors, as well as being a doting "Aunt Lily" to the young Loc Luu. Nat also spent a good deal of time with the boy and, in support of Trung Luu's cultural education of his son, managed to extend his own rudimentary knowledge of the Vietnamese language first acquired in Navy language school.

With Nat's influence, the young Loc Luu also gained an appreciation of history. It was a time when the Western nations, including the United States, were competing to extend their hegemony throughout the world. Nat explained how France, building upon the efforts of early missionaries to bring Christianity to the lost souls of equatorial Africa, Guiana and Indo-China, was able to subjugate the indigenous people and impose colonial rule in those regions of the world. He explained how a natural historical pattern initially evolved, and was then refined and ultimately exploited: the local population at first tolerated, and in some cases, welcomed the early missionaries. Trade initiatives began, followed by settlers. Before long, however, the native people realized that their culture and freedom were being threatened and the interlopers were no longer welcome. Skirmishes erupted, and boatloads of soldiers were sent to maintain order and protect the missionaries and nationals as well as interests of French investors at home. Centuries-old feuds among local neighboring tribes were exploited. At the slightest provocation, native leaders were tracked down and killed. Ultimately, a harsh colonial government was installed.

Nat made it clear that this pattern of colonial conquest was not limited to the French. Britain had accumulated its vast empire in much the same way and, after the American Revolution, U.S. Government policy regarding native Americans was not markedly different. American expansion abroad got a late start, due in large measure to the country focusing inward following the massive disruption surrounding the Civil War. With Britain, France, Germany, and the Dutch dividing up the remaining previously unexploited lands around the globe, the American government began to consider the projection of U.S. power to locations where the hold of the present colonial landlord was tenuous, as in Cuba and The Philippines, then held by Spain.

Nat and Loc Luu would spend many afternoons together discussing these and other historical events, but in their frequent talks, Loc Luu harbored a particular fascination with the country of his ancestors. He would barrage Nat with penetrating questions. For example, how could the Vietnamese insurgents, from the earliest days of the French occupation, sustain an ultimately successful guerilla war against the repressive government in charge while others, notably the Native Americans, were unable to do so? In the course of future events that Nat would relate to Loc Luu, why did the United States withdraw its early support for a free Vietnam after World War II? President Roosevelt initially supported self-rule for Vietnam, but ultimately gave in to the demands of U.S. allies to restore French authority. And knowing the decades-long resolve of the Vietnamese people to govern themselves and their final success in overthrowing the French, how could America purposely step in with anything other than a naive expectation of victory? Their discussions would often continue for hours, enhanced by

Nat's unique historical perspectives. Inevitably, their dialog would end with consideration of the questions that even Nat was unable to answer: what would be the final outcome? What would be the course of events in the history of Vietnam and the rest of the world after 1968?

One day in late September, Trung arrived at work early as usual, well before the rest of the staff, and was surprised to find that Nat was already in his office. On his desk was an enlarged map of the eastern United States, showing the mid-Atlantic states of Virginia and Maryland as well as Pennsylvania. When Trung came in, Nat placed on the desk the pair of metal dividers he had been holding.

"You're here awfully early. Are you and Lily planning an autumn getaway, perhaps to watch the leaves turn in the forests of northern Pennsylvania, or perchance take a barge cruise on the Erie Canal?" Trung was smiling broadly.

Nat began to laugh, "No, Trung, but I have a question for you."

"Go on." Trung Luu sat down.

"I remember your father telling me about his first days in Washington, when he and your grandmother arrived there after running away from the rubber plantation in Vietnam. He said it was the year 1828 in Washington."

"That's right. What about it?"

"Did he ever tell you what month and day it was, when they showed up?"

Trung thought for a minute. "Not directly, but I remember him saying that Grandmother was very upset in the days after it happened. To console her, he told her that the big celebrations going on in the city were in honor of their arrival. She didn't believe him, of course. He found out later that the parades and other events were part of the 4th of July celebrations in the Capitol. So they must have arrived around the 1st or 2nd of July, or maybe the end of June. Why is that important? What are you thinking?"

"Well, I think there is a definite pattern here: Look at this map. I've marked Washington DC and also the point just west of Gettysburg where I was shot down on June 30th and found myself in 1863. And here," Nat pointed at the map, "is Montross, Virginia, where your father told me that *his* father found himself sometime in 1793 or 1794, or thereabouts. The three places are all in a straight line. But not only that, the distance from Montross to Washington is exactly the same as from Washington to Gettysburg. And the differences in time between the events seem to be exactly the same as well. Mine was thirty-five years, practically to the day, after your father's arrival in 1828 and your grandfather's was just about thirty-five years before then. Not only that, but when my airplane was shot down, it was 1968 in Vietnam and remember that it was 1933 when your father and grandmother disappeared from the Vietnamese countryside. Again a difference of—"

"—of thirty-five years. That's very strange."

"And I don't believe it's a coincidence. Now look at this: if I extend the line north, further into Pennsylvania, and mark out the same distance, I end up with a fourth point right about here—near the town of State College. If I am correct, that should be the location of a fourth event which should occur next year, about June 30th."

"And so, your thinking that maybe some folks from Vietnam in the future—from, I guess it would be the year 2003, will magically appear in northern Pennsylvania, next June 30th?"

"Not as a certainty. Only if someone happens to be at the particular place and time in Vietnam when this—this time disruption—this convergence event—takes place." Both Nat and Trung stood silently, considering the theory that Nat had presented.

"Wait a minute," exclaimed Trung Luu. "You're not thinking about people showing up here from Vietnam next year—you're thinking of using it to leave here—to get back to the future, to the year 2003!"

"Why not? What's to say it can't go in both directions? If I can be at the right place and time in Pennsylvania next June 30th, why can't I get translated from there to Vietnam in the year 2003?"

"That's crazy. Even if it were possible, it would be risky. How do you know where you'd end up? You could drown in the Sea of Japan or who knows where. And whom would you have back there in 2003? Your parents? I'm sorry, Nat, but they will probably be dead by then. Besides, you'd be at a huge disadvantage. Being a man with knowledge of coming events is one helluva lot better than being a stranger in the future, knowing only the past. The world will undoubtedly change enormously between 1968 and 2003."

"I can't argue with that, but if Lily will agree to go with me, we're going to do it!"

FIFTY-FOUR

WHEN NAT LAID OUT THE PLAN to Lily, she was simultaneously excited and terrified by the prospects. He had told her much about the wonders of the twentieth century—of airplanes and fast cars, and the advances of radio—beyond Guglielmo Marconi's wireless telegraph invented three years earlier—and the miracle of television that would come later; of medical progress and the terrible wars and the weapons that made them possible. She wanted to see these things for herself. The dangers that he outlined to her as distinct possibilities were indeed frightening, but after a few days, her chief concern was the disappointment that she knew that Nat would feel should it not come to pass. What if they went to the predicted convergence point, as they were now calling it, at the appointed time and still missed it by miles, or days, or missed it simply because it didn't occur at all?

Despite all of the doubts and concerns, advance planning for their adventure began in earnest. It had been four years since Nat had set up a trust account in the name of his parents, Wendell and Rose. This was done shortly after he and Lily attended the funeral of Nat's great-grandfather, Edwin Booth, who died in New York City. The funeral was an eerie experience for Nat. He had seen Edwin on the stage—just once—at a New York production of *Hamlet*. The lead role in this play had over the years become the actor's hallmark. Edwin's son, Nat's grandfather, had died in the year that Nat was born, so to see him as a young man, twenty years younger than Nat, mourning the loss of *his* father, was a particularly emotional experience for Nat. As Lily had expected, Nat decided in advance not to disrupt the solemnity of the occasion with even a suggestion as to his true identity, choosing instead to describe he and Lily as long-admiring fans of the deceased.

The long term trust account for Wendell and Rose Booth was set up for continuing management by Khronos Trust Services, but with the added proviso that if the Luu family at any time ceased to be actively engaged in the business, that management of the account would be transferred to a Swiss bank that Khronos had long used as a trusted European affiliate. Detailed instructions within the trust papers called for the delivery of trust assets to the Booth family during the month of July 1969, a year after Nat's disappearance. The benefactor was to remain anonymous. A similar trust account was now established with Lily Booth and/or Nathaniel Booth as beneficiaries. But Trung Luu had expressed some concerns: there was no absolute assurance that the written directives would be explicitly followed after he was no longer around. After all, human beings—subject to all of the usual temptations—would be charged with carrying out those directives.

Under Nat's tutelage, Trung Luu and Loc were well-prepared for the opportunities as well as the cataclysmic events that would unfold during the first sixty years of the new century: growth of oil and steel in lock-step with the developing auto industry, office and factory automation, a period of economic hardship after the Great War followed by a short period of great prosperity, Black Friday at the New

York Stock Exchange in 1929 and the world-wide depression that follows, the start of World War II in Europe and the attack on Pearl Harbor, the advent of the nuclear age and the cold war which would result in tremendous growth of defense-related industries, or depending upon your point of view, the military-industrial complex.

Nat and Trung agreed that within fifteen years at most, Loc Luu would probably be taking over the reigns of the firm—maybe running the company for another forty years. But after that, who could know what might transpire? Nat conceded that it was unlikely that Loc would be around even for the planned future delivery of trust assets to Nat's parents in 1969, so planning beyond—out to the year 2003—seemed especially risky.

"The trust account for you and Lily is a good idea," offered Trung, "but I think you need a back-up, just in case things go badly."

"What kind of back-up?"

"Buried treasure. You know, like pirates might use. We could hide, say, twenty-five thousand in gold. Only you and Lily and I would know where it was. According to what you've told me, it would be worth close to a half-million dollars in 1968. Probably a lot more by 2003."

"So it would be like an insurance policy—something Lily and I could rely on in event that assets in the trust account disappeared."

"Exactly."

FIFTY-FIVE

BY LATE JUNE 1898, Nat and Lily had made several trips to the expected convergence point near State College, Pennsylvania. Earlier that year, Nat had purchased the four sections of farmland, some 2,500 acres, surrounding the expected departure point. The seven farm families that were displaced were paid handsomely for their land, leading to all manner of speculation concerning the new owners—the wealthy couple from New York City. The latest rumor was that the land would become a private hunting preserve. A week earlier, it was a posh hotel and health spa, and before that, everyone was certain that oil-drilling rigs would soon be appearing in the unplanted fields.

"Do you think you'll be able to get by here for a few days without the usual conveniences—no lights or plumbing?" Nat and Lily were examining the wood cook stove in the old farmhouse.

"I'm looking forward to it. It will give me a chance to brush up on my culinary skills. You always favored my cooking, didn't you, Nathaniel?"

"Of course, dear, but it's been years since you've cooked anything."

"I'm sure you'll be pleased."

"I'm sure I will. And isn't it great to get away from the city for a while?"

"Ye-Yes." Seconds earlier, they were joking with each other, but now Lily started to cry and Nat put his arms around her. "It's just so sad. We may never see our friends again—and our beautiful home."

"We don't have to do this, you know. We can go back to New York and simply live out our lives there."

"No, I want to go, and I know that you do, too."

FIFTY-SIX

BASED ON HIS OWN EXPERIENCE from thirty-five years earlier, Nat believed that the most likely day for the beginning of the hoped-for convergence event was Saturday, June 30th. As to the duration of the "open window", he had very little to go on—a few hours was probably the most he and Lily could hope for. Trung and Loc Luu, who would be seeing them off, arrived at the Pennsylvania farmhouse on Friday morning, June 29th. That evening, Lily had served a fried chicken dinner and was now cutting into the apple pie she had baked earlier in the day. For the first time, she was dressed in the Levi blue jeans that Nat had bought and had re-tailored especially for her.

"I like your time-traveling outfit, Lily. You look good." Nat was being sincere. She did look good.

"You're sure the women where we're going will be wearing these—these miner's pants?" she asked, tugging at the tight outside seams on her legs.

"Absolutely, but mainly, you wouldn't want to find yourself in a Vietnam jungle wearing a long dress over your petticoat!" The talk of travel and Vietnam had gotten Loc's attention once again.

"Why do you and Lily want to leave us, Uncle Nat?"

"We don't really want to leave, Loc. It's just something we've got to do. For me, it will be like going home after being away for a long, long time."

"I guess you won't even be able to write to us."

"No, but we'll be thinking about you often."

"I'm going to miss you."

"We'll miss you, too," offered Lily.

"Hey, you people." Trung reached for the slice of pie that Lily was offering. "This is beginning to sound like a funeral. Cheer up." Trung looked at Loc. "Nat and Lily may not be going anywhere."

"That's right. Now eat your dessert. And no complaints about the pie crust—I burned it a little."

"The pie is excellent, my dear. You haven't lost your touch!"

When they had finished, Loc volunteered to help Lily clean up the kitchen while Nat and Trung retired to the creaky wooden porch overlooking the farmyard. It was dark, and only the persistent croaking of hundreds of frogs provided evidence of the marshy pond some fifty yards away and the narrow stream that fed it. Just above the horizon, Nat could see the pattern of stars known as "the teapot"—the constellation Sagittarius in the southern sky. Overhead, the summer Milky Way glowed brightly, stretching across the heavens from North to South.

"These last few days, I've been trying to think of anything I may have forgotten—anything else that might help you run Khronos in the years ahead." The old rocking chair squawked in protest as Nat leaned back.

"I think you've given me a pretty good lesson, Nat. I have enough notes—I could probably write a history text."

"My part was easy. You always had the tough job of interpreting it and selecting the right investments. I guess the most important thing will be to get out of the markets before the downturns, and not get back in too early. For example, the big market crash in October 1929 will be only a marker for the Great Depression to follow."

"I don't expect to be around by then, Nat."

"Well, whoever is in charge—Loc, I guess—Loc will need to know. Valuations will continue to slide for three or four years and won't get back to pre-crash levels for several years. This will be true for stocks and real estate. If cash is available, he will do very well picking up investments in 1933 and 1934. Property owners will be especially desperate by then and he will be able to acquire some choice real estate. Loc should look for improved properties in Manhattan and other big cities. For vacant land, tell him to wait until the end of the war in 1945. Then jump in, buying up acreage in the suburbs of big cities like Los Angeles. The men coming home after the war will be looking to buy homes and start families."

"What about the next twenty years—anything else I should know?"

"You may be tempted to invest with some of the aircraft pioneers, but I would stay away. The Wright's will spend years trying to sell their airplane to the U.S. Government, and I really don't remember much about any of the others. Several Europeans, as I recall. Autos will get strong, but a lot of the smaller companies will go under. Stick with Ford. Chevrolet will do well later and eventually become General Motors. But no matter which auto companies survive, you won't go far wrong with big oil and steel, at least until the U.S. enters the war in 1917. Most important, be sure to diversify. Don't put all the money in one industry, no matter how tempting that may be."

"I'd say we've done pretty well up to now, Nat. Thanks to you."

"Listen. You've always been the brains behind Khronos, and without your persistence, I'd probably still be herding reporters at the *Washington Times*." Just then Lily came out on to the porch.

"I don't mean to disrupt this meeting of the Investment Advisor's Mutual Admiration Society, but I wanted to say 'Good Night'. I'm going to bed."

An hour later, Trung and Loc turned in, leaving Nat on the porch. When Lily awoke at 5 AM, Nat was not in the bed and she felt a brief flutter of fear in her chest. She ran out to the porch.

"My God, Nat. You scared me. I thought you were gone. Why didn't you come to bed?"

"I'm sorry, Lily. I don't want to miss this thing. It may be thirty-five years before we get another chance."

"You need to get some rest, Nat. You go on into bed. I'll stay up and I'll wake you if I see anything strange going on."

But nothing out of the ordinary occurred that morning, nor during the following afternoon. By nine o'clock that evening, Nat was clearly discouraged. He had hardly touched his supper, and without waiting for the others to finish, excused himself and walked the entire perimeter of the farm on the off chance that the convergent point was beyond the boundaries of his land. He saw nothing. When Nat returned to the farmhouse, Trung did not bother to ask if he had witnessed anything of significance.

"What's to say it has to occur today, Nat. Loc and I were going to leave for New York in the morning, but we can wait a couple of more days."

"Thanks, Trung. But if it doesn't happen soon, I don't believe it will happen at all. I guess we could wait another day. It can't hurt. At this point, though, it looks like Lily and I will be going back to New York with you." By midnight, everyone but Nat was asleep.

FIFTY-SEVEN

B Y THREE AM, Nat stopped struggling against the sleep that had been trying to overtake him for the last hour or more. He was dreaming. Lily, Trung and Loc were in a rowboat in the middle of the pond. Lily was in the back of the boat, calling out to him, pleading for him to hurry while Trung was rowing the boat furiously away from him. Nat's arms and legs were so heavy that, much as he tried, he couldn't get out of his chair on the porch. A wind came up, blowing hard against his face. Lily and the boat were now shrouded in a wispy white fog. She was still calling out his name, but he couldn't see her any more.

"Nat! Nat! Wake up! It's starting!" It was Lily's voice, now very close. Nat looked up and saw Lily and Trung standing next to him.

"I was dreaming—", Nat said, not yet fully awake.

"Well, this is no dream: look out there!" Trung pointed out beyond the pond. The white fog was being drawn into a slowly expanding and revolving vortex with a glowing white center. It reached a mile or more up into the sky. The wind blew harder and lightning bolts could be seen on the horizon all about them. As they watched, Loc came out from inside the house, rubbing the sleep from his eyes.

"I'm scared, Papa."

"It's going to be all right, Loc. Don't worry."

"Lily. We've got to go." Nat picked up the duffel bag he had prepared the day before containing a change of clothes for him and Lily, water, some food and a cache of gold coins. "Take care of your Dad, Loc." He hugged the boy. Trung kissed Lily on the cheek and then hugged Nat.

"Goodbye, my friend."

"Goodbye, Trung." Nat took Lily's hand and they stepped off the porch.

"Goodbye Lily and Nat," the boy called out. Lily turned around to look at Loc.

"We love you."

Trung and Loc watched from the porch as Nat and Lily ran across the unplanted fields toward the bright white swirling fog. The wind was whipping their clothes against their bodies, threatening to tear them off. In a few minutes they reached the edge of the vortex that was now moving slowly away from the farmhouse in a southerly direction. Seconds later, Nat and Lily Booth disappeared into the bright glare emanating from the center of vortex that marked the centroid of the convergence event.

FIFTY-EIGHT

"I CAN'T SEE A THING, NAT." The stark brightness was overwhelming.

"Just hold on to my hand and keep running." Slowly, the blinding white light began to dissipate. A mottled pattern of shadows, at first barely visible on the ground, became increasingly more distinct. Nat looked up and discovered the source to be sunlight filtered through the overhanging vegetation. The heat was stifling and the air felt heavy with humidity. Nat and Lily stopped running and held each other closely as they surveyed the tropical jungle that surrounded them.

"I think we can safely say that we are no longer in Pennsylvania," Nat offered.

"You didn't tell me it would be so hot." Lily unbuttoned the sleeves of her blouse and rolled them up. Nat retrieved a water canteen from the duffel bag and offered it to Lily.

"Here, take a drink." He had also removed two straw hats from the bag and was now wearing one of them. "And put this on." A few feet to his left, the vegetation seemed less dense and he moved in that direction.

"Don't you leave me, Nat!" Lily was frightened, as she could no longer see him.

"I'm right here. Don't worry." Nat stretched out his free hand and Lily grabbed it. He pulled her toward him and they both stepped into the middle of an overgrown foot path.

"Well, this is a bit of luck," Lily said. "Which direction do we go?" Nat looked down the trail in each direction, then up at the sun, which was directly overhead.

"I'd say we should head south, if I knew which direction south was!" Looking down the trail once again, he said, "Let's go this way. The trail seems a little wider in this direction." Nat led the way, carrying the duffel bag. Lily followed close behind with the palm of her right hand resting on Nat's back.

After twenty minutes the trail had become better defined and the jungle vegetation seemed thinner: fewer trees and vines and more tall grass. They stopped to rest when they came to a clearing.

"Do you think we're in Vietnam, Nat?" Lily asked. Nat took a drink from the canteen.

"Looks promising, but we could also be in Central or South America, or Africa, or maybe even Florida."

"I think it's kind of creepy; can we keep moving?" Nat took her hand.

"Let's go."

The trail seemed to go on without end. Where the overhead vegetation was sparse, the grass on both sides of the trail had grown thick and tall. In some places, it was nearly as tall as Nat. They had seen some animal life including small monkeys in the treetops and a few snakes. Lily thought she heard a wild pig behind some of the tall grass, but didn't actually see it. Except for the trail itself and the apparent use of a machete or similar bladed tool to keep it clear, they had seen no evidence of human presence whatsoever. The sun was no longer straight overhead, but lower in the sky and on their right. They had been walking in a southeasterly direction.

"Do you want to rest for a few minutes?" Nat stopped and turned around to Lily.

"I'm fine. Let's keep going, unless you need to rest. I hope we won't have to be in this jungle after dark!"

They continued on. Up ahead, the trail, which had been nearly flat or slightly downhill for the past hour and a half, now sloped steeply higher. Here the trees and vines were much thicker again. The trail became increasingly difficult to follow and then, it suddenly ended. They came out of the dense brush and vegetation and found themselves on a narrow asphalt road that ran nearly perpendicular to the trail they had been following. Lily pointed at a small metal sign behind them that marked the beginning of the trail. "Is that in Vietnamese? Can you read it?"

"Yes, it's in Vietnamese, but I'm not sure what it says— something like 'reserve' or 'preserve', but I'm not sure."

"Which way do we go?"

"I think that south is this way." The roadway was wide, but only a narrow strip in the center, barely wide enough for a single car, was paved. On each side of the paved strip was a lane-wide shoulder of packed red clay. Nat could see tire tracks in the clay—definitely a good sign.

The gray clouds came over them suddenly. The rain was light at first, but after a minute it began to come down hard, and then harder yet. They were soaked, and except for the cover of the rain forest, there was no protection from it. Soon, it was accumulating on the pavement faster than it could disperse. They splashed through a river of water that was an inch deep. "At least it's warm!"

"What did you say?" The rain was now falling straight down, in sheets, and Nat couldn't hear her.

"Never mind," she shouted back. But they both heard the automobile horn behind them. When they turned, the headlights of a jeep-like vehicle with a black canvas top were glaring at them. A young Asian man had his head partially out of the driver side window. A girl, perhaps eighteen years old, was in the passenger seat.

"What you people doing out here?" The young man shouted at the two of them. Nat approached the door of the vehicle.

"We got lost. We need a ride into town."

"What town? No town aroun' here," the young man exclaimed. "You better get in car now." The young man opened the door and climbed out of the vehicle. Then he folded the driver seat forward and motioned for Nat and Lily to get in quickly. Lily got in first and Nat followed, seating themselves in the two small jump seats in the back of the jeep. When the young man was seated once again behind the steering wheel, he turned to face the two strangers. "My name Thanh. This my girl friend, Lieu Nguyen."

"Hello." The girl smiled at them.

"Hello," offered Nat. "I speak only a little of your language. My name is Nat and this is my wife, Lily. We need to get to Saigon."

"O.K." offered Thanh. "We go to Ho Chi Minh City."

"No. We want to go to Saigon."

"You don't understand. Same place, same place. Name Saigon changed to Ho Chi Minh City long time ago." Nat looked over at Lily.

Thinking out loud, Nat commented to no one in particular, "Well, I guess I won't have to ask who won the war!" He turned back toward Thanh. "O.K. Thanh. How far is it to Ho Chi Minh City. And can you take us there?"

"Almost 400 kilometers. It will take all day. How much money you got?" Nat reached into his pocket and held up a twenty dollar gold piece.

"This is one ounce of gold. How much is an ounce of gold worth?"

"Maybe 350 American dollars." Thanh's eyes were fixed on the coin.

"Now, this is an old U.S. gold coin and is probably worth much more than the gold content. It's yours. All you have to do is take us to Ho Chi Minh City. We need a guide for maybe tomorrow and the next day. I will give you another coin like this for each day that you help us."

"We do it." Thanh grabbed the coin and put it in his shirt pocket, then turned toward Lieu Nguyen. The couple exchanged several words in Vietnamese. They spoke very rapidly, and Nat couldn't follow the conversation— something about her job, but the young lady was obviously upset about making the long road trip at this time.

"Is there a problem?" Nat asked.

"Lieu supposed to work in morning. I tol' her to call in sick. She work for her father—no problem."

"Are you sure?" Nat reached forward and placed his hand on Lieu's shoulder. She turned, smiling.

"No problem. Everything O.K." Lieu looked at Lily. "Lady like music?" Lieu handed a thick album of music CDs to Lily. "You pick CD, O.K.?" Nat and Lily looked at each other with the same question on each of their minds: What is a "See-Dee"? Lily unzipped the black fabric album with polyethylene sleeves containing the shiny colored flat disks. Lily had never seen anything like them before and was curious. Suddenly, Nat had a sinking feeling in the pit of his stomach. The first album he saw was *Meet the Beatles* and this and the rest of the CDs in the album looked remarkably similar to the 45 rpm records he was familiar with as a teenager.

"My God," Nat thought to himself. "Did I get back here before I left? Before 1968? No. Impossible. Remember, the war is over. . . Ho Chi Minh City. . . ."

"Thanh. Lily and I have been out here for a long time. What is the date today?"

"Today July 1ˢᵗ," Thanh answered.

"And the year, Thanh?" Nat hesitated. "What year is it?"

"You don' know year what this is?" Thanh glanced up at Nat in the rear view mirror. "You funny man. This is two-thousand-three, you know." Thanh muttered some words in Vietnamese that Nat could not quite hear.

Nat smiled at Lily and turned the album pages to *The Beatles 1* CD and pulled it out. Examining it closely for a moment, he realized that this was not a conventional phonograph record. He remarked to Lily, "You'll like these boys. They're English." He handed the CD to Lieu. As she inserted it in the player, Nat remarked to himself that he never really cared for eight-track tapes. This looked like a real improvement.

When they came to the main highway, the rain had stopped and Thanh pulled over. "We put top down, O.K.?" Without waiting for an answer, Thanh had loosened the windshield latches and began to fold back the canvas top of the old Soviet army jeep. Thanh tied down the fabric at the back of the vehicle and jumped back in. "Now you get better look at my country."

On the road, Thanh talked almost incessantly. He explained that he and Lieu were from Nha Trang, on the coast. Neither of them had much formal education. Thanh made a fair living buying and selling used cars and Lieu worked at her father's wholesale fish market. They had spent the earlier part of the day at Xuan Huong Lake in the Central Highlands of the country, near Dalat. After the rain started, they decided to cut their little excursion short and were heading home when they came upon Nat and Lily. Thanh had a lot of relatives in the United States. He said that most of them lived in Orange County, California.

"How is it that they came to America?" Nat asked.

"Several my uncles were officers in South Vietnamese Army during the war. I was born in 1973, just two year before end of war. Before North Vietnamese Army and VC take Saigon, Americans fly my uncles and families out of country so they be safe. Viet Cong kill many left behind who help Americans during war. My mother escape with me to small village in Mekong. We stay there for three years, until safe to return to city. My uncles and their families do well in America. American government help them start businesses in Westminster, California. They send my mother money from time to time. Maybe someday I go to university school in Los Angeles. Maybe UCLA."

"Tell me, Thanh, why do you think that the South and the Americans didn't win the war?"

"You know, I was just small child—so I don't know for certain. In government school, students learn that Vietnamese people were victorious over criminal Americans and traitors in the South because cause was right and North people were better fighters, but I was not able to go to government school. In my school, we are taught that the North won because South Vietnam government was corrupt, and people tired of war no longer care who run government. American people get plenty tired, too, with so many Americans killed."

"How many, Thanh? How many Americans were killed before the war was over?"

"More than 50,000." Nat shook his head from side to side, slowly in disbelief. Lily put her arm around his shoulder. "Don't feel so bad, Mister Nat. Many more Vietnamese die in war. Maybe two millions. Maybe more. No one know for sure." Thanh paused while passing an ox cart on the narrow road, then continued. "But most people not talk about war much anymore. That was thirty years ago. Now we have Coca Cola and McDonalds." Thanh pointed at the CD player. "—and The Beatles, just like you."

"Yes", added Nat. "And Ho Chi Minh City."

Thanh slowed down as they reached the next village. "Maybe we get food to eat. O.K.?"

"Great idea, Thanh," Lily offered. "I'm starving!"

Thanh stopped the jeep in front of an open-air restaurant. The hand painted sign read "Café Victory." In the patio area, they were greeted by the hostess, very striking in appearance and about the same age as Lieu. Thanh tried to feign a lack of interest as the hostess slowly slinked ahead of them, leading the party of four to an empty table. But he knew he was found out and began to laugh, holding his side, after taking a sharp jab in the ribs from Lieu's elbow.

"That's quite a dress," remarked Lily.

"Yes, it is!" offered Nat. "Maybe Lieu will help you pick out a new wardrobe tomorrow, Lily. Some of the things we packed for you look like they're a hundred years old." Nat winked at her.

At the table, the hostess spoke directly to Thanh, and he translated. "What you want to drink?"

"Cold beer," Nat said without hesitation.

"I guess I can let mine sit and warm up," offered Lily.

Thanh spoke to the hostess, then to the Americans. "You like Heineken?"

"Heineken is good, Thanh." The hostess walked off with the order. Nat looked around, observing the other patrons. A young couple with two small children at one table, one middle-aged couple at another, and a young man by himself at a third, reading a newspaper and smoking a cigarette. He had finished his meal. The smoke smelled good to Nat.

"Hi, peoples. My name Charlie. I got your beer here." The waiter, about Thanh's age, served the four cold green bottles, wet with condensation. "You want I get you glasses." Before anyone else in the group had a chance to respond, Thanh waved a 'no, thanks' with a raised open right hand, forearm resting on the tabletop. Now Charlie spoke to Thanh in Vietnamese and Thanh relayed the information in English.

"What you like to eat? How about fish? Fish good here." Thanh shifted glances between the two Americans.

"Fish would be good," Nat offered as he looked at Lily. She was nodding in agreement. "Why don't you order for us, Thanh?"

"You like cooked fish, or maybe some raw fish?"

"Cooked, if you please." Lily spoke up without hesitation. Thanh rattled off several sentences to the waiter, who then promptly disappeared. Lieu leaned over and whispered in Thanh's ear. Thanh responded out loud, but spoke so fast that Nat could not catch what he was saying. Thanh seemed irritated.

"What's the matter, Thanh?"

"Lieu worried about restaurant bill. I tell her not to worry. No problem. I pay."

"Well, thank you, Thanh." Then Nat reached into his pocket and pulled out a stack of gold pieces and looked at Lieu.

"Don't be concerned, Lieu. Thanh will pay for this meal. Tomorrow, we will change some of these coins into dollars and dong and Lily and I will pay for everything in Saigon."

"Ho Chi Minh City." Lily corrected him. Lieu smiled and looked down, feeling embarrassed.

Charlie returned to the table with a busboy, both of them carrying plates full of hot grilled fish and cold mậm —-raw fish—plus vegetables and steamed rice. "This looks wonderful," declared Lily, "except for that raw fish." Lily wrinkled her nose, looking at the mậm.

"You should try it, Miss Lily." With Thanh's mouth full, she almost didn't understand him.

"No, thanks."

Nat passed the large bowl of sticky rice to Lily. "Thanh," he said, pointing to the young man's plate. "Where I come from, we called that 'bait'."

Thanh had a quizzical expression on his face. "Bait." Nat repeated. "You know, like you put on a hook to catch fish."

"O.K. I understand now." Thanh laughed and then related Nat's comment to Lieu in Vietnamese. She missed the point, but smiled politely anyway.

By the time Charlie came back to check on them, the two couples had consumed everything except for some of the rice. Thanh ordered two more beers for the men, leaned back in his chair and offered the strangers a cigarette and took one for himself. Nat accepted; Lily declined.

"Mister Nat." As Thanh held the flame of his butane lighter to the end of Nat's cigarette, Charlie returned with the beers. "Maybe you explain something to me?"

"If I can. What is it?"

"I jus' no understand. How come you guys don't know about end of war and Ho Chi Minh City? Then you ask me before what year it is and also you got no American paper dollars or Vietnam dong. All you got is old American gold money. How come that is? Thanh no understand."

"Well, I guess that's an honest question, Thanh. All I can tell you is that Lily and I have been isolated for a number of years—sort of in our own little world, and we had no access to current news reports or other sources of information."

"But all this time, where were you at?"

"Sort of between Vietnam and the USA."

"You mean, like on an island?"

"Well, I guess you can say that. It's like we've been on an island for the last thirty-five years."

Thanh raised both hands, palms facing Nat with fingers extended, in mock surrender. "That's O.K., Mister Nat. As long as you got the money, you don't need to tell Thanh nothing. Now we go. Maybe we get to Ho Chi Minh City before dark." Thanh stood and looked at the guest check that Charlie had left and threw a pile of bills on the table. The two couples got back on the road, heading south. Within ten minutes, Lily was asleep with her head on Nat's shoulder.

FIFTY-NINE

Ho Chi Minh City, formerly Saigon and once known as the "Paris of the Orient" was an old, but certainly not an ancient city. The settlement on the Sai Gon River in the Cuu Long Delta had its beginnings in the 17th century. The French influence began with the arrival of colonialists in 1858. Nearly 100 years later, in 1954, the French forces withdrew, but the French influence continues to the present day. During the occupation, Saigon was the capital city of the country known as French Indochina. As a consequence of the departure of the French, the country was partitioned North and South and Western concern for the future of Vietnam shifted to the United States. Saigon became the capital of South Vietnam and the city prospered under a steadily increasing level of American military presence and dollars.

But it all came to an end after nearly twenty more years of further struggle. The fate of South Vietnam was sealed with the signing of the Paris Peace Accords in 1973, marking the beginning of the end of U.S. presence and support for the South. On April 30, 1975, on the same day that the last helicopter evacuating U.S. Marines lifted off from the abandoned American embassy for the safety of the U.S. Seventh Fleet waiting offshore, North Vietnamese tanks crashed through the gates of the Presidential Palace. The city was surrendered in a short radio address by South Vietnam's President Duong Van Minh later that afternoon. Saigon became Ho Chi Minh City, not for the vanquished president, but in honor of the man who led the struggle, first for independence with creation of the Viet Minh and then for the reunification of his country. Ho did not live to see the final victory of his North Vietnamese army regulars and Viet Cong guerillas. He died in 1969 at the age of 79, but his successors held fast to Ho's vow to reject any peace proposal that resulted in continued partitioning of his country. His heirs were not, however, as willing to comply with Ho's wish that his body be cremated and his ashes scattered about the country he loved. Instead, the embalmed body of the dead leader was displayed in a glass mausoleum in the Lenin tradition.

"So, Mister Nat. You been here before?" It was nearly dark when they entered the outskirts of the city.

"Yes, Thanh. Many years ago. I'm surprised that it doesn't look a whole lot different after 35 years."

"Many more people in Vietnam now. Population more than double from before the end of war, but Ho Chi Minh City not get much bigger." The biggest difference that Nat noticed was the absence of the U.S. military. No army trucks at all, and the few old U.S. jeeps he saw had been repainted in non-military colors. Overall, the traffic congestion seemed about the same. No U.S. military vehicles, but a lot more cars than before. "How about we check in to Majestic Hotel? You know it from before?"

"Yes, I know the Majestic, but Lily and I really don't want to attract any attention. How about you find us a nice small hotel in a quieter district—one where nobody will notice us."

"O.K. Mister Nat. Thanh know jus' the right place."

Lily was now awake with eyes wide open. Up until now, there had been little other than the sleek, fast automobiles on the highway to Ho Chi Minh City that belied her 19th century frame of reference. But now there were the bright lights of the city. Certainly, she had seen electric lights before, but not on this scale or in all these colors.

Thanh found a parking space just a half-block from the Hotel Giang on Bui Vien Street. The De Tham area of the city seemed to attract more foreigners—that is, non-Asians—than Nat would have preferred. He saw a lot of European couples, mainly young tourists with backpacks, who were obviously traveling on a budget, but at least he didn't hear any American voices as they made there way to the hotel check-in. Inside, Thanh booked two adjoining rooms on the ground floor and, at Nat's urging, advised the clerk that they would probably be staying for two nights.

It had been a long day for Nat and Lily. At the door to their room, Nat turned to Thanh. "We're going to turn in for the evening. We have a lot to do tomorrow. How about we meet you and Lieu at the coffee shop next door at 8 o'clock in the morning?"

"Very well, Mister Nat. We see you in the morning. Have a good evening, Miss Lily."

"And Thanh—"

"Yes, Mister Nat?"

"Thank you for helping us out today."

"No problem, Mister Nat. We happy to help you."

SIXTY

THE ROOM WAS rather austere, but clean. Nat didn't expect a view from the solitary window, and he wasn't disappointed: it looked out on the alley at the rear of the building. Across the brick pavement was the open back door of a restaurant. Nat could hear two cooks just inside the doorway arguing, or a least speaking excitedly on an unknown subject of obviously high mutual interest. They were speaking too fast for Nat to pick up any more than a few words. It was hot, and when Lily asked about the large vented box below the window, he said, "It's called an air conditioner. I'll show you what it does." Nat pressed the blue plastic button switch and the fan came to life. Then he twisted the thermostat knob to maximum cool and listened for the tell-tale sound of the air conditioner compressor starting up. Lily sat on the floor with her back against the bed, directly in front of the flow of air with her eyes closed, and hands up and open, taking in the cool breeze.

"I think I'm going to like it here in the 21st century!" Nat kissed her on the cheek, then rose and walked to the bathroom door, switched on the light and looked in. "What's the bath look like, Nat?"

"Come and see."

"I think I want to stay right here on the floor, forever."

"Come on, Lily. I'll draw your bath water."

"If you insist." Lily jumped up and joined Nat in the bathroom. She looked around, unimpressed.

"What's the matter, Lily?"

"Well, it's not that much different from our master bath at home, now is it?"

Nat turned on the hot water spigot above the free-standing bathtub. "What did you expect?" He began to chuckle when he realized he was about to get defensive over the contents of this circa 1960 bathroom in the face of his wife's apparent nineteenth century indifference.

"Oh, I don't know. Maybe hot and cold running servants?"

"How about this?" Nat grabbed the portable hair dryer that was mounted on the wall above the sink and switched it on. "After your bath, you can dry your hair. Just be careful not to drop it in the water; it's electric. Zzzzzzz." He grabbed her arm as he made the electrical sizzle sound and she jumped back.

"Nat! Don't"

"Sorry, Lily. You take your bath. I'm going to check out the TV."

"The what?"

"TV. You know, television. Remember, I told you about it. Like radio, but with pictures?"

"Oh yes, I remember now. I shan't be too long. Now get out." Nat closed the bathroom door, walked to the armoire housing the 25-inch Samsung color television and switched it on. He picked up the remote control and sat on the bed. Flipping through the channels, virtually everything was in Vietnamese or French. Finally he came upon a CNN feed from Hong Kong in English and scooted himself back to the head of the bed.

Nat didn't recognize the elderly gentleman at the microphone of what appeared to be a press conference, but the voice certainly sounded familiar. The speaker was complaining that the Administration had misled Congress regarding the reasons for going to war in Iraq. "Iraq?" thought Nat. "Why were we at war with Iraq?" Finally, a text caption was displayed on the screen: "Sen. Edward Kennedy, (D) Massachusetts." Nat remarked to himself that despite the years, some things don't really change. Ted Kennedy had already been Senator for two years when Nat joined the Navy in 1964. Now, nearly forty years later, he was still there. In the next twenty minutes, Nat learned that a man named 'Bush' was the current occupant of the White House, that the United States had been engaged in fighting in both Iraq and Afghanistan and although the major fighting of the war was believed to have been over, we were still losing men to guerilla fighters and insurgents and that all this seemed somehow related—according to some and unrelated according to others—to an earlier event referred to simply as "Nine-Eleven."

The thought of U.S. involvement in another guerilla war elicited a vague sense of physical discomfort in Nat. He remarked to himself that the Soviets were no doubt aligned against us or maybe even in it up to their eyeballs, especially in Afghanistan. He wondered if the Cold War had heated up any time in the last 35 years and if we had got into it with the Soviets in Europe, something that the Pentagon had been concerned about since the end of the World War II. He should have asked Thanh about it, but then again, maybe it was best not keep drawing attention to their total ignorance of modern history. There was no other word for it. Nat counted eight, no nine, presidential elections that he had missed. He didn't even know who ran in 1968, having intended to support Bobby Kennedy until he was shot a few weeks before Nat's adventure in time travel had begun.

Nat had been so absorbed by Headline News that he was unaware that Lily had finished her bath and had begun watching from the bathroom doorway. After a few minutes, she approached the screen and touched it. Lily withdrew her hand momentarily, surprised by the mild jolt of electrical charge that had built up on the television monitor, but then cautiously returned it to the screen again, as if to touch the face of Wolf Blitzer. "This is wonderful." She said. "Is this man making some kind of important announcement? Where is he speaking from?"

"No, it's just a routine news program. He's kind of like a newspaper reporter, only he is reading the news out loud instead of writing for the paper."

"So he's like the town crier?"

"Exactly right, Lily. Only I think the program must be coming from the United States. Even the commercials are in English."

"What's a commercial?" she asked just as an advertisement for Lexus automobiles appeared on the screen.

"This, my dear, is a commercial. The man speaking in the background wants you to purchase one of these fine automobiles. Although I must admit, I've never heard of this make of car." The Lexus commercial ended and another one began; this one with a scene from a veterinarian's office.

"Medicine for dogs?" She was incredulous.

"Oh, yes. If we wait long enough, I'm sure we'll see some commercials for all kinds of things like dog and cat food, soap, beer, travel. Even ads for newspapers. You can expect to find commercials for practically anything that is sold anywhere."

"So the makers of these products pay the television owners to talk about them? Like an advertisement in a newspaper?"

"Something like that. They pay the television stations that broadcast the programs. A television program can be seen by millions of people, so it might cost thousands of dollars for a one-minute commercial."

"So millions of people are watching the very same thing that we are seeing now?"

"Either this program or a different program on a different channel."

"Really? Are there many different channels?"

"Around here, there seems to be a lot. When I grew up in Richmond, we had only a few stations. I remember WTVR Channel 6. This program is on Channel 36. There is a button below the screen that changes the stations. Try it and see if there is something else you would rather watch." Lily pressed down on one of the buttons. The channel didn't change, but suddenly Wolf Blitzer was speaking very loudly. She backed away from the set, covering her ears.

"Why is he shouting at us?" Nat scrambled off the bed and turned down the volume.

"Here, Lily. Use this instead." He gave her the remote control. "Try the buttons next to these up and down arrows. This is called a 'remote controller'. Our neighbors in Richmond had one, but there's had a long wire connecting it to the TV set. This one is wireless." Lily slowly advanced the channels, eyes fixed on the changing images: infomercials on exercise equipment and food processors, soap operas, news broadcasts and weather programs. She didn't spend a lot of time on any one channel. Once she got an idea of what was being presented, usually with some input from Nat, she advanced to the next. At one point Lily became interested in what appeared to be the broadcast of a wedding ceremony. She was shocked when she saw a young man outside the glass doors of the church, desperately shaking them and calling out the bride's name, "Elaine!"

"Look at this." she said. "Can you imagine if some ne'er-do-well tried to ruin our wedding like that? I'd have been embarrassed to death. The poor girl, what must she be thinking?"

"I don't know if you're reading that right, Lily. It looks to me like maybe she really doesn't want to marry the groom. I think she might end up with that young man, Ben."

"No. Really?" They watched for few minutes as Dustin Hoffman disrupted the entire ceremony and started swinging a large cross at members of the wedding party and guests.

"That's right. I wouldn't be surprised if that young man used that cross to lock everyone in the church, and then he and the bride run away together." Seconds later, they saw it on the television screen, just as Nat predicted. Lily socked Nat on his upper arm.

"Very funny, Nathaniel Booth. I know you weren't there, and this isn't one of those news reports, is it? So, what are we watching?"

"Remember the Kinetoscope parlor that I took you to on Broadway a couple of years ago? You looked into the machine and watched the short moving pictures?"

"Yes, I remember, but there was no sound and I don't remember seeing any color in those pictures."

"The motion pictures like this one simply build on what Thomas Edison and some other folks invented years ago. Someone wrote this story as a screenplay—like a regular play, only it's been recorded on film instead of playing before a live audience. This one is called *The Graduate*. It came out the last year I was in the Navy, so it's pretty old. It's a good one, though. Someday we'll watch it from the beginning."

"I'm really tired. Can we go to sleep now?"

"Sure, Lily." Nat opened the covers of the bed, but before turning out the light, he switched back to CNN and turned down the volume so that Lily wouldn't be disturbed. He needn't have worried. A minute after her head hit the pillow, Lily was asleep. After a few minutes, a sports program came on. Nat switched off the set and closed his eyes.

SIXTY-ONE

"YOU WANT REGULAR COFFEE or maybe some espresso coffee?" Thanh was interpreting again.

"Just two regular coffees, with cream. And get some of those French pastries, Thanh. They look delicious." It was barely 8 AM and the little coffee shop was packed with patrons. After ten minutes Thanh and Lieu returned to the small table and four stools that Nat and Lily had been saving for them. "This is going to be a busy day, Thanh. We have a lot to do."

"No problem, Mr. Nat. What you want to do first?"

"First we need some cash. Dollars and dong, but mainly dollars. What we need to find is a rare coin dealer." Thanh rose and excused himself. The other three watched as Thanh introduced himself to a well-dressed businessman near the end of the coffee ordering line. After a minute, Thanh returned to the table.

"There is gold coin dealer close to here. Only two streets away. We go now." The other three rose and followed Thanh out of the coffee shop. When they were all outside, Thanh turned and looked at Nat. "And we no need Vietnamese dong. Everyone in my country happy to take American dollars."

It took less than ten minutes to reach the Do Long Rare Coin Galleries. The proprietor, Mr. Bay Le, spoke perfect English and addressed Nat. "Mr. Smith. Is that what you said your name is?"

"Yes."

"Well, Mr. Smith, these coins are quite interesting. I can offer you five-hundred dollars each. That is more than one hundred dollars above the gold content value." Mr. Bay Le was examining six Liberty Head double eagles that Nat had placed on the counter. The glass cases in the store contained hundreds of coins, mostly gold and platinum, from all over the world.

Nat shook his head, apparently unimpressed with the offer. "Mr. Bay Le, these are nearly perfect specimens and many are from years with very low mintage."

"Mintage records show little correlation with value," Bay Le countered. "Because many of the coins were melted down by your government, it is impossible to know how many of each date and mint mark remain. Most collectors acquire these as type coins, with little concern for particular dates. But I will acknowledge that the condition of the coins may perhaps merit an additional premium. I could go as high as $600 each. How many pieces do you have all together?"

"Twenty." Nat replied. "And if you can take them all, I will accept your offer." Mr. Bay Le began examining the remaining coins with a loupe. Nat looked over at Thanh and noted that Thanh was holding the gold piece that Nat had given him the previous day. "And my associate here has a similar piece that he would like to sell also."

"Very well." Mr. Bay Le disappeared into the back room and returned a minute later with a stack of hundred dollar bills. He began to count them out in front of Nat.

"Wait!" Nat raised his right hand and looked over at Thanh. "These bills look awfully strange!" Nat was uncomfortable with the caricature appearance of Ben

Franklin on the bills. He picked one up to examine it more closely.

"Not to worry, Mr. Nat." Thanh was trying to reassure Nat that the bills were legitimate. "This new money just fine. Everything be O.K."

"Shall I proceed, Mr. Smith, or have you changed your mind?" Bay Le stopped and picked up the bills he had already counted out. Thanh gave Nat a nod.

"Go ahead, Mr. Bay Le. I guess I forgot what the new bills look like. I'm sorry." Bay Le started over, counting out one hundred and twenty of the bills to Nat in twelve stacks of ten bills each and six more bills to Thanh. When he was done, Nat made one stack of the bills, folded the stack in half and stuffed the wad into the pocket of his trousers. Nat and Thanh left the coin store and joined Lily and Lieu, who had been waiting outside.

"How did you do, Nat?" Lily asked.

"Six-hundred dollars each—more than I expected."

"It's a good thing. Everything seems terribly expensive. Lieu and I were looking in the window of the women's clothing store next door. The dresses were very nice, but when she told me how much things cost in dollars, it was startling!"

"You know," Nat began. "With Lieu here to help, I think now would be a good time for you to pick out some new traveling clothes—maybe three or four outfits. Remember that you have an airplane ride tomorrow."

"How could I forget?" She smiled weakly. Some time ago, Nat had explained what flight in a large passenger aircraft was like. Every time he mentioned it since then she felt a flutter of anxiety in her stomach, especially since she understood that she would be flying without him.

Nat pulled the wad of bills out of his pocket and began to count out money. "First, Thanh. Here is six hundred for your salary for today, plus another two hundred to cover expenses from yesterday and the hotel bill." Thanh's palm was open as Nat counted out the money.

"Thank you, Mr. Nat."

"And Lily, take this for now." He handed her a stack of bills. "Get clothes for your trip." Then he turned to Lieu and pressed three hundred dollars into her hand. "That is for you, Lieu, for whatever you want." He looked at Thanh. "Please explain to her, Thanh. Ask her if she will go with Lily and help her pick out some things for her trip: Dresses, shoes, stockings, underwear. Even a purse. But it all has to fit in one suitcase. Find one. Maybe there's a luggage store around here. From what I've seen, you should be able to find just about anything anyone would need."

NAT WAS CORRECT. The De Tham Street area was saturated with small shops and street vendors offering everything from bootleg videos and CDs to custom tailored suits. "Help her pick some nice things out, and don't spare the cash." Thanh had to repeat the translation to Lieu. She didn't hear a word of it the first time through; just standing there with her mouth open, staring at the hundred dollar bills that Nat had shoved into her hand.

Nat continued. "It must be nearly 10 o'clock." Thanh looked at his watch and nodded. "Why don't you ladies meet us over there—" He pointed at a small bistro across the street. "—at two PM? Thanh and I have a couple of things to do while you ladies are shopping." Lieu apparently understood Nat without waiting for Thanh's translation. She took Lily by the hand and the two headed back to the women's store. Nat then turned to Thanh. "I need you to help me find someone who makes official documents. We need a British passport for Lily. Where can we find such a person?"

"That's a tough one, Mr. Nat. Thanh is not, as you say, well-connected here in Ho Chi Minh City like in my home town." He paused in thought for a few seconds. "But let me call friends from Nha Trang, my home." Although he had seen plenty of them in the last twenty-four hours, Nat could hardly hide his fascination for the small, portable telephones that, according to Thanh, were called 'Sell Phones.' Nat didn't understand the term, but decided not to ask. Thanh spoke to one friend for about five minutes, then placed another call to a number his friend had given him.

Nat searched Thanh's face for some encouraging sign. Minutes passed, then one more call, and then another. Nat watched as Thanh checked the time on his wristwatch, then—finally—he looked directly at Nat, smiling. Success was confirmed after thirty seconds more on the phone when Thanh gave Nat a 'thumbs-up' sign. Thanh switched off his phone and put it in his pocket.

"That man can get us passport for Lily. Five hundred dollars."

"We need a British passport," Nat reminded him.

"We get whatever you need. British passport, American, French, German. Whatever you need," Thanh repeated. "You have photograph of Miss Lily, for passport?"

"Yes. I have several." Nat had portraits and passport-size photos of Lily taken at a New York City studio before their departure. "Where do we go? And when?"

"We take my car and go now."

SIXTY-TWO

I T WAS A THIRTY MINUTE STRUGGLE through the late morning sea of scooters and small sedans to the pre-arranged meeting place on Danang Avenue, on the east side of the city. As soon as Thanh stopped the car, the man leaning against the brick façade of the French bakery discarded his cigarette and approached the passenger side of Thanh's jeep.

André, their document connection, was half French and spoke excellent English. "Do you have the money?" André leaned into the car window.

"Could we first see some examples of your work?" Nat came right to the point. André pulled sample American and British passports from his coat pocket and handed them over. Nat hadn't seen an American passport in years and never a British one up close, but they certainly looked like the real thing. Nat passed them back with five one-hundred dollar bills, each of which André examined carefully.

"You have a suitable photograph?" Nat handed André three small portrait prints of Lily. "Color is better. Don't you have a color photograph?"

"Those are all I have. Pick one."

"O.K. This one will work. Now you need to write some information down for me." André passed a yellow legal pad to Nat. "Please print very clearly. My document people will make the passport with the information exactly as you write it. First, the full name, place and date of birth." Nat wrote quickly, but carefully. When he got to Lily's birth date, he honestly and absentmindedly wrote 'February 5, 1850', but then quickly scratched out the year and wrote '1963' instead. Lily, he thought, didn't look a day over forty. André had a few more personal questions, then asked about visas. Nat thought for several seconds before he spoke.

"Show one for Hong Kong with an entry for a month ago, and of course, for Vietnam for last week. And don't forget: we need a U.S. visa as well." Nat had handed back the yellow pad and André was taking notes.

"What about supporting documents? If she is traveling, she will need a separate photo ID or driver's license and maybe a credit card."

"How much?" Nat asked.

Because you are such a good customer, only two hundred more. I'll bring them with the passport. You can pay me then. And give me another one of the photographs. We can reshoot it for the driver's license. Remember to tell—" He looked down at the pad for Lily's name. "—Miss Freemont—tell her that the credit card is strictly for show. She won't be able to use it."

"Understood."

"I'll be back here with your documents in three hours." As André turned and disappeared up Danang Avenue, Nat and Thanh exited the jeep.

"How about one of your smokes, Thanh?"

"Sure, Mr. Nat." Thanh handed Nat his half-empty pack of Marlboro reds and butane lighter. Nat raised himself on to the hood of the jeep and lit up.

"Do you think he'll be back?"

"Of course, Mr. Nat. André is businessman."

Sixty-Three

"SO, YOU ARE HAPPY, Mr. Nat, with the passport?" André had returned with the documents at the appointed time, and Nat and Thanh were now headed back to the 333 Café, where they were to meet Lily and Lieu.

"I couldn't be happier. And look at this British driver's license. They were able to add color to the black-and-white photograph of Lily. Even this American Express Card looks genuine. You've been very helpful, Thanh." Thanh smiled broadly, obviously pleased with the praise that Nat was heaping upon him. "Tell me something, Thanh."

"Yes, Mr. Nat?"

"You seem to be a very capable person. And I am sure that your car business is very successful, but I am curious. How come you never finished your schooling? You could have gone on to the University and become a doctor or lawyer, or a corporate businessman." Thanh laughed out loud.

"Things here in the South are better now, but not too long ago it was much different. After unification, many people come from North, many were Party members."

"Communist Party members?" Nat interrupted.

"Yes, Party members and relatives. They take most high paying jobs in government, schools and business. Many in South are left with no job or only bad jobs with low pay. If anyone in family was part of the ARVN, you had it much worse. Many children like me not allowed to attend government schools."

"I guess there are carpetbaggers after every civil war."

"I don't understand, Mr. Nat."

"Never mind. It's just too bad. You have a lot of talent; you could have gone far with a better education. Anyway, what time is it? Are we going to be late meeting the women?" Thanh was nearly stopped dead in the traffic.

"Maybe we be a few minutes late." Thanh shrugged his shoulders.

By the time Nat and Thanh reached the 333 Cafe and parked, they were nearly an hour late. Lieu and Lily were sipping Mai Tais, which Lily was obviously very much enjoying. But before the men had a chance to sit down, Lieu lit into Thanh, scolding him severely for being so late.

"Lieu, please don't be upset with Thanh. It's my fault. We were waiting for these." Nat handed Lily the passport and other pieces of identification.

"Why do I need this?" Lily was holding up the driver's license. "I've never driven an automobile."

"It's used for identification. You won't be showing your passport much after you get to the states. Did you get a separate billfold with that purse?" Lily nodded. "Put it in there. Now, before we order lunch, let's see your new wardrobe, Lily."

"Well, how is this, to start?" Lily stood up and turned around slowly, showing off her figure in a pale yellow pantsuit and a bright orange and white large print blouse.

"I approve" Nat exclaimed. "What else?" Lily reached into a bag near her feet and pulled out a short, bright red dress.

"Lieu liked this one so well that I had to buy one for her, too, only in green to go with her beautiful eyes. What do you think?" Nat nodded his approval. "Everything else has already been packed away. Do you want to see it?"

"What about underwear?"

Lieu answered for Lily, "Miss Lily have plenty of new underwear. I think you like, Mister Nat."

"I think you'll like it, too," added Lily. "But it's all packed away also. I'm sorry."

"That's O.K. You'll have plenty of time to surprise me with your new wardrobe when we're home." Before Nat had finished speaking, Thanh turned from the table to shoo away a pair of street urchins who had entered the café peddling packages of chewing gum, cigarette lighters and silk handkerchiefs, but Nat called them back. "Give them a couple of bucks, Thanh. I'll pay you back." Thanh grumbled some unintelligible words in Vietnamese, but complied with Nat's request.

When the waiter appeared, ready to take their order, Nat pointed across the table at Thanh. "Why don't you order for us again? You've been doing such a great job of it." Thanh smiled broadly, then rattled off orders as the waiter wrote furiously to keep up with him. When the waiter left, Thanh lit a cigarette and turned towards Nat.

"Mr. Nat, how about we find some new clothes for you after we eat?"

"Are you suggesting, Thanh, that my outfit is less than stylish?" Nat raised his arms and looked down at his khaki-colored shirt and trousers in mock self-examination.

"No, No, Mr. Nat. Please—not to be offended. I mean that you should have new clothes for traveling with Miss Lily now that she look so elegant."

Nat took a cigarette from the pack that Thanh had left on the table, lit it, took a deep drag and exhaled slowly before replying. "Lily and I are going to be leaving for America very soon, but we won't be traveling together. Lily is leaving first. In fact, after lunch, we need to make reservations and buy her ticket." Thanh glanced over at Lily and, noting that she didn't seem surprised by Nat's revelation, had to assume that it wasn't news to her. There was an awkward minute of silence until the waiter reappeared with their drinks. Thanh raised his beer bottle and tipped it towards Nat.

"No problem, Mr. Nat. Whatever you and Miss Lily want, we do."

SIXTY-FOUR

DIAMOND PLAZA is a twenty-two story steel and glass showplace; the prestigious address of more than a hundred professional and corporate offices and retail businesses in District One of Ho Chi Minh City on Le Duan Boulevard. Construction by the Hoa Binh Corporation began in 1997 and was completed in 1999. One of the businesses on the ninth floor is the local ticketing office for Korean Air Lines. The young woman ticket agent behind the counter spoke impeccable English.

"Let's review your itinerary, Miss Freemont." Nat and Lily stood at the counter; Thanh and Lieu were waiting outside on the mezzanine. "You will be departing Tan Son Nhut Airport here in Ho Chi Minh City early tomorrow morning at 1:15, Korean Air Flight 682, arriving Seoul at 8:10 AM, connecting with United Flight 884 at 11:00 AM and arriving Chicago at 11:45 am the next day after a stop over in Tokyo." At this point, Lily's mouth was wide open. She hadn't understood a word the agent was saying. Nat squeezed her hand in an effort to reassure her. "There you will connect with United 614 at 1:00 PM and arrive at Reagan National, Washington DC, at 3:45 PM. Any questions?"

"Yes." Nat spoke up. "Reagan National? I'm sorry, we haven't been in Washington for a while. What airport is that?"

Without a hint of condescension in her tone, the agent explained that Reagan National Airport was formerly known as Washington National Airport, close to the city, and renamed in honor of the former President of the United States. "Is there anything else I can help you with?" She asked.

"No thank you, I think we've got it. You've been very helpful."

"Enjoy your flight, Miss Fremont, and thank you for choosing Korean Air." The agent handed Lily's tickets, itinerary and passport to her. Lily opened her purse and stuffed the documents inside as Nat led Lily away from the counter.

"I don't think I can do this, Nat." Lily was clearly upset.

"Of course, you can."

"No, I don't think so. Why can't we travel together like we always have?"

"You know why, Lily. I can't just show up in the United States after thirty-five years. How would I explain it? Besides, it will be easy. We'll get you safely aboard the first airplane. From there, you just follow this itinerary. And if you get confused, just ask someone who looks like they are in authority. I have confidence in you."

"I wish I did." Outside the airline office on the ninth floor mezzanine Thanh could see that Lily was very unhappy.

"What's wrong, Miss Lily?" She didn't answer.

"Lily's a little uncomfortable about the trip," Nat explained. "She's never flown before." Thanh immediately registered a quizzical expression on his face.

"So you arrive in Vietnam by boat?"

Nat ignored the question. "We are going to have a late night tonight. Are you and Lieu going to be up for it? Lily's plane leaves at 1:30 AM and she needs to check in about three hours early."

"Lieu is tired. She want to go back to hotel. I will drive you and Miss Lily to the airport tonight by myself."

Lily had two hours to pack and rest back at the Hotel Giang before they had to leave for the airport. Nat went over her flight itinerary again and explained how she would need to change planes in Seoul and Chicago, but not in Tokyo. It didn't do much to set her at ease, but she accepted it.

"So, you're telling me, Nat, that I will be in Washington in two days? Really?"

"Yes, but you're only going to be traveling for a little more than twenty-six hours."

"So, I will arrive about 3 o'clock in the morning? Right?"

"No, it will be in the afternoon. Remember that Washington is on the opposite side of the earth, so it is about twelve hours later there than here." He wasn't sure she understood. "When you arrive, you'll be told where to retrieve your bag. You'll need to show someone your baggage claim ticket."

"Where do I get that?"

"We will get it tonight when you check in. They will take your bag at the check-in counter and give you a claim ticket. After you get your bag in Washington, just walk out to the street and take a taxi to the National Hotel. If you can't get a room there, just leave a message at the desk. I will come and get you or at least try to contact you there as soon as I can. You need to wait in Washington until you hear from me."

"All right." She sighed.

"You have plenty of cash; don't worry about money." Nat had kept only the few hundred dollars that he owed Thanh plus a few dollars extra. Lily would carry two hundred in small bills in her purse, while the rest—about seventy one-hundred dollar bills—were safely tucked away in the light fabric money belt under her dress.

At the curb on Bui Vien Street, Lily gave Lieu Nguyen a tearful hug while Nat and Thanh waited inside the Jeep with engine running. She got in and waved a final goodbye, and then they were off for Tan Son Nhut.

SIXTY-FIVE

THEY ARRIVED at Tan Son Nhut airport just about in time. Traffic had been a little heavier than Thanh had predicted, both through the city and on the highway to the airport. Thanh dropped Nat and Lily off at "departures" at the main terminal building which now handled all international flights. He agreed to return for Nat at the same location just outside the Korean Air ticket counter at 1:30 AM, right after Lily's scheduled departure. There were only three travelers ahead of Nat and Lily at the check-in counter when they walked in. Within five minutes they were at the counter.

"Could I have your ticket and passport, please?" Lily placed the documents on the counter. "Thank you. You have bags to check through to Reagan National?"

"Just one." Nat first mistakenly attempted to pick up the wheeled bag by the extendable handle before realizing it. Pushing it back in, he then grabbed the other—the correct—handle and placed the bag on the agent's check-in scale.

"I need you to fill out this baggage tag with your current address and telephone number." Lily slid the tag and pen toward Nat. He filled it out, listing the National Hotel as Lily's address and entered the only phone number he remembered—his old Richmond residence phone. "We expect to depart on time, Miss Fremont. Your flight will be called for boarding about forty-five minutes after midnight. Gate 21. And thank you for choosing Korean Airlines."

"Excuse me." Nat had a question for the agent. "I see that you have a sign at the entrance to the gate area stating that only passengers are permitted beyond that point. Is that correct? Does that mean that I cannot wait with my wife at the departure gate?"

"That is correct, sir. I'm sorry, only passengers are allowed in the gate area."

"And why is that?"

"Airport regulations, sir. It is a security matter. I don't believe there is an airport anywhere in the world that allows anyone but passengers at the departure gate since 9/11." There, he heard it again. Those two numbers: nine, eleven. He still didn't know what those two numbers meant.

As they stepped away from the counter, Lily asked, "What's happening, Nat? What is she saying?"

"It's not a problem, Lily. It's just that when I last flew on a commercial airline, anyone could get to the departure area. It was only in getting on the plane that you had to be a ticketed passenger with a boarding pass. See the blocked off area up ahead? You'll need to go through there by yourself."

"What are they looking for?"

"Weapons, I think. They don't want anyone to try and take over the aircraft while it's in the air."

"Why would anyone want to do that?" Now Lily sounded worried.

"They called it 'hijacking'." A man in a suit walking quickly past the couple heard Nat say the "h-word" and gave him a dirty look. "Sometimes it was as simple as someone wanting to be taken to a country that the airplane wasn't scheduled to go. People have also taken over airplanes in order to make a political statement. It becomes big news. But don't worry. Nothing is going to happen to your airplane. Just get in line there and do what they tell you. When you get through this security area, look for the area marked 'Gate 21'. That's where you will be getting on the airplane when they call your flight number. It's 682. See here." Nat pointed to the boarding pass. "The gate number and the flight number are printed right here."

"O.K. I can do it. I love you." She looked up at Nat's face and kissed him.

"I know you can. I love you, too. Wait for me in Washington. I'll be there in a few days." Lily joined the line of passengers, briefly stalled at the beginning of the security check-in area. Soon the line began to move quickly. Before stepping through the metal detector, Lily turned to look back at Nat. He waved. A minute later and she was gone, lost in the throng of similar travelers, all clutching boarding passes and looking at the signs directing them to their departure gates.

Back in the observation area of the main terminal, Nat could see three Korean Air jets lined up, but only the center one appeared to be surrounded with activity. Nat waited at the window as a provisioning truck came to the aircraft followed by two trains of carts full of passenger bags. It was forty-five minutes before the jetway boarding ramp was finally retracted and the aircraft lumbered out to the staging area for take-off. Five minutes later, Lily was gone.

Thanh had taken a catnap for about an hour, but was waiting for Nat as promised at the curb outside the Korean Air check-in counter at the appointed time. "Where we go now, Mr. Nat? Back to hotel?"

"Do you have a few hours, Thanh?" I want you to take me somewhere, but it's far too early. Maybe we can get a couple of drinks, or maybe just some coffee."

"How about we get drinks now, then coffee later? I know good place."

It was still too early for the city to wake up, but there were signs of it stirring. Delivery scooters and trucks were threading through narrow streets and garbage trucks were picking up the black plastic bags piled high on street corners and outside storefront doorways. A few street merchants were already sweeping the few square feet of bricks that would define their market location for the business day. "These folks have it pretty tough," thought Nat. He could not help but think how their life is probably harder here in the twenty-first century than his was in the nineteenth.

Thanh parked the jeep outside the Mekong Bar on Dalat Street. Inside, Thanh ordered beer and Nat bought a pack of Marlboro cigarettes from a pretty bar attendant.

"I want to thank you again, Thanh." Thanh shrugged his shoulders. "Thanks for helping Lily and me these last few days, and thanks also for not asking us too much about how we got here and what we are doing."

"I think that it is your business, what you do here. You pay me well. I no see that you do anything against the law, except maybe getting Miss Lily's travel documents. You don't smuggle drugs or anything like that, I don't think." Thanh lit one of the cigarettes.

"I really can't tell you much, but I feel I owe you something. Let me explain. Thirty-five years ago, I was a U.S. Navy pilot. My plane was shot down. I don't know what happened to the other man who was flying with me, but as for me, I'm sure my government believes to this day that I was killed. Exactly where I've been and how I got here is something that I won't try to explain, but the fact is that I wasn't here—or back home—for the last thirty-five years. In fact, other than what I've managed to learn in the last few days, I don't know what has gone on in the world since the day I was shot down." Thanh sipped his beer, listening intently.

After a minute, Thanh spoke up. "I think was very strange when you ask me what year it was. I think maybe you a little bit crazy."

Nat smiled, then they both began to laugh. "Maybe I am, but I need to ask you about a few more things. First, I need to know, what is 'nine-eleven'?"

Thanh admitted that he was no great follower of the news and world history, but over the next two hours, he told Nat what he could about the World Trade Center attacks and the subsequent events, including American military excursions in Afghanistan and Iraq. Nat asked about the 1970s and 80s, especially about the end of the Vietnam War. Here, Thanh could provide more details as he related events closer to home. As Thanh spoke, Nat was amazed to learn of the breakup of the Soviet Union and the normalization of relations with China. When he asked about technical advances, Nat could appreciate how cellular telephones had become so popular, but he had a tougher time understanding about personal computers and what the internet was all about.

They dozed for an hour after more beer and cigarettes. About 6 AM they were awakened by the bartender who wanted to sweep the floor beneath their table. Still half-asleep, Nat and Thanh moved to another table and asked one of the girls if they could order breakfast.

SIXTY-SIX

THE AMERICAN CONSULATE in Ho Chi Minh City is at 66 Dalat Street. Nat had to give Thanh the address, but Thanh had no problem finding it, barely twenty minutes after they finished an impromptu breakfast at the Mekong Bar.

"Take it all, Thanh. I only need twenty dollars. I probably don't even need that much." Thanh was parked on the street, maybe fifteen feet from the entrance to the building.

"You sure, Mr. Nat?" Thanh was stuffing the bills that Nat had thrown on the passenger seat into his shirt pocket.

"Absolutely. I'm still an officer in the U.S. Navy. I'll let my government figure out the best way to get me home, at their expense." Nat was now outside, leaning into the open passenger side window of the vehicle. "Goodbye, my friend."

"Goodbye, Mr. Nat." Thanh extended his hand toward Nat's and shook it. Nat stepped back on the curb and watched as Thanh drove off, then turned and walked to the iron security gate outside the Consulate Office and rang the buzzer. An elderly Vietnamese gentleman appeared, speaking with only a slight accent.

"May I help you?"

"I'm an American citizen and need to speak with someone in authority." The man opened the gate and motioned for Nat to enter.

"Your name, sir, that I might give it to the officer on duty?"

"It's Nathaniel Booth. Lt. Commander Nathaniel Booth, U.S. Navy." Nat was led to a reception area, but no one was on duty at the large U-shaped reception desk.

"Please wait, sir. I'll get someone to help you. Do you have your passport with you?"

"I don't have a passport," Nat offered unflinchingly. The old man disappeared. Minutes later, a young lady in a gray business suit appeared behind the counter.

"Commander Booth?" Nat was resting his elbow on the counter, but had turned away and was unaware of the woman's presence until she spoke.

"Yes."

"How do you do?" She extended her hand. "I'm Loretta Dunbar, the Deputy Officer in Charge. I understand that you've lost your passport?"

"No, that's not correct."

"You believe it was stolen, then?" The deputy's smile had turned to a serious frown.

"No, no. It wasn't stolen." A sense of exasperation was overtaking him. "Look, I was a Navy pilot—"

Before he could continue his explanation, Miss Dunbar interrupted. "Yes, we have a lot of veterans visiting Vietnam these days." Nat raised his hand to his forehead, waiting quite impatiently as she went on. "I believe it's a good thing for both countries; it can't help but heal the old wounds left from the war. But I need to ask you a few questions about your missing passport."

Reaching into his shirt pocket, Nat pulled out his dog tags and slammed them down. "My passport isn't missing, Goddamnit!" Miss Dunbar was startled by the loud slap of the metal dog tags striking hard upon the counter between them and raised her hands to her ears. Nat leaned over the counter, practically in her face. "I never had a passport. I was shot down thirty-five years ago and was captured by the enemy. I escaped just two days ago."

The deputy raised the index finger of her right hand as if to make a point. "Excuse me for one minute, Commander Booth; I need to make a call." She picked up the phone and dialed a three-digit extension. "Yes, Mrs. Shigaru. We have a situation here. Can you come to the reception desk? Immediately?"

SIXTY-SEVEN

"YOU SOUND DEPRESSED, ROGER. What's the matter?" Amanda took another sip of iced tea. She sat across the table from Roger Atwood in a booth at Jake's Sports Bar. Amanda had finished the tuna sandwich with fresh fruit; Roger had eaten only half of his cheeseburger and had barely touched the French fries. Two of the three big screens were showing the Yankees vs. Red Sox game that started just before noon. It was the top of the fourth inning and the Yankees were ahead two to one. An ESPN anchor was interviewing a black female tennis star on the third screen, on the wall directly behind Roger.

"I guess I am a little depressed. It looks to me that we've come to a dead end concerning Khronos, and I don't see that we're going to find out anything more about Nathaniel Booth."

"You don't think Rose will be disappointed, do you?"

"I don't know, Amanda."

"Well, I don't think so. Look, we've learned a lot. We know that Nat survived a prisoner of war camp and escaped in 1865. He founded Khronos Trust Services and apparently operated a successful business until he retired in 1898. That means that he probably lived a pretty good life, a life nearly four decades longer than Rose first believed. Why would she be disappointed?"

"We've found out virtually nothing about his personal life. Was he married? Did he have children and grandchildren? Maybe some of his great-grandchildren are alive today. We don't know, and I have no idea how we could find out."

"What about his retirement—in California? We might be able to follow that up." Their server, skimpily dressed in navy blue shorts and a gray sports bra, came to the table.

"Can I get anything else for you?"

"We're finished, but how about some more iced tea?"

"Certainly." The smiling server picked up their plates and disappeared.

"Where would we start? California is a big place." The heaviness in Roger's voice irritated Amanda, but she tried not to show it.

"I think that something else is bothering you, Roger. I think it's volume three of that damn book." Now her irritation was showing.

"What? So you think I'm disappointed because we just missed out on having in our possession a history of the next thirty years? How could you possibly think that that would upset me?" Amanda did not appreciate the sarcasm.

"You're really an ass, you know." She rose from her seat in the booth. "I'm going back to the hotel—by myself!" She turned and started to walk away, but Roger slid out of the booth and grabbed her hand.

"Please wait. I'm sorry. Please—sit with me." Amanda tossed her purse on the table as she sat back down.

"Roger. You need to know that I am having a hard time dealing with your moodiness. This has got to change soon or it will be all over between us."

"I understand. I promise to do better."

"You're sure?"

"Yes."

She stared at him for several seconds, as if contemplating whether or not to believe him. "O.K., then, about those volumes. How do you think that Loc Luu got a hold of them back in—what was the date he wrote inside—1933?"

"Yes, it was 1933. There must have been another convergence event connecting that year with one sometime after the copyright date on the history volumes. Someone brought those books to Loc Luu. I think we can rule out Nathaniel Booth and his partner; they would have been too old."

"Maybe Loc himself was involved. He might have gotten caught up in the convergence, grabbed the books, and then returned to 1933, kind of like Link Hayes. By Link's own account, he found himself in 1863 for less than one day."

"You may be right, Amanda." The server returned and filled their glasses. "I guess we should put together what we know for Rose and then let her make the decision about pursuing it further. What do you think?" Amanda was no longer looking at Roger. She was looking past him, reading the news crawl at the bottom of the ESPN screen behind Roger. "Amanda, what do you think?" He repeated the question.

"My God, Roger, turn around and look at that!" Amanda was pointing at the crawl at the bottom of the television screen. Roger turned to see just as the text message was repeating:

> BREAKING NEWS . . . PENTAGON SOURCES REPORT TODAY THAT A VIETNAM-ERA U.S. NAVY PILOT MIA HAS BEEN FOUND SAFE AND IN APPARENT GOOD HEALTH. NAVY PILOT MISSING SINCE 1968 IS UNDERGOING DEBRIEFING AT U.S.

CONSULATE IN HO CHI MINH CITY, VIETNAM. PILOT'S NAME WITHHELD PENDING NOTIFICATION OF FAMILY.

"Do you think it might be—?"

"I don't know. I wouldn't rule it out." Roger rose and walked to the bar behind them. "Bartender. Would you mind changing the channel to CNN or Fox News? There's something big happening."

"This is a sports bar."

"I understand, dammit, but this is important." The bartender rolled his eyes as he threw down the towel he had been using to wipe down the bar. Then he knelt down in front of the receiver that controlled the input to the third video monitor. Roger and Amanda stood and watched as the changing monitor images flashed before them.

"That's good. Stop there," Roger called out to the bartender. By now a half-dozen patrons from the sports bar had gathered nearby to see what the excitement was all about. The Fox News reporter was repeating the story without adding much in the way of additional details, but then stopped speaking momentarily as he raised his hand to the earpiece in his right ear.

"I am just now getting some additional information. We have been told that the pilot's name is Lieutenant Commander Nathaniel Booth, from Richmond, Virginia. His Navy A6 Intruder was shot down over North Vietnam thirty-five years ago, on June 30th, 1968, while attached to the air wing of the *USS Enterprise*." When the television screen displayed a photo of the pilot—the same photo of Nat in uniform that Rose had given to Roger and Amanda—Roger let out a whoop.

"Yes!"

The reporter continued. "Pentagon sources report that despite repeated inquiries throughout the years, that the

Vietnamese government has consistently maintained that they never held Commander Booth as a POW. The crash site of the downed aircraft had never been found." The reporter paused again. "We are continuing to get more late breaking news concerning this incredible story. We have just been told that the pilot's mother, Rose Booth, has spoken to her son by telephone this morning." When Roger looked over at Amanda, she was wiping tears from her eyes.

Mai Tran, unnoticed earlier as she eavesdropped on the couple's conversation from the next table, had now moved to the rear of the sports bar and was on her cellular phone. "James. You need to turn on Fox News. Our 150 year old MIA is no longer missing."

SIXTY-EIGHT

As Roger Atwood looked about, he couldn't help but notice that the luncheon setting in Rose Booth's garden was even more sumptuous than at the first meeting with Amanda and Lincoln Hayes at the Booth home several weeks before. In order to accommodate the extra guests, the round glass garden table had been replaced with a heavy wooden one, long and narrow, covered by an ivory linen table cloth heavily embroidered in silver thread. The matching trim on the china had been polished to a brilliance surpassed only by the mirror finish on the sterling flatware. The lead crystal was deeply cut and looked heavy. Robert the butler had just finished filling the larger goblets with ice water and was now passing between the guests, pouring from a bottle of two year old Orvieto.

Rose Booth sat at the table's head, with son Nat at her right and Amanda on her left side, next to Roger. The old woman smiled broadly, listening with great pleasure as Amanda related the experience of first hearing about Nat in the sports bar. Nat, and Lily, who sat directly across from Roger looked on, as did Lincoln Hayes, who was seated next to Lily. On Roger's left side, Junius paid no attention at all, apparently captivated by the distorted reflection of his own face in the bright metal blade of the butter knife he was holding.

As Robert filled the last glass at the table, Rose spoke up. "Be sure to pour a glass for yourself, Robert, and please ask Maria and Carmen to join us for a minute." Robert disappeared into the kitchen alcove and returned shortly with Maria Rosario, the matronly cook, and her daughter, Carmen the maid, in tow. The three of them stood near the table facing Mrs. Booth, each holding a half-filled glass of the straw-colored wine. Rose cleared her throat and began. "I wanted you all to be here to celebrate this special time with me. Long ago, I'd given up all hope that this day would ever come to pass. Thirty-five years are gone, but there is no regret in my heart, for my beloved son, who was lost, is now found." She raised her glass in Nat's direction as did the others, both seated and standing. "Welcome home, my son. I love you so." She paused, and all followed her lead, sipping from the crystal goblets. Robert gestured toward the kitchen and followed as Maria and Carmen returned there to finish preparing the meal. Rose continued, "And welcome also to my new daughter. I thank the Lord for my good fortune." She smiled fondly at Lily, who returned it in kind. Lily squeezed Nat's hand that she had been holding since Rose began the toast. "My thanks, also, to Professor Atwood and Amanda who have been working so hard for me these last few weeks."

Roger nodded in acknowledgement of Rose's kind sentiments, but inside he couldn't help his feeling of mild ambivalence. In his mind, Nat's sudden and dramatic reappearance overshadowed, even devalued to a large extent, the detective work that he and Amanda had undertaken. He felt like a researcher who had spent years developing a potentially ground-breaking theory or discovery, only to have someone else publish the same results ahead of him. Deep down, he understood that harboring these feelings was irrational, perhaps a symptom of character weakness, and he was determined not to share them with Amanda or anyone else. He reviewed in his mind the events of the last several days as Robert began to place the chilled plates of Caesar salad in front of Rose and each of her guests.

IT HAD BEEN FIVE DAYS since the announcement of the block buster news concerning Nathaniel Booth. Roger and Amanda had tried in vain to get through to Rose Booth all that afternoon. Unable to contact Rose by phone, they had made the decision to fly to Richmond and were at La Guardia Airport when Rose called Roger's cell phone. Mrs. Booth confirmed what Roger and Amanda had suspected: that Rose had been deluged by phone calls and a veritable invasion of news vans to her Richmond home from virtually every media outlet, both local and from the greater Washington DC area. Rose explained that she had received a visit earlier in the day from two officials from the Pentagon. They brought news that there was a possibility that Nat was alive and asked Rose a lot of questions. A call was placed from Rose's home to the U.S. Consular Office in Ho Chi Minh City and she and Nat were able to speak to each other for the first time. It was not until that phone conversation and more questions from the officials that the Pentagon released a statement to the press.

Rose was told that Nat would be undergoing a comprehensive physical examination and some intensive military debriefing for at least another day before he would be flown to the U.S. mainland, and so there was no reason for Roger and Amanda to rush back to Richmond that evening. Roger concurred, especially since he was scheduled to deliver the third in his series of guest lectures at Long Island University the very next day. He had intended to cancel his appearance, but now Roger and Amanda would rebook their flight to Richmond for the next day, after the Tuesday afternoon lecture. Before she hung up, Rose indicated that the government had expressed some concerns regarding Nat's claim that he had been held captive all these years, and so she cautioned Roger that it might be best if they did not disclose to anyone just yet any of the information that they had discovered concerning Nat's life after his 1968 disappearance.

Roger and Amanda arrived in Richmond on Tuesday evening and telephoned Rose the next morning from their motel room. Since last speaking with them, Rose had learned from the Navy Department that Nat was expected to arrive sometime on Thursday. The time was still indefinite, but the location would be Naval Air Station, Oceana, about one hundred miles southeast of Richmond. The Navy would be sending a car to pick up Mrs. Booth and Lincoln Hayes in time for Nat's arrival. During a second phone conversation with her son, Rose learned about Lily; that she was in Washington DC by herself awaiting Nat's return to the United States. At Rose's request, Roger and Amanda agreed to drive up to Washington, pick up Lily and bring her with them to the air station in Virginia Beach for Nat's arrival.

FOR LILY, the last few days were a continuing adventure in future shock that had begun the day that she and Nat were swept up in the convergence event at the Pennsylvania farmhouse. With the benefit of Nat's advance briefing and taking cues from the passengers boarding ahead of her, Lily had found her assigned window seat on the Boeing 777 and was able to relax for a few minutes before takeoff. She gave the flight attendant her rapt attention as the emergency procedures were dutifully recited and closed her eyes in response to the full-throttle roar of the engines and the g-force acceleration that pressed her back into her seat as the aircraft rushed down the runway. But once the plane reached cruising altitude, Lily began to enjoy her first flight experience.

After landing in Seoul, she had plenty of time to make her connection for the one-stop flight to Chicago. This was a good thing, because she managed to get lost for a time in the terminal and actually stepped outside by mistake and had to re-enter through the security check-in. By mid-ocean, boredom had begun to set in, evidence that Lily was fast becoming a seasoned traveler. The aircraft change in Chicago proceeded without incident, and when the 737 began its final approach into Reagan National, Lily smiled as she recognized a few familiar landmarks on the ground below. The day was cloudless and the dome of the Capitol gleamed in the bright sun; the Washington Monument stood majestically in the distance. Having slept for only a couple of hours during the long second leg of her flight, Lily was tired but the bustle around her and new sights and sounds at every turn kept her going as she followed the other passengers to the baggage claim area. No hitches or glitches, thankfully. Even finding a cab outside the baggage claim was no problem, but once on her way downtown, she was horrified to see the steadily mounting charges on the taxi meter as they jumped with each fifth of a mile. She had to remind herself of what Nat had often told her before: "When you see things priced in twenty-first century dollars, think of them as pennies back in 1898."

After checking in at the National Hotel and tipping the bellhop who had brought her bags to the smallish room on the third floor, Lily began to unpack. Half way through, she stopped and sat on the edge of the bed, feeling a sudden overwhelming sense of fatigue. "I'll close my eyes for just a minute," she thought to herself as she scooted herself to the center of the bed.

She awoke to the sound of the ringing telephone. Nat had told her to expect his call, and she reached excitedly for the handset. The last vestiges of the fog of sleep were gone in an instant.

"Nat, is it you?"

"Is this Lily?"

But she didn't recognize the voice on the line. "Yes, but to whom am I speaking?"

"Lily, my dear, this is Nathaniel's mother, Rose Booth."

She was startled by the response. Naturally, Nat had told Lily all about his family, but before they left the Pennsylvania farmhouse in 1898, they had talked about it and Nat clearly had no expectation that he would find either of his parents still living in 2003. Her mind began to race. Why wasn't it Nat that was calling her? After several seconds of silence she spoke up. "Is there something wrong? Has something happened to Nat?"

Rose could hear the panic in Lily's voice and spoke calmly to reassure her. "Nat is fine, my dear. I spoke with him a short time ago and he asked me to call you. He would have called you himself but they are—well, let's just say that his freedom to communicate is being limited to some extent for now. I was told that Nat is being taken to Maryland as we speak."

"Maryland? I understood that he would be coming here, to the hotel in Washington."

"Some government people need to speak with him first. They want to do that at Fort Meade. He'll be close by, but it will be another day or so before we can see him."

"He'll be coming here after that?"

"We're going to be meeting him on his arrival, so I'm sending someone for you—a couple, actually—so that you can be there when Nat's plane arrives. I'm looking so forward to seeing my son and meeting you, my dear."

"And it will be good to meet you as well, Mrs. Booth."

"Please, please call me Rose."

"Very well, Rose. And the couple who will be coming for me?"

"Yes, my dear. It will be Professor Atwood and his associate, Amanda Marshall. They should be there for you about this same time tomorrow." Lily looked outside for the first time since she was awakened by Rose's call. She realized it was morning and that she had slept through the night.

"Until tomorrow, then."

"Yes, Lily, tomorrow." After hanging up the phone, Lily sat back to consider her conversation with Rose Booth. Tomorrow or the next day she would be reunited with Nat. She smiled to herself, happy for the unexpected good fortune that her husband would soon see his mother after thirty-five years.

SIXTY-NINE

ASIDE FROM THE MESSAGE CENTER, the conference room was the only guaranteed secure location in the U.S. Consulate office building in Ho Chi Minh City. These two rooms were swept for bugs on a daily basis. While the United States and the Republic of Vietnam enjoyed cordial diplomatic relations of late, there was always the risk that one or more members of the support staff, all of whom were Vietnamese nationals, were in fact agents tasked with learning what they could of U.S. State Department plans and policies to be used to advantage by the Vietnamese government or military or to be traded off as useful information to regimes that were less friendly to the United States.

Captain Lawrence Edwards, U.S. Naval Attaché in Japan, had flown in on short notice from Tokyo at the request of the State Department. Mrs. Emi Shigaru, U.S. Consul General in Ho Chi Minh City, had made the initial request to Washington concerning the matter of Commander Nathaniel Booth. Nat sat between the two of them at the large table inside the closed and locked door of the conference room. Captain Edwards, mid-forties, jet black hair with graying only at the temples, projected an aura of authority considerably enhanced by his dress white uniform and expanse of colored ribbons. His gold-braided hat was on the table in front of him.

"Look, Commander," Captain Edwards was speaking forcefully, "I understand that when you first walked in here off the street, you were intimating that you had been held prisoner for the last thirty-five years and that you had just escaped from your captors. Is that correct?"

"Yes, that's true."

"And now you are changing your story. You have given Mrs. Shigaru and me some fanciful account of how you were somehow translated in time and space from Vietnam in 1968 to nineteenth century Pennsylvania, to the Civil War Battle of Gettysburg, no less? And then, back again to present day Vietnam?"

"Yes. Also true."

"And why is that? Why the change in your story?"

"Well, Captain, I guess I made the questionable presumption that the true facts of my disappearance and subsequent reappearance might possibly hold some national security significance and that it just might be in the best interest of my country to limit disclosure."

"You mean, to do your duty as a loyal American Naval officer?"

"Exactly." Nat ignored the sarcastic tone of the Captain's retort.

"Let's cut the crap, Commander."

"Just a minute, Captain." Emi Shigaru was now leaning over the table in the direction of the Captain who sat directly across from her. With both forearms resting on the polished mahogany and eyes fixed on the Captain's, she continued, "I'll remind you that this is an interview, not an interrogation. Commander Booth is not on trial here."

"Not yet," the Captain quickly interjected.

Nat responded angrily, "Just what is that supposed to mean?"

Emi Shigaru was not about to let Captain Edwards take charge over the situation. He may have been Commander Booth's superior officer, but he certainly was not in command over her. Despite her youthful appearance, Mrs. Shigaru was a Senior Foreign Service Officer with an impressive career history, having earned numerous meritorious citations for her work. This was her office and she intended to exercise her legitimate authority. "Let's just tone it down a bit, shall we? Now, Captain, are you suggesting some wrongdoing on the part of Commander Booth?"

"Let's just look at this thing logically." The Captain was now speaking softly and more slowly. "We know that Commander Booth and Lincoln Hayes, his Bombardier/Navigator, were shot down in 1968. No argument. The account of events that I was given before leaving Tokyo states that after Hayes bailed out of the aircraft, there was an explosion and no sign that Commander Booth survived the ordeal. He was officially listed as missing in action, presumed dead. Despite repeated inquiries by DoD, the Vietnamese government claimed to never have held Commander Booth as a POW. Are you with me so far?"

"Yes, go on," Nat replied and Emi Shigaru nodded in agreement.

"Now fast forward thirty-five years." The Captain looks directly at Mrs. Shigaru. "Commander Booth shows up on your doorstep suggesting at first that he has been held captive all this time by the government here or by, God knows, some renegade military organization, and that he managed to escape a few days ago. Then a few hours later confides to you and me that the initial account of his captivity and escape was really just some cover story. The purported truth, which he held back for reasons of national security, is that he has spent the last thirty-five years as a nineteenth century investment analyst." The Captain pauses for a response from Nat or Mrs. Shigaru, but there is none.

Captain Edwards continues, "Now my training as an engineer and a Navy officer tells me that when analyzing some mysterious occurrence, the most logical explanation is usually the most likely as well. To give you a down-to-earth example, last week my wife's diamond earrings and gold bracelet disappeared on the same day that our housekeeper left work early. We have neither seen nor heard from the woman since. I guess it's possible that space aliens came into our home, stole the jewelry and kidnapped our housekeeper, but logical reasoning leads us to believe the more obvious explanation."

"So tell us, Captain. What does logical reasoning tell you about my case?" Nat's arms were folded in front of him.

"Simple, really. Obviously, you got out of your plane before it blew up. You were probably picked up by an NVA patrol and turned over to some political command, maybe with Soviet advisors. They put pressure on you—maybe even tortured you—and you broke, turned on your country and cooperated with the enemy. You've probably spent the last 30 years at some Russian military intelligence agency in the Urals." Now Nat was standing, his face was red and the raised index finger of his right hand was shaking, but Captain Edwards continued. "After you could no longer provide them with any useful information, they could have put a bullet in your head, but for some reason, maybe so that you could be a double agent, they brought you back to Vietnam and released you."

"That's a Goddamn lie. I would never betray my country," Nat shouted. Emi Shigaru raised an open hand in Nat's direction.

"Commander, please sit down, and Captain Edwards—" Before she could continue, the telephone on the table behind Mrs. Shigaru's chair began to ring. "Excuse me." She answered the phone, "Yes, what is it?" Pause. "What do you mean, he's insisting?" Pause. "Very well, send him in." Emi

Shigaru hung up the telephone and turned back to the conference table. Thankfully, Nat was back in his chair. "Gentlemen, we have a visitor."

There were two light raps on the door of the conference room and Emi Shigaru rose and unlocked the door. The man who entered was holding out a U.S. Government I.D. His husky and over six foot high frame towered above the diminutive Consul General.

"My name is Freundlich." he stated with overemphasis on the first syllable. "I'm with NSA. And you are Consul General Shigaru?"

"Yes, I am."

The NSA man looked at Nat, "And you must be Commander Booth?" Nat nodded. Freundlich then turned towards the Captain. "And who, sir, are you?"

"Captain Lawrence Edwards, Naval Attaché."

"Very well. Mrs. Shigaru, can you tell me what is going on here?"

"Commander Booth presented himself at the information desk this morning, claiming that he had been held as a POW here in Vietnam for thirty-five years and that he had recently escaped his captors."

"I'm aware of that much, go on."

"I immediately called my superior at State in DC who notified the Pentagon. I received a call later that Captain Edwards would be sent from Tokyo and not to discuss the matter further with anyone else. However, before Captain Edwards arrived, I received another call from Pentagon officials who were apparently calling from the home of Commander Booth's mother in Richmond."

"You were able to speak with her, Commander?"

"Yes, I was."

"And then you arrived here, Captain?"

"Correct."

"What's your take on this, Captain?"

"Booth changed his story—said he wasn't a POW after all—or at least not a prisoner of the Vietnamese. He claimed to have been caught up in some kind of time warp and spent a couple of years as a prisoner of the Civil War Union Army starting in 1863, then the next thirty-odd years in Washington and New York until another time warp brought him back to the present. He said that—." Freundlich didn't let him finish.

"O.K. That's enough. Now listen carefully to what I'm about to tell you. This applies to any and all information pertaining to the arrival, statements of, and discussion with Commander Nathaniel Booth since his arrival at the Consulate General Office here in Ho Chi Minh City this morning." Freundlich removed a card from the breast pocket of his suit and began to read. "The aforementioned information constitutes material falling within the purview of the United States National Security Agency and has been deemed to be vital to the security interests of the United States. It is classified as TOP SECRET - SENSITIVE. The disclosure, transmission or further discussion of this information with unauthorized persons or entities constitutes a felony under the Security Laws of the United States of America, punishable by fines and prison terms of up to 10 years on each count. Do you fully understand the meaning of the statement that has just been read to you?" Freundlich returned the card to his pocket. "I need to hear an audible acknowledgement from each of you. Now." All three answered in the affirmative.

"O.K." Freundlich continued. "This meeting is over. In fact, it never happened. Consul General Shigaru, you will refer all further inquiries concerning Commander Booth to the State Department. Captain Edwards, you are to return to Tokyo immediately. Commander Booth, you will accompany me to Hawaii for further debriefing. When that is completed, you will be flown to Virginia for the reunion with your family. We are leaving immediately."

SEVENTY

I T WAS NEARLY 8 PM local time when the car carrying Nathaniel Booth and Fred Freundlich approached the security gate leading to the General Aviation Annex at Tan Son Nhut Airport. Freundlich held out a diplomatic passport, which the guard examined carefully, returned it to the NSA agent, and motioned for the driver to proceed through the gate. Freundlich had called ahead to the crew of the waiting aircraft, so when the car pulled up on the tarmac next to the Gulfstream IV, the engines were already whining at idle. Within minutes, the sleek aircraft was making a wide, rapidly climbing turn over the city suburbs, racing away from the setting sun in the direction of the South China Sea.

"I keep wanting to turn around to see who else is on this airplane," Nat commented to his fellow traveler. Freundlich removed his sport coat and sat back in one of the two oversized captain's chairs in the passenger section.

"I told you it would be just the crew and us two," replied Freundlich. "Are you surprised that your government is making such a big deal over your sudden reappearance?"

"Quite frankly, yes."

"Let me tell you something, Commander. It's been more than thirty years since we got out of Vietnam. You'd think that the country would be over it, but we're not. You can bet that as we speak there are folks in Washington deciding exactly what information will be given to the public and the best way to do it. You will probably become the story of the year."

"You're not serious!"

"I'm absolutely serious. But for now, there's a shower aft and I've brought a change of clothes for you. We've got plenty of gourmet TV dinners aboard and you can help yourself to the adult beverages."

"That shower sounds good."

Freundlich continued, "It will be about four-and-a-half hours to our first refueling stop."

"That would be, Guam, I'd guess." Freundlich nodded. "What's the range on this baby?"

"Four thousand."

Nat was heading to the rear of the aircraft when he stopped and returned to where Freundlich was sitting. "Just a minute. What did you mean by our *first* refueling stop? There shouldn't be another stop before Hawaii."

"We've had a slight change in the flight plan. We're headed for the east coast. Depending upon what you tell me, we may end up at NSA headquarters in Fort Meade for further debriefing. Maybe or maybe not."

Nat sat back in his seat. "Well, before you start on me, Freundlich, you're going to have to answer a few questions." The agent nodded. "For starters, I thought that NSA was concerned with code breaking and cryptology. Why the interest in my situation?"

"You're essentially correct. NSA has two primary missions. Signals intelligence has been our traditional role, but more recently, a department was established to counter cyber threats and to maintain internet security. It's called the 'Information Assurance Directorate.'"

"Cyber—what? And the internet? What's the 'internet'?"

"You really have been out of touch with things, haven't you? Here's the short history and description: During the last years of the cold war the Defense Department needed a military communication network that would be invulnerable to disruption in the event of nuclear war. Before the internet, it would have been fairly easy to isolate a military base from its command structure simply by severing the communication links between them. Now imagine a giant grid that overlays all of our bases and military commands throughout the world. You could blow away huge sections of the grid, but as long as there was a grid path, even a circuitous one, between the nodes on the grid, then communications would remain intact."

"So, does it work?"

"Fortunately, we've never had to operate in the extreme case, but it's become so successful that the internet now carries all types of commercial and personal communication as well. We call it electronic mail, or email for short. But even more significant, the internet serves as a giant distributed store of information. Companies all over the world describe their products and services in text and pictures, all displayed on screens—similar to television screens—on personal computers. You can buy virtually anything over the internet, from prescription drugs to pornography."

"Thanks for the update, but you still haven't answered the main question. Why is the National Security Agency interested in me?"

"O.K. That's fair. Let me try to explain. It's true that the facts surrounding your disappearance in 1968 and your recent reappearance are beyond the scope of NSA's stated mission, but we have sections that do a lot of basic scientific research in subjects that even I am unaware of. I'll tell you what I know, but first I'm going to take a leak and grab a couple of brewskis from the reefer."

Fred Freundlich returned to his seat several minutes later and popped open two cold cans of Heineken, passing one to Nat. After taking a long pull from the beverage can, he began. "First, I'm sure you understand this, but let me make it perfectly clear just in case: everything I am about to tell you is highly classified. You must not disclose it to anyone, not even your wife."

"How do you know about my wife?"

Freundlich chuckled. "We placed a tap on your mother's phone within a couple of hours after you announced yourself at the Consulate. That *is* our business, you know." Nat nodded. "I was meeting with some folks in Ho Chi Minh City on an unrelated matter, but I got the word to hot foot it over to the Consulate and check out your story and put a lid on it. That is, if it met with certain criteria." Freundlich waited for the anticipated response from Nathaniel Booth.

"Such as . . ?"

"Quite simply, if you breathed so much as a single word to suggest that some cosmic space-time event was in any way related to your disappearance. Here's why: About ten years ago we received a report of some strange happenings in the Ukraine from years before. The local police raided a long-abandoned farm house outside their small town and ended up in a fire fight with three soldiers who were holding up there. Two of soldiers were killed outright and the third was mortally wounded, but when the cops came in they were surprised to find that the soldiers were wearing German army uniforms—World War II uniforms. And these weren't Eastern Front uniforms. These guys were dressed in desert warfare garb. Before he died, the wounded man kept mentioning Tobruk."

Nat interjected, "Part of Rommel's Afrika Corps, circa 1942."

"Exactly. When the KGB got wind of it—this was in 1977 or 78, before the breakup of the Soviet Union—they came in and locked-down the town, flew the bodies out, and threatened every one who knew anything to keep quiet or else. The cops who participated in the raid were never heard from again."

"If that's the case, how did we hear about it?"

"From a Russian immigrant. A Dr. Tushenkov who was working at a Soviet Army research facility before he emigrated. He claimed that the autopsies performed on the Germans indicated that all three men were in their twenties and that enlistment records captured by the Russian army in Berlin at the end of the war confirmed that these guys were the real thing. The Soviets poured a ton of money into researching this in hopes of developing a valuable intelligence tool at the very least, or ultimately, maybe a way to alter future historical outcomes. When the Soviet Union ran out of money, the research was suspended. Tushenkov claims it was because the big wigs could see no pot of gold at the end of the rainbow. Even given that they might be able to control this thing, they saw no practical value to bringing people from the past to the present, and there was no evidence to suggest that time travel in the other direction had ever occurred or was even physically admissible from the mathematics. That is, until you came along."

"Then you believe my story?"

"I'm keeping an open mind. After all, I recognize that the potential could be enormous."

"Could be. My experience indicates that this thing is predictable, but controlling it or developing some kind of machine to exploit it—well, I just don't see it happening. When I was sucked into the past, back to 1863, I had no idea what was happening. I got caught up in this convergence event because I was present at the right time and place when it occurred, probably just like those German soldiers. Coming back from the past, I sought out the particular time and place where I thought it might reoccur, but again, I was just along for the ride. I had absolutely no control over what was happening. And about trying to change the future course of history, forget it. I tried to do just that, but failed miserably."

"Tell me more. This is getting good!"

"I spent almost two years in a Union Army prisoner of war camp—two different ones, actually. I escaped the day after Robert E. Lee surrendered to General Grant, and I headed to Washington DC. They called it Washington City in those days. I arrived there the day before President Lincoln was shot and tried to stop John Wilkes Booth. I even met and spoke with him, but I was unable to stop him. I've come to believe that I always have been part of the historical record. That is, if anyone had seen fit to record the small mark I may have made in the thirty-five years I spent in the nineteenth century, we could go to a library somewhere and look it up."

Fred Freundlich leaned back in his seat and closed his eyes for a minute to consider what Nat had just said. When he opened them again, Nat was in the galley at the back of the plane, checking out the available frozen fare that Freundlich had boasted about.

SEVENTY-ONE

ESPITE THE 115 DEGREE HEAT, Nat would have preferred to have stayed in the hanger a while longer checking out the Joint Strike Fighter that was parked inside than to climb back into the G4. The trip had been fatiguing. Four-and-one-half hours to Guam and then eight more to Honolulu for more fuel and a crew change. Then five more hours here to Edwards Air Force Base before they would continue on for the last leg of the flight. Freundlich apologized for the long flight with multiple stops, but the longer range G5 assigned to his section was engaged, in transit to an undisclosed Mid Eastern country. Nat was anxious to get to Virginia, but was not disappointed when Fred told him that they would be laying over a day at Edwards. Before landing yesterday, Freundlich explained that they would be picking up another passenger and Nat assumed that the man who was now walking in his direction with Fred was Leonid Tushenkov.

"I have been very much looking forward to meeting you, Commander Booth." The accent was Russian, but barely perceptible.

"This is Dr. Tushenkov." Before Fred Freundlich had finished with his introduction, the stocky Russian had thrust his hand toward Nat's and shook it firmly.

"Pleased to meet you, Doctor," offered Nat. Tushenkov looked a few years younger than Nat, shorter, but with a full head of black hair, streaked with gray and combed straight back.

"Let's get going, gentlemen. Our aircraft awaits." Freundlich gestured for his two traveling companions to lead the way out of the hanger door to the stairway hatch of the G4 waiting at the edge of the runway. Minutes later the aircraft was climbing to its cruising altitude of 32,000 feet for the cross-country flight.

Over the next two hours, Dr. Tushenkov questioned Nat in detail about the strange events surrounding Nat's last mission over Vietnam and his translation in time and space. Tushenkov scribbled notes in a black book as Nat spoke. The doctor was especially interested in the physical manifestations of the convergence event: the electrical storm and loss of power on his aircraft, the blinding white light, and eventual realization that his plane was flying inverted over the nineteenth century countryside. The doctor apparently cared little about the details of Nat's internment and escape from the prisoner of war camp, but Tushenkov became very excited when Nat began the story of his encounter with John Wilkes Booth and the failed attempt to save the life of President Lincoln.

"Tell me, Commander, what was your motivation in attempting to save the life of the President?"

Nat felt that the answer to the doctor's question was self-evident. "Why wouldn't anyone try to prevent a crime that was about to take place, if they had the power to do so?"

"Yes, but did you consider beforehand what the result of your actions might have been had you been successful?" Nat was disturbed by the tone of Tushenkov's question. It was almost as if the doctor was chastising Nat for daring to intercede.

"I'm not sure I understand the question. Are you suggesting that I was wrong to try to stop the assassination?"

"Commander Booth, you should know that American history is not a subject with which I am very familiar, so I cannot begin to speculate what might have been the subsequent course of events had Abraham Lincoln not been shot in April 1865. But let me give you an example from Soviet and European history. Historians from my former country often lament over the failed attempts to assassinate Adolph Hitler during the Second War. 'If only someone had put a bullet in that madman's head in 1941', they would say, 'the war would have ended years earlier and so many lives could have been saved!' But research conducted at the institute at which I worked years ago suggests differently. In 1941, Hitler broke the Non-aggression Pact that had been signed with my country. Breaking that treaty required the Wehrmacht to engage in a two-front war, something that Hitler's generals had always warned against. Most historians would agree that that event was the single most important cause of the downfall of the Third Reich. Researchers at my institute developed special tools to assess the most likely course of events in the face of a hypothetical history-changing occurrence, as the assassination of Hitler most certainly would have been. We called it Action-Reaction Outcome Analysis and our research concluded that if Hitler had been eliminated before he gave the order to commence his operation Barbarossa, the code name for the invasion of the Soviet Union, that the Non-aggression Pact would never have been broken by Germany. It would have probably been extended instead. A peace treaty would be signed with Britain guaranteeing permanent German occupation of the rest of Europe and North Africa. The United States would grudgingly accept the brokered deal for peace in Europe.

With only a Pacific war to contend with, America would be able to bring Japan to her knees in early 1944 without the use of the atomic bomb. In fact, bomb development in the U.S. would be put on the back burner, until, that is, Germany tested its first nuclear weapon in the Libyan Desert in 1946 or 47. There would be no United Nations, no State of Israel, and by 1950, Germany, the United States and the Soviet Union—my country again using stolen U.S. technology—would be engaged in an unprecedented three-way arms race. In the estimation of my analysts, within ten years the arms race would inevitably end with a world-wide thermonuclear exchange threatening the very existence of human life on this planet." Nat and Fred Freundlich were both captivated by the doctor's presentation of this alternate historical scenario.

"That's pretty startling. And you are confident of your group's conclusions?" asked Fred.

"Most assuredly. I believe that one well-intentioned German citizen could have set into motion a series of events which would have led to the destruction of the earth as we know it. It's a classic application of the Law of Unintended Consequences."

"Very interesting," offered Nat, "but from my experience, I don't believe it's possible to alter an historical outcome."

"But are you not basing that belief on the single experience of your failure to save President Lincoln?" From his tone, it was clear that Tushenkov did not want to accept Nat's premise.

"Not just the President," replied Nat. Then he spent the next several minutes telling Dr. Tushenkov and Fred Freundlich the story of Jennie Wade and John Wesley Culp and Nat's encounter with John Wesley during the Battle of Gettysburg. When Nat was finished, Tushenkov sat with his eyes closed and finger tips of his two hands pressed together, carefully considering Nat's story and it's implications.

"If you are correct," began Tushenkov, "If we are unable to rewrite the historical record, then the chief military value of all this will be considerably reduced. I would say that it would have minimal value outside the area of military intelligence." For a few seconds, Tushenkov considered his own stated conclusion, he then continued. "I believe—" He turned toward Fred Freundlich, "—that we are done with Commander Booth for now. Commander, will you be staying in Virginia for the near term?"

"With my mother in Richmond, I'll probably be staying there at least for the next few weeks," Nat offered.

"Then if we need you, you wouldn't mind coming to NSA at Fort Meade?"

Nat was puzzled. "Not a problem, but I thought that's where we were headed today?"

Fred Freundlich quickly interjected, "If Dr. Tushenkov says we are done for now, we are done." Fred headed to the front of the aircraft to advise the pilot and co-pilot of the destination change. When he returned from the cockpit, Freundlich handed Nat a single sheet of paper.

"I just received this from Headquarters." He handed the paper to Nat. It's a suggested cover story that some folks at NSA developed for you."

"Suggested?" Questioned Nat.

"Absolutely. This was still a free country, last time I checked. You can tell the news media and anyone else anything you want. We simply feel it would be best for all concerned if we limited disclosure of the exact truth in this case."

Nat read over the summary and considered the bullet points that were presented:

- SUBJECT BOOTH WAS SHOT DOWN AND CAPTURED BY THE VIET CONG IN EARLY JULY 1968.

- SUBJECT HELD AS THE SOLE PRISONER IN A MAKESHIFT MILITARY PRISON IN THE SOUTHERN HIGHLANDS AREA OF VIETNAM.

- SHIPPED OFF TO HANOI AFTER THE REPATRIATION OF MOST OTHER U.S. POWs AND HELD THERE UNTIL 1995.

- RETURNED TO THE SOUTHERN HIGHLANDS AND TURNED OVER TO EX-MILITARY DRUG LORDS. FORCED TO WORK IN AN ILLEGAL DRUG PROCESSING PLANT.

- ESCAPED FROM HIS CAPTORS AND TAKEN TO HO CHI MINH CITY BY VIETNAMESE CIVILIANS HE ENCOUNTERED AFTER HIS ESCAPE.

Freundlich allowed Nat several minutes to read over and consider the cover story summary. "What do you think? Can you sell that? Do you want to? Talk to me."

"I guess so," Nat offered reluctantly.

SEVENTY-TWO

I T WAS JULY 4TH and drizzling lightly on the National Mall. Two days earlier, Nat had disembarked from the G4 at Oceana Naval Air Station not knowing who or how many people would be greeting him. Thankfully, there was no sign of the press. A little disinformation planted by the Navy Department had sent all of the news crews to BWI in Baltimore. It only bought him a few hours. Once the press discovered that they had been snookered, they converged on Rose's home in Richmond. They wanted video of the Vietnam vet and a statement, and were not going to leave until they got exactly that. Without getting too specific, Nat read a brief written statement, then invited a few questions. Yes, he acknowledged that he had been shot down thirty-five years earlier, but that he was happy now to be home in Richmond. It was true he had been held in two different POW camps, but was especially gratified by the reunion with his mother upon his return. No, he couldn't go into detail about his captivity, but was pleased to see that his A6 flight partner, Lincoln Hayes, was also waiting for him on the tarmac upon his return. In summary, Nat didn't give the news people very much information concerning his whereabouts for last thirty-five years, choosing instead to answer questions about what had happened in the last few hours since his arrival home; questions that were never asked.

The Armed Forces Chorus was singing on the Mall that day, protected by a canvas portico set up near the west wall of the Vietnam Memorial. The chorus could be easily heard by visitors coming to the Wall from the direction of the Lincoln Memorial. Nat and Lily stopped to listen to the velvet voices above the hiss of the drizzle.

"This is the most beautiful rendition of that song I have ever heard," whispered Lily before the chorus had finished even the first verse of *The Battle Hymn of the Republic*. Nat just smiled and squeezed her hand more tightly. Before the last verse was over, the pair continued toward the entrance to the West Wall.

"How do you find any name?" She asked. "There are so many."

"My mother said it was on Panel 54 West, at about the middle." The chorus now began to sing Nick Glennie-Smith's and Randall Wallace's *Mansions of the Lord*.

"There it is!" exclaimed Lily. NATHANIEL L. BOOTH was inscribed about eye-level in the polished black granite. "What's the meaning of the little cross in front of some of the names? Most of them have diamonds in front."

"I don't know what it means," replied Nat.

"I do." reported a voice from behind them. Nat and Lily turned to see an elderly couple standing arm-in-arm. The man continued. "That 'plus sign' means 'Missing'; the diamonds are 'Killed in Action'. If a missing soldier is later determined to have died, you will see a diamond inscribed over the plus sign."

Nat was now only half listening to the man. Captivated by words he had never heard before, Nat simply could not turn his attention away from the chorus of voices until the last verse of *Mansions* had come to an end.

Lily noticed that the woman had been listening to the chorus as well; she began to cry openly as her husband explained the symbols. "You've lost someone close?" Lily asked.

"Our son, Robert. They found his remains just three weeks ago. We've come from Saginaw."

"I'm so sorry," offered Lily.

"Robert's been gone for so many years now. We always knew this day would come—eventually. I shouldn't be crying like this." The old woman buried her face in her husband's coat as they turned to walk away.

"Oh, sir!" Lily called out to the man. He turned.

"Yes, what is it?"

"How would they mark the name of someone who was missing, but later found to be alive?"

The man drew a round outline in the air with his finger. "A circle. A circle would be carved around the plus sign. But you won't find any of those on the Wall. Until a few days ago, no one marked as missing in action had ever come back alive." Lily squeezed Nat's hand as the older couple turned away from them once more.

SEVENTY-THREE

"YOU MAY BE RIGHT. Remember that it was just two months ago that the President announced with considerable fanfare that major combat operations in Iraq were over. We all saw the big 'Mission Accomplished' sign. But now we are hearing that a guerilla insurgency may be emerging there." Roger Atwood was commenting on the statement of a student seated at the back of the room. She was suggesting that the situation in Iraq was beginning to look more and more like the U.S. experience in Vietnam from forty years earlier. Roger continued, "Here's an example for you. From what I understand, U.S. forces have been quite capable of entering a sector and neutralizing the insurgents effectively, but as soon as our troops leave, the insurgents are back in control. This is really no different from what happened in South Vietnam at locations away from the major cities." Roger waited for a follow-up statement from the woman. When there was none, he went on. "By early 1970, it became evident to most Americans that no real progress was being made in the war; public opinion had reached the tipping point and moved steadily negative. Within three years, we were out of Southeast Asia and the communist governments prevailed in Vietnam and Cambodia. Those governments wreaked real havoc on their people in the years immediately following. Will the same thing happen in Iraq? It's really too early to tell." Atwood looked at his watch. "Let's take a short break. Be back here in about ten minutes and we'll continue the discussion."

This was the third in the series of six weekly lectures that Roger had contracted with Long Island University at the C.W. Post campus on Long Island's "Gold Coast." In the lectures, Professor Atwood hoped to present an in-depth survey of post World War II conflicts, comparing and contrasting with each other and the U.S. Civil War.

IT WAS THE MIDDLE of the afternoon and across town on the Brooklyn-Queens border, Nat and Lily Booth were on a foot path in the old section of the Evergreens Cemetery.

"I know it has to be around here somewhere, but everything looks so different," said Nat. "There's a lot more foliage."

The Evergreens Cemetery was founded in 1849 and serves as the final resting place for more than a half-million souls. The grounds provide majestic views of the Atlantic Ocean to the south and the Manhattan skyline to the north. The name "Evergreens" comes from the thousands of pines that were imported from the Catskills, replacing most of the native cypress trees that originally covered the land.

"I think it's more in this direction," offered Lily, pointing towards the south. The last time they had seen the mausoleum that Trung Luu had erected for the Luu family, it was not quite finished.

"I believe you're right. I think I see it behind those trees." When they reached the mausoleum, Nat had to walk around to the front of it to be sure. There carved into the stone fascia above the Greek columns was the name 'Luu'. "This is it." Nat waited for Lily to catch up, then guided her down two narrow steps to the iron gate entrance to the tomb.

On the right side of the gate was an imposing antique padlock, rusted to a uniform dark brown shade, securing the gate with an equally rusted length of chain. Nat reached overhead and felt for a gap behind the stone lintel, then brought down a large key, thoroughly encrusted with an unsettling amalgam of dirt, dried tree debris and cobwebs. Lily watched patiently while Nat whisked away what was loose using his free left hand, only to find the cobwebs clinging to his fingers. A sharp flick of his wrist finally sent the debris flying. Nat grasped the lock and slid the keyhole cover open with his left thumb, then thrust the key inside with his right hand.

Click-click. First to the left, then right, the key barely turned. There was no expected and satisfying ka-lunk of the spring-loaded tumbler giving way. Nat tried once again, this time with more force. Click-click.

"What's the matter, Nat?"

"I think it's frozen with rust."

"You can't turn it?"

"I don't want to break the key off inside. Let me try again." This time he pulled the lock and chain towards himself first. Before he could even turn the key, the shackle gave way, pulling entirely out of the lock case. "So much for security." Nat removed the chain and swung the gate open. The screech of protest from the rusted hinges was so loud that Nat looked behind him to see if anyone was close enough to hear.

Inside, the light was dim; the diffuse rays passing through the gate opening behind them being the sole source of illumination inside the chamber. It was several seconds before their eyes adjusted to the reduced light level.

Eight caskets could be made out in the dim light. Lily was drawn to two smaller ones near the wall to their right. Nat lit his butane lighter to read the brass plaques on the side of the caskets, the tops of which were covered in fine dust.

"Derrick Jr. April 24, 1974 to May 13, 1978," Nat read aloud.

"It must be painful to lose a child so young," cried Lily.

"This one died the same day. Amber—nine years old." Nat moved to two larger caskets nearby. "Same day for Derrick Luu and Brenda. There must have been an accident."

"How terrible for the whole family to perish at once!"

Near the wall to their left there was a single casket. "This one is Van Luu—your piano player, Lily."

"He was a nice man, and he could certainly play that piano! I didn't know that Trung intended to have his father disinterred and moved here from Washington." Nat stepped to the far side of the tomb to read the plaques on one of the three remaining caskets.

"This is little Loc," Nat sighed. "He was ten years old when we left two weeks ago." Lily put her arm around Nat.

"He lived a long life, Nat." Nat brushed the dust from the brass plaque that showed Loc Luu died in 1960. Finally they stood in front of the remains of Nat's best friend and business partner, Trung and Trung's wife, Kim. "There's nothing to say. It's hard to understand that they have been gone for more than eighty years." Nat was examining the elaborate wood turning that ran the entire length along the bottom of Trung's casket. There was an identical turning on the other side of the casket as well. Nat firmly grasped the ornate knob at the foot end of the turning and twisted. It came off in his hand. This he repeated at the opposite end of the turning, near the head of the casket.

"There's a steel rod behind you against the wall, Lily. Would you bring it here?" Nat was bent over now, looking directly into one of the two circular shafts that ran the entire length of the sarcophagus. When he brought the lighter close to the opening, the reflection from the yellow metal inside was unmistakable. "It's here!" Nat quickly moved around to opposite end of the casket and opened the empty briefcase he had been carrying. "Put the end of the rod into the shaft opening and push towards me when I tell you."

The large gold coins—all Liberty Head Double Eagles—
fell into Nat's open palms as Lily pushed with the steel rod
against the horizontal stack of coins from the other end of
the casket. It took all of the strength that Lily could muster.

Nat laid the coins into the open case, side-by-side like
rows of plastic Backgammon markers. When they were done,
there were five neat rows of about 120 coins each, almost
forty pounds of gold, in the aluminum case. Although the
total face value at twenty dollars each was no more than
twelve thousand dollars, the current spot gold price meant
they were worth maybe $350,000 for gold content alone, but
Nat knew that the numismatic value was nearly double that
amount.

"What about the other side of the casket?" Lily asked.

"I looked at it. Probably contains a like amount, but it
should be safe here. Besides, I don't think we'll be able to
carry any more of the coins." He closed the case and emitted
a short grunt as he lifted it to his side. "I hate to leave the rest
of the gold here, but this thing is heavy."

"We can come back any time," offered Lily. She knew
that Nat was still upset after learning that his mother knew
nothing of the *second* trust that Nat had set up. It was to be
their nest egg when they returned from Nat's 35 year sojourn
in the past. There was no trace of the investment account that
Nat had every reason to believe would have been worth
millions today.

"I suppose you're right." The couple stood quietly
surveying the casket remains of the Luu family members for a
minute, then turned and left the tomb. Nat secured the gate
as best he good, knowing that anyone who wanted in would
need only to pull firmly on the shackle of the lock. But he
also understood that it was highly unlikely that anyone other
than he and Lily would ever set foot inside again.

SEVENTY-FOUR

BACK ON LONG ISLAND, Roger Atwood was nearing the end of his lecture. A student had posed to the professor a direct question concerning Atwood's personal position on the continuing conflict in Iraq.

"I can state unequivocally that I am neither for nor against it." The audience laughed, and Roger raised his hands as if to quiet the room. "Seriously, I hate to see the loss of life, but if our military can keep this early insurgency from expanding and a suitable political solution can be worked out soon, the U.S. action in Iraq may prove to have been a grand success."

A few of the students began to boo, then someone called out over the fading volume of their disagreement, "Don't you think they're lying to us? They probably knew all along there were no WMDs. It was a big mistake to get into this war."

Professor Atwood was quick to reply. "Who knows? Who can say what the final outcome will be? Someone out there may know, but I certainly don't."

The young Asian woman in the back row of the lecture hall stopped her note taking and looked up at the professor. She slid her writing pad to the side, revealing the brown cloth-bound book that was concealed below it. After first assuring herself that no one near by was watching, she opened the book as she had done many times since acquiring it only weeks before and flipped past the photographs showing the World Trade Center towers streaming columns of black smoke. She then perused the photos that followed, a pictorial history of the world in an event-filled first third of the twenty-first century: Aerial photos of several cities in Europe, North Korea and the Mid East devastated by atomic weapons of terror, or in some cases, by a vengeful thermonuclear response. The signing of peace treaties in New York City. Scientific achievements in energy production and conservation. Economic disaster and recovery. It was all there. "Someone, indeed, knows what lies ahead," thought Mai Tran as she smiled to herself.

Author's Notes

EARLY IN THE PROCESS of conducting research for this project, consideration was given to the inclusion of historically real, but largely unknown, personages in interaction with the created fictional characters. There are thousands of individuals in official and unofficial war records, most of them obscure to history, who nonetheless risked and often gave their lives for the country or cause in which they believed. There were many others whose imprint on history may not have been made on the battlefield, but whose life's struggle is nonetheless worthy of our respect.

What is to be gained from using the historical account of real people where entirely fictional characters could have been substituted? For the reader, the knowledge that their lives are part of the historical record adds some measure of realism to the fictionalized characters around them. Acknowledging their contribution or sacrifice will hopefully help keep them a little longer within our collective memory. The reader is reminded, however, that this is a work of fiction. The incidents and character portrayals included in this book are purely fictional, a product of the author's imagination, and are in no way intended to reflect the true character, actions, conversation or opinion of these individuals. Any exceptions must be attributed to coincidence.

In contrast, the following information is believed to be an accurate, though woefully incomplete, historical account of those individuals:

• Sergeant Andrew Wyatt, Company B of the 26th North Carolina Troops was from Wilkes County, North Carolina, and enlisted on September 21, 1862. He was killed in action at Gettysburg on July 1, 1863.[1]

• Captain William Wilson was a member of Company B of the 26th North Carolina Troops from Union County, North Carolina. He enlisted on June 5, 1861, at the age of 20. Captain Wilson was killed in action at Gettysburg on July 1, 1863.[2]

• Lieutenant William Richardson was age 26 when he enlisted in the 26th North Carolina Troops on June 5, 1861. He was from Union County, North Carolina and was killed in action at Gettysburg on July 1, 1863.[3]

• Basil Manly was a Lieutenant in the 1st North Carolina Artillery, serving bravely in many Civil War battles including Gettysburg in the artillery battery that bore his name ("Manly's Battery"). He was promoted to the rank of colonel by the end of the war and later served as mayor of Raleigh, North Carolina.[4]

• Jennie Wade, Jack Skelly and John Wesley Culp knew each other in Gettysburg well before the Civil War began. Jennie, whose full name was Mary Virginia Wade, was the only known civilian to be killed during the Battle of Gettysburg. A bullet that passed through the door of the house struck her while she was in the kitchen baking bread for Union soldiers. The account of Wesley Culp taking a message for Jennie from his wounded friend, Jack Skelly, cannot be substantiated and probably did not occur. John Wesley Culp was killed on July 3, 1863, during the Union counter offensive after the Confederate assault that took place on his uncle's farm, at Culp's Hill. Jack Skelly died on July 12, 1863, from wounds sustained during the Battle of 2nd Winchester.[5]

It is not known when the dramatic love story version of this tale first began to circulate, but it was true that Jack and Jennie were engaged to be married. Details of Jennie's life and death tend to vary among available sources, including some, as in the story line, that present a less than flattering account of her character. The exact truth may never be known.

• Walter Addison was a private in Company A, Breathed's battery of Stewart's Horse artillery and spent six months incarcerated at the Point Lookout, Maryland, and Elmira, New York, POW camps. Although the story portrays Private Addison as one of the early internees at Point Lookout and that he had been wounded at Gettysburg, he did not in fact become a prisoner until the summer of 1864, after the Wilderness Campaign. In response to a large number of articles that appeared after the war describing Confederate atrocities perpetrated against Union prisoners, Private Addison wrote a detailed account, published in 1889, of his experience in the two Northern camps.[6]

• John R. King, born in Marion County, Virginia, was a member of the 25th Virginia Infantry and fought in several Civil War battles, including Gettysburg. He was captured by Union forces at the Battle of the Wilderness in early May 1864. King was taken to the Point Lookout camp later that month and transferred to Elmira in August 1864. He was released in June 1865 and in 1916 wrote a detailed account of his experiences as both a Confederate soldier and a prisoner of war.[7]

• Washington Traweek was a member of the "Jeff Davis" Artillery, captured by Federal troops at the Battle of Spotsylvania in May 1864. While the story account of the tunnel escape from Elmira Prisoner of War Camp is set in April 1865, Traweek was one of about ten prisoners who made a successful escape from Elmira on October 6, 1864. After making his escape, Washington Traweek returned to

Alabama, eventually retiring to the Home for Confederate Soldiers and Sailors in Biloxi, Mississippi, where he died in 1923. [8]

• Major Colt was the Union Provost Marshall in charge of the Prisoner of War Camp at Elmira, New York, for a time while John King was incarcerated. Unlike many reports of cruelty in the Northern camps, John King's account suggests that Colt and his assistants, Captain Mungery and Captain Peck, treated their charges well, although they could often do little to improve rations or living conditions. [9]

• John and Nathaniel Ballard and another man whom history records simply as "Doty" were believed to be the first white settlers in the area of Columbia Township, Bradford County, Pennsylvania. An account of the early history of Columbia Township was published in The Bradford Reporter, Towanda, Pennsylvania in February 1884. While the story herein suggests that Doty and the Ballards gave up their claims due to the harsh living conditions of the wilderness, this is not a fact that can be substantiated by historical records. Rebecca Cantrell is a fictionalized character, created solely to advance the story line. [10]

• Jonathan Lewis joined the Ohio Volunteer Infantry in May of 1864. He was only fifteen years old, but claimed to be eighteen in his enlistment papers. Although his unit was never engaged in providing security for the President, Private Lewis was issued special orders and sent to Washington. He was a guard at the White House, assigned the duty of keeping unauthorized persons away from a well pump where the President would often obtain a cup of water when outside on the White House grounds. In an interview years later, Lewis recalled a time when President Lincoln said to him, "Son, you are too young to be a soldier."

It is ironic that on the morning of Lincoln's assassination that the President signed into law a bill establishing the Secret

Service. The original role of the agency was to stop the widespread counterfeiting of U.S. currency. It was not until 1901, after two more presidential assassinations, that the Secret Service would be assigned the responsibility of protecting the lives of American presidents.[11, 12]

• Clara Harris and Major Henry Rathbone, the guests of President and Mrs. Lincoln on the night of the assassination, were married in July 1867. Clara was the daughter of New York Senator Ira Harris who had been elected in 1860. Major Rathbone scuffled with John Wilkes Booth in the State Box seconds after the attack on President Lincoln. Booth slashed Rathbone on the arm with his Bowie knife. It is believed that the struggle caused Booth to become unbalanced when jumping from the State Box to the stage, resulting in a fracture to his ankle.

Rathbone suffered from depression and paranoia in the years following Lincoln's assassination and resigned his army commission in 1870. He irrationally considered himself responsible for the President's death and may have suffered from the effects of Post Traumatic Stress from his war experiences. In 1882, Rathbone was appointed as Consul General to Germany. Two days before Christmas 1883, Rathbone shot and stabbed his wife to death in a paranoiac rage. He spent the rest of his life in a German asylum for the criminally insane and died in 1911.[13]

• Edwin Booth, the brother of presidential assassin, John Wilkes Booth, was born in Belair, Maryland, in 1833. From a young age, he aspired to become an actor. Surprisingly, his career was interrupted only temporarily by the crime of his infamous brother, and he went on to achieve international acclaim. His most famous role was as Shakespeare's Hamlet.

Edwin Booth was married twice and had one daughter, Edwina (1861- 1938) and no known male heirs. Thus, the story account of Wendell Booth, Nathaniel's father, as the grandson of Edwin is purely fictitious. Edwin Booth died in New York City on June 7, 1893.[14]

• Vital Jarrot, prominent businessman, financier and public servant, was born in Cahokia, Illinois on September 10, 1805. He was a member of the original board of directors of the St. Louis & Illinois Bridge Company founded in 1855. This firm is credited for planning and construction of Eads Bridge over the Mississippi River, completed in 1879. Jarrot became financially destitute as a result of the Panic of 1873 and was drawn to the Black Hills in the Dakota Territory by accounts of vast gold deposits reported by General George Armstrong Custer. He was unsuccessful at gold prospecting and died penniless in Rapid City, South Dakota, on June 5, 1877. [15,16]

• Nguyen Thai Hoc led an uprising against French colonial forces in Vietnam in February 1930. For decades prior the French had maintained a stranglehold on the country, exploiting cheap coolie labor on farms and vast rubber plantations. The February uprising was doomed to fail before it began and on June 17, 1930, Nguyen Thai Hoc and twelve of his comrades were executed by French authorities in Yen Bay, a provincial capital north of Hanoi. The French method of execution at that time was by guillotine. According to some accounts, Nguyen Thai Hoc was the last to be executed and requested that he be allowed to die on his back, facing the blade. Although the uprising failed, the sacrifice of these men strengthened the determination of the Vietnamese to overthrow their colonial rulers. The thirteen heroes of Yen Bay are commemorated in Vietnam each year on the anniversary of their deaths.

As the Second World War approached, leadership of the independence movement fell to Ho Chi Minh. During the wartime period, a tangled web of shifting alliances within the country continued the struggle for independence in the face of external pressure from China, the reality of a Japanese occupation, and ongoing colonial claims of the puppet Vichy Government in France. U.S. President Roosevelt strongly supported the notion of a free Vietnam, but his successor gave into British and French pressure to restore France's colonial rights at war's end. After several more years of fighting, Ho's guerilla and military forces under the direction of General Giap eventually ended French occupation in the north after the French defeat at Dien Bien Phu, on May 8, 1954.

It is difficult to speculate as to how the subsequent political landscape of Vietnam might have changed if a leader like Nguyen Thai Hoc, rather than Ho Chi Minh, had been able to lead the country to independence. Clearly, it was Ho's early exposure and dedication to Soviet-style Communism in the 1920s plus lack of support from the U.S. Government at a critical time that eventually led to a final freedom for the country of Vietnam that unfortunately still denies many fruits of that freedom to her people. [17,18]

Thomas Settimi
Lake Arrowhead, California

REFERENCES

[1] http://www.26nc.org/history/KIA/cobkia.htm
[2] Ibid.
[3] Ibid.
[4] http://aotw.org/officers.php?officer_id=866
[5] http://arar.essortment.com/jenniewade_psx.htm
[6] http://www.angelfire.com/ny5/elmiraprison/addison.html
[7] http://home.jam.rr.com/rjcourt52/cwprisons/king.htm
[8] http://www.angelfire.com/ny5/elmiraprison/
[9] http://home.jam.rr.com/rjcourt52/cwprisons/king.htm
[10] http://www.iarchives.com/lds_04/pdf/lds_04_story-of-
bradford-co_0469.pdf
[11] http://www.shelbycountyhistory.org/schs/arcives/civilwar
archives/jlewiscwara.htm
[12] http://www.nps.gov/foth/linsecur.htm
[13] http://www.spartacus.schoolnet.co.uk/USACWharrisC.htm
[14] http://www.theaterhistory.com. Original source:
Encyclopedia Britannica, Eleventh Edition, Volume IV.
Anonymous. Cambridge: University Press, 1910. p. 239.
[15] http://216.125.204.247/Cahokia_Beginnings/Romantic/
Colonel%20%Vital%20Jarrot.htm
[16] http://www.eslarp.uiuc.edu/ibex/archive/Cahokia/
inscriptions.htm
[17] http://www.vietquoc.com/17-6spir.htm
[18] http://www.vietnam-tourism.com/vietnam_gov
/e_pages/Dulich/touspot/dienbienphu.asp